"A success . . . *The Rainy City* is a solid debut for a promising detective series."
—*Long Island Newsday*

"Emerson's first book, *The Rainy City*, convinced me that he was destined to rank among the best of the new generation of American private eye writers."
—*Chicago Sun-Times*

"Impossible to put down; I constantly wanted to know what would happen next, but at the same time I never felt that the surprises were being pulled out of a hat. Emerson plays fair, concealing the result like a master magician."
—*The Drood Review*

"More than a dozen colorful characters, major and minor, male and female, upstanding and lowdown, cross Black's trail. All come to life. Some stay that way."
—*The Register-Guard* (Eugene, OR)

"The writing is clean, the dialogue crisp and neat, and the plot appealing."
—*Northwest Review of Books*

*Please turn the page
for more rave reviews . . .*

"Emerson is carving his own special niche among a new generation of private eye writers."
—*The Washington Post Book World*

"Earl Emerson and Thomas Black only get better and better! Emerson's plotting is original, suspenseful—so well done that the richness of his writing seems almost a bonus. Black and his cohorts and enemies are real enough that sometimes I think I recognize them on Seattle's streets. Earl Emerson has taken his place in the rarefied air of the best of the best!"
—ANN RULE

"Emerson's sense of creating lean plot and dialogue improves with each book."
—*The Seattle Times*

"Emerson is at the top of his game, and very few are better."
—*Mostly Murder*

By Earl Emerson:
Published by Ballantine Books

VERTICAL BURN
INTO THE INFERNO

The Thomas Black novels
THE RAINY CITY
POVERTY BAY
NERVOUS LAUGHTER
FAT TUESDAY
DEVIANT BEHAVIOR
YELLOW DOG PARTY
THE PORTLAND LAUGHTER
THE VANISHING SMILE
THE MILLION-DOLLAR TATTOO
DECEPTION PASS
CATFISH CAFÉ

THE RAINY CITY

Earl Emerson

BALLANTINE BOOKS • NEW YORK

A Ballantine Book
Published by The Ballantine Publishing Group

www.ballantinebooks.com

Library of Congress Catalog Card Number: 19-95402

ISBN 0-345-41405-5

Manufactured in the United States of America

First Ballantine Books Edition: June 1997

OPM 10 9 8 7

"God help all men on rainy afternoons."
—Raymond Chandler

1

ON SATURDAY SOME GHOUL MURDERED MY dog.

It surprises you when they do something like that.

I expect to be flattened by snarling eighteen-wheelers on the freeway. I expect to be lunged at by booze hounds with broken beer bottles in taverns. I expect to be slapped by loose women who aren't quite as loose as I thought. But it surprises you when some jerk caves in your dog's skull on a rainy Saturday evening.

I had squandered the day polishing off a dismal case.

A pipe fitter with long arms and long teeth named Bruce Lemay hired me to discover what his girlfriend played at while he worked the night shift at Lockheed. I found out and even turned down a modestly tempting opportunity to play at it with her. When poor Bruce received the news he flew off the handle.

He launched a sloppy right cross at my chin and then boasted he was going to sue me for slander.

The right cross missed, and he missed again when he tried to plunk down into a chair after I Frisbeed a packet of photos at him. The three-by-five's were nothing grandiose. I had once immortalized a state representative *flagrante delicto* with another man's wife while he

1

sprayed Reddi Wip on her nude body from a pressurized can.

These were nothing like that, just simple snapshots of his bosomy Amanda hoisting brews with three different bozos on three different nights. She had sworn to Bruce she had been in bed with a migraine each of these nights. Maybe one of Bruce's pals was named Migraine. I could not really blame the grimy pipe fitter for growing irate and taking a poke at me.

"How come this kind of stuff always happens to me?" Bruce Lemay moaned. "My ex ran away with our meter reader. Can you believe that? The electric meter reader, for christsakes."

I drove my Ford pickup home in the dark. The streets were awash under a solid, slanting November rain. It was funny. I didn't even like dogs.

He wasn't much; never had been. Only a jaunty little mutt who found and adopted me four years ago. I'd even trained him to do all his numbers next door under Horace's hydrangea. The city was full of mutts. Hell, they were cheap. I could fetch another one tomorrow. The pound gassed eighty a day.

As I angled up the driveway, the truck's headlights cut a brilliant swath through the downpour and I saw him sprawled under the Adolf Horstmann like a discarded rag doll. A length of pipe which I later assumed to be the murder weapon lay next to his stiffened legs. It was hard to tell how long he'd been gone because everything was soaked by the rain, everything damp and slick to the touch.

Leaving the Ford's headlights on to bleach the scene, I fetched a spade from the garage and buried him deep.

Next spring I would sink a Whiskey Mac over him. Roses always grew tall and luxurious over graves.

If you're a private detective and somebody plays lead-pipe polo with your dog, you have to rake over your memory and the cases you've handled recently. You have to wonder who might be sporting a grudge. I could think of some people, but they were out of town or at the crossbar hotel. Bruce Lemay's check was the first sniff of professional money I'd had in six weeks. It was too soon for him to be stalking through my yard killing pets. I had only quashed his romance with Amanda an hour earlier.

Mine was a modest frame home off Roosevelt in the University District: two bedrooms upstairs and a bachelor apartment in the basement which I rented to a student. My needs were few, my life tranquil except for an occasional messy divorce case. My truck was thirteen years old and squeaked in places I could not find with a grease gun. I pedaled a bicycle when the Seattle rains abated. Having been a cop for almost ten years, I was living largely off the LEOFF pension system. I had been a good cop. In those days I knew it all. I was going to be the chief one day.

After horsing down a cold meat loaf sandwich, I submerged my weary bones in a hot bath and scrubbed and listened to the blather of a talk show on the radio, lazily watching the soapy water slosh around my limbs.

I might have dived straight into bed, but there's a certain stink that clings to you when you bury something.

Kathy doesn't knock and enter so much as she slugs the door and barges in. Familiarity will do that. I recognized her wooden clogs on the basement steps which led directly to my kitchen. Before I could escape, she was sitting on the closed lid of the throne beside me, fretting. Kathy was the student, first year law, who rented my basement.

On her way through the kitchen, she had snatched up my dog's collar, along with a bell she had given the mongrel several years ago for some forgotten occasion.

"What's this?" Kathy said, clicking off my radio and dangling the collar. A newspaper clipping was crimped in her other hand. "Where's a-mutt-named-Jeff?"

"In the rose bed."

"It's raining."

"He's dead. Murdered," I said.

"Dead?" Kathy frowned, cooed, and thought about it for a few moments. "That's awful. Who . . . ? J.D.s?"

"Somebody came into the yard and whacked him with a piece of pipe. You didn't see anything funny today, did you?"

Kathy shook her head and pondered the development. "Why would anyone kill your dog?"

"Maybe for no reason. Maybe for laughs."

"Horace next door wouldn't do it, would he?"

"Naw. He's just a grump. He'd toss Ex-Lax in the mutt's dish, but he wouldn't have the nerve to kill him."

"One of your cases?"

"I've been thinking about that. Maybe you've noticed. I haven't been real busy lately."

"You haven't?" A musical note of hope infused Kathy's voice.

"What's on your mind?" I asked, draping a flowered washcloth across myself.

"That looks ridiculous," said Kathy, without glancing away from the newspaper clipping in her hand. She had obviously pawed and perused the clipping repeatedly, but she sat and read it again, word by word. "You don't have to display any false modesty around me."

"What's false about it?"

"I know you love to show off, Thomas. I know it."

"Sometimes I wish you wouldn't catch me this way. What do you do? Hear the tub running, wait five minutes, and then dash upstairs?"

Kathy ignored me.

She was wearing one of her more traditional outfits: thick knee stockings, a tweed skirt, and a tightly knit navy-blue sweater without the benefit of a brassiere underneath. She had small, buoyant, rounded breasts that men loved to stare at. Her long, dark, and wavy hair drifted past her shoulders and danced with the electrical charges it got after being brushed.

She focused her violet eyes on me and said, "I've got a case for you. If you'll take it."

"Who's the client?"

She gnawed at the inside of her cheek and said, "That's just it. I don't know. I suppose *I* would be."

"I'll get dressed and we'll talk about it." When Kathy didn't budge, I scuffed some water across my legs, hoping the noise would break the standoff. "You have the advantage of me here."

Apparently she hadn't heard, or if she had, it hadn't fazed her. She handed me the crumpled newspaper clipping. I read it, trying to keep from getting it wet. A mere three lines:

Persons having information on the whereabouts of Melissa Crowell Nadisky please contact us at 555-5249. A reward of $2,000 has been posted.

"So?"

"She's a friend, Thomas. *My* friend. I went to school with her. Actually, we roomed together for a quarter. She was . . . well, anyway, I phoned the other day and Burton said she had been missing since last Sunday. That's six days she's been gone. Then I found this ad in the paper."

"Burton?"

"Her husband."

"Okay, she's missing."

"Can you find her?"

"If she hasn't gone too far. The question is, do I want to find her?"

"Thomas, don't be difficult. Something awfully suspicious is going on here, and I want you to find her before . . ." Kathy hesitated. I had seen the look on her face in the past.

"Before what?"

"It's only one of my silly feelings."

I had learned long ago there was more to Kathy's "silly feelings" than most people were ready to accept. If you wanted to call them something, you could call them premonitions. She never flaunted the ability. It was just something eerie that was a part of her.

Once, driving on the freeway with her, she suddenly slumped forward and began weeping. When I questioned her, she said she was shook up about the accident ahead of us. On that particular sweep of interstate, you could see for miles. The road ahead was clear. Totally clear. Three minutes later, we rounded a curve and rolled past one of the most grisly motorcycle accidents I had ever seen.

When I told her to look, that she'd been right, she

clasped her face in her lap, saying that she didn't want to see the "woman in red."

Two bikes had spilled. Two males and their female passengers had been thrown to the pavement. Three of them were dead. A woman in the remains of a red touring suit was being worked on by two perspiring paramedics and a team of firemen. I knew their motions were perfunctory, recognizing their haste as a mere public display. Only a miracle was keeping the woman alive. A miracle from hell. If fate were related to decency she would have expired with the others.

Call it clairvoyance, intuition, ESP, Kathy had a real dose. She wasn't particularly fond of it, but she availed herself of it when it suited her.

"So you think something's the matter? Something more than a woman running away?"

"I do. I can't say what, but I'm worried. Real worried."

"Is this one of your 'feelings'?"

"It sure is."

"What did her husband say? He worried?"

"With Burton it's hard to tell. I almost have the suspicion he knows where she went."

"Look," I said, rearranging the washcloth, "if they're only having a lovers' spat . . ."

"I talked to her father." Kathy became animated, her violet eyes widening and absorbing me. "He must be the one behind that newspaper blurb. Don't you think? Why would he tell me he wasn't worried and then put up two thousand dollars to find her? Does that make any sense?"

"Kathy," I said, swirling the water around my knees. "I'm getting cold."

She looked at me blankly for a moment, then tossed me a towel, failing to remove herself from the room.

"You'll find a pen and paper in the other room," I said. "Write down everything you know about her. List her friends. Where she works. Schools she went to. Everything of a factual nature. You'll be surprised. It'll probably only take you a minute or two." I was fervently hoping it would take at least a quarter of an hour.

Bounding into the other room on her noisy wooden clogs, Kathy shouted over her shoulder, "I knew you'd help me. I knew it."

"No promises. I'll look. That's all."

Kathy stuck her head back around the corner as I was getting up. I hastily wound the towel around my middle. "By the way," she said, "it does too float."

"What?"

"You know. And your face is turning pink."

"I don't know anything," I said, disgruntled.

"It floats."

"Who said it didn't?"

"You did. You told me once they don't float." Then she was gone, giggling to herself, a mere whiff of her perfume lingering to taunt me.

"Me? I never said any such thing." But I was talking to the walls.

2

"HI HO, SAM SPADE. GET YOUR TRENCH coat off the nail. You and I are going to look for the lost Princess today."

She was garbed like a clown, in white face with a red bulb nose, baggy black canvas trousers, and a tiny, black top hat. It is not every day that a clown wakes you up carrying a pan of hot biscuits and a jar of homemade blackberry preserves. I crawled out of bed and got dressed. Gobbling biscuits smothered in jam, we sat at the kitchen table, our chairs shoved up against the baseboard heater, sharing the waves of heat that feathered upward and tickled our backsides.

Kathy Birchfield had been leasing my basement apartment for almost four years. From time to time, one of us splurged on a Sunday morning breakfast for the other, generally at a time when we wished to discuss Saturday night's companions. Not many men could truly call a woman their best friend, but I could call Kathy mine.

We had met at the university in a history course I was taking for the police department and she was taking on her way to a bona fide law degree. The professor was a neat-freak, insisting that we all sit in precise alphabetical order. That's how we met. Thomas Black. Kathy

9

Birchfield. Three times a week for three months we sat side by side, scribbling notes and whispering. It was the year I left the department, no longer destined to be chief, and I needed someone to lean on, needed her badly.

My life had capsized, my brain flipped inside out, feeling the way a wet T-shirt does when you pull it off. Kathy had seen me through some ugly times. She had always been staunch, no matter what shape her own life was taking, and I owed her. It was partially on the basis of our history that I was so easily persuaded to poke into the affairs of her missing friend. That and the fact that Kathy had a premonition about her. If Kathy thought you were in trouble, you were in trouble.

Along with the biscuits and blackberry preserves, Kathy hauled up an enormous glass pitcher of apple juice. As we ate she gradually filled me in on Melissa Crowell Nadisky's life.

"How about if we mosey over to Burt's and then you can drop me off at Eloise's birthday party? She's having four clowns there, all told. Why don't you come? It'll be fun."

"We'll see what happens at Burton's first. Besides, four clowns might be more than I can handle. I have enough trouble with just one sometimes." Kathy grinned impishly, folded her palms under her chin as if framing a flower and batted her eyelashes. It made me laugh in spite of myself.

As she clambered into the truck, the mound of fresh wet earth beside the Adolf Horstmann caught my eye. I surveyed the neighborhood. Who the hell would have slipped into my yard—in the rain yet—and brained my dog? Being a reasonable man, I had to believe there was a reason. I wondered whether I would ever find out.

"Melissa was one of those ugly ducklings you see arriving at college and blooming right before your eyes," Kathy said. "She was so shy and backward when I first met her that she almost seemed retarded. That's a terrible thing to say, but it's true. What do you think, Thomas? Think we can find her?"

"Does her husband want us to look?"

"I don't know what Burton wants."

"What about mom and pop? You saw them? What did they say?"

"I only met *him*. He's a fancy Dan executive for one of those big conglomerates. He might even own the company for all I know. I told him . . . I suggested to Mr. Crowell how strange it was that he didn't care where his daughter was. He got real annoyed when I mentioned I had a private detective friend who would find her."

"You happen to mention my name?" I glanced across the seat at her.

"I don't remember. What do you think the chances of finding her are?"

"It's more likely she'll come back on her own. On the other hand, some people who run away want to be found. So they don't go far and they don't put much thought or worry into covering their trail."

Kathy was silent for a long while. When I looked across at her, she was examining the close rows of pre-war housing we were passing near the zoo. For a moment, I admired her clean profile below the top hat.

The missing woman's husband lived in Ballard and the drive was a short one. Kathy and I wouldn't have long to talk. I pushed in the choke on the Ford. The motor coughed.

"I only had the one . . . whatever you want to call it.

Just this one-time feeling that something too awful was going to happen."

"To Melissa?"

Kathy cleared her throat. I could see where the white paint ended just above the hollow at the base of her neck. "I don't know. Maybe it has something to do with her little girl. But it has everything to do with her disappearance. It's all connected somehow."

"You didn't tell me she had a little girl."

"Angel? She's three. She's a darling. Gosh, I hope this costume doesn't scare her."

"I have a feeling there are a lot of things you haven't told me. Last night you started to go into something about Melissa and then you stopped yourself. What was it?"

"You caught that?"

I grunted. "What was it?"

"In college Melissa was so bashful at first, you almost had to feel sorry for her. Then she went through a phase. It must have been about her junior year. She became a . . . kind of a tramp. Nothing else you could call it. Then she settled down and was quiet again. I wasn't seeing much of her at that time, but I heard about it from mutual friends."

"You mean she dated a lot of different guys?"

"She dated *every* guy, practically. And the way I understood it, she slept with all of them."

"How did people know these things?"

"Melissa didn't care who knew. She'd tell you if you asked her."

"When did she marry this fella, Burton?"

"I don't know. I lost touch for a few years. Three years ago? Four years? About the time I moved into your basement. She dated him off and on ever since I knew her. But I always had the feeling there was nothing hot and heavy to it. You know, one of those guys a girl keeps on the back burner for a weekend when nothing else turns up."

"Just like you and me?"

Kathy squinted at me and thrust her fingers into my ribs through my cocoa-colored ski coat. "Give me a break," she said.

"So what do these people do for a living?"

"Burton's a poet."

"Are you talking 'poet,' as in poetry?"

"He's a real poet. He's been published in everything, even the *Atlantic*. He's quite good."

"Does he find that supports his family?" I asked, semi-facetiously. I had written some poetry once.

"Unless they've changed, they don't have a lot of bread and butter on the table. They're on food stamps. Burton works part-time when he can get it. Last I heard, he worked this summer for a month in Alaska doing something with crabs. But that was months ago and he hasn't had anything since. Melissa keeps the house together. She used to work at a dime store down the street from their place. Recently, I think she was out of work."

"Did she graduate?"

"About the time Angel was born. She's got a teaching certificate. You know about how valuable they are these days. That and fifty cents will get her downtown on the bus."

"What's your feeling on this? You never explained what you think will happen. The premonition."

"You don't want to hear it."

"But I do. I trust your feelings. You may not always be right on the button, but you've been close enough to make a believer out of me. If you said it was time to sell my mother, I'd have to pack her up and stick an ad in the *Times*."

For several moments Kathy debated whether or not to articulate her thoughts, then decided against it. "We'll find her and then things will work out."

"Okay, but if both Burton *and* her father don't want me screwing around, it's no deal. It's tough enough locating someone when you have the family pitching for you. With the family on the other team? No deal."

"Are you good at finding people, Thomas?"

"I'm good."

Kathy lapsed into a world of her own and I suppose I started thinking about my dog's assassin. Perhaps someone thought the mutt was Kathy's. Maybe some pervert was after her. I decided to break up the somber mood by switching on the Bible thumpers. Though she had been raised in a strict religious atmosphere, Kathy had forsaken all organized worship and loved to mock her past. The radio dial was loaded with proselytizing preachers on this cloudy, windswept Sunday.

"What if Burton's not home?" Kathy asked suddenly.

"Sunday morning?" I looked at my watch. "Not yet nine-thirty? Are you kidding me? And miss Brother Andy Bob? Even the mayor is home in front of the tube. Hallelujah, Brother! Amen, Sister! Praise the Lord Jesus!"

I rolled the dial and tuned in several evangelical speakers. Each seemed more vociferous and impassioned than the last. Everyone had Sunday fever. After a block, Kathy caught the infection and we were swamping the cab with amens! and hallelujahs! Kathy giggled like a child concealing a pocketful of snitched cookies. It's contagious when someone you know and are fond of laughs with you. Anyone hearing us would have thought we had both gone over the wall at Western State, one of the local loony bins. Kathy sang out, "Praise the Lord, kiss the devil, and shine my boots!"

The mirth stopped when we got to the street the Nadiskys lived on.

I swerved in the nick of time. It was one of the new, smaller Cadillacs swooshing up the street toward us. The other driver was determined not to give an inch.

Hunched over the steering wheel of the oncoming vehicle was a large, angry man. He had grizzled hair and bushy caterpillar eyebrows. The speeding Cadillac was crowded with faces, among them a middle-aged woman, a small towheaded girl in her lap.

When a car comes at you fast enough to kill everyone involved, you don't have much of a chance to reconnoiter. All I saw clearly was a strobe-light glimpse of the infant blonde. She looked as if she were in a state of shock, as if Santa had just puked on her. She sucked her thumb madly, a tattered blanket pressed up against the opposite side of her face creating a giant, formless ear muff.

Kathy pulled her hands off the dashboard where she had impulsively reached to brace for an accident. "That was Angel."

"Melissa's kid?"

She nodded. "I think that was her grandfather at the wheel."

"If he eats like he drives he'll choke to death."

The Nadisky homestead was around the corner a block away. The houses were all tiny, cramped, squarish, but it was easy to single out the Nadisky place. It was the only yard where the grass grew past your knees. The only place that had an overturned, rusted wheelbarrow canted against the front porch. The only bungalow with water-spotted sheets tacked in the windows where drapes should have been. The only house on the block where the front door stood wide open.

A late-model, tan sedan was parked at the curb, the motor chugging, puffballs of exhaust meandering up the sidewalk. More out of habit than reflex, I stopped behind the sedan and scrawled the license number down on the tablet I kept in the glove box.

"Is that their car?" I asked, realizing even as I spoke that the spanking-new undented sedan did not match the condition of the house, or the rest of what I'd gleaned about Burton and Melissa.

Kathy was already on her way up the stairs toward the front stoop, a clown on the run. "They don't own a car," she said over her shoulder. "Burton doesn't drive."

I scooted across the truck seat but didn't catch Kathy until she had already plumbed deep into the residence. It was cold inside, as if the door had been open for a spell. The living room was a shambles, not dirty so much as messy, littered with children's toys, clothes, and sections of the Sunday newspaper. I caught up with Kathy at the entrance to the bedroom—just in time to keep her from taking a blow to the mouth. It was quite a little scene.

Holder was there. So was Burton. Holder wore a nattily tailored sport coat, slacks, and handmade Italian shoes. He stood facing three-quarters away from the doorway, backhanding the hell out of Burton Nadisky. I had seen Holder at work before. He loved violence. He was the sort of guy who ate popcorn raw. There were few people he couldn't slam across the room using the back of his hand, probably me included.

"Stay down," ordered Holder.

Burton was splayed across a tangle of bloodstained sheets, his face looking like a piss-poor club fighter's last performance. Holder was a mulatto, six-foot-three, about twenty-two, a flamboyant dresser. He had been a boxer once. He was a good eight inches taller than the disheveled Burton.

Scrabbling off the bed, Burton lurched to the open doorway. His face was crimson. As if swatting a fly, Holder slammed him onto the floor. The impact made a sickening crunch.

"Now stay down, boy. Don't you know the score?"

Moving like a sack of rocks, Burton sniffled and began to roll over, presumably so he could crawl, the last vestiges of strength sapped from his trembling legs.

"Leave him alone!" shouted Kathy. She was gutsy— but stupid. Holder would knock her into next Tuesday.

She prepared to pounce on Holder. She might have made a little headway. She might have reached almost to his armpit before he broke her jaw. Already, I could see him doubling up his enormous fist.

I grasped Kathy around her slender waist and flung her to the right of the doorway. Nothing less would have dissuaded her. I had forgotten how little she weighed.

"Stay out of this," I commanded. Kathy shook her head, cleared the cobwebs, and looked at me the way a cat who had been kicked off the dinner table might.

A lump was noticeable in the center of Holder's back under the tight-fitting turquoise sport coat, a lump which corresponded to the spot in which some people carry their hip holsters. Holder was too dangerous to mess

with. He had been only partially aware of us in the
doorway, his mind dwelling on other things, but now we
were fodder for the machine.

Burton Nadisky managed to worm his way to my feet.
Holder moved to drag him back.

"Uh uh uh," I said, putting more menace into my voice
than either I or Holder had expected. "Enough is enough.
Burton, you don't want to go out there. Your daughter is
long gone." He sank his head to the floor, giving out a
low groan.

"Holder? If you want to stop this man from catching
his in-laws, why not go out and move that car in front?
That's the only thing he could possibly use. Burton here
doesn't own a car. You think he's going to catch them on
foot?"

Holder glowered at me darkly, straining to recall my
name. We had clashed on a case about a year earlier. He
was awful with names. He snapped his fingers repeatedly
as I picked up a wire clothes hanger from the rubble. I
said, "Black. Thomas Black."

"You the private eye who messed with that divorce
case a mine."

"Good memory."

"I owe you on that one." He was trying hard to recall
precisely how much he owed me. If I was lucky, he
wouldn't resuscitate the entire story.

I fiddled with the wire coat hanger and twisted it into a
long shepherd's crook.

"I'm sure your employer would love for you to stay
here and stir up all sorts of trouble. We've got friends
coming right behind us. It might work out better if you
left now. What do you think?"

The mention of additional friends goaded Holder. More

people meant more witnesses. He was already cutting it too close. He stepped gingerly over Nadisky and strode past me like a man carrying a mess in his britches. He stopped and stared quizzically at Kathy, who was still on the floor, her red bulb nose askew. Holder conjured up a queer, disjointed face and used it on her. You'd think the man had never seen a clown before.

When he turned to walk out of the house, I fish-poled the wire coat hanger out and dropped the sharp crook of it into his coat pocket. As he kept walking, the hanger ripped the pocket off his coat. I let go of the wire. It swung from the remnants of his pocket for a moment and then tinkled onto the floor. Holder swirled around, his eyes tiny dots of brown death.

"Sorry," I said, smiling smugly. He examined the pocket flapping at his hip. I wouldn't be the bull that locked horns with him, but I'd be the gnat that made his ass itch.

"Isn't that Dave and Jim outside right now?" blurted Kathy, thinking quickly.

Holder glared at me.

"Ain't life a bitch," I said.

Holder considered the situation, then marched through the front door without bothering to hold the pieces of his gaudy sportscoat together. A spectre in tattered turquoise.

3 BURTON'S MOANS WERE THE SORT THAT hurt to listen to in the beginning, then rapidly became irksome, then disgusting, and finally, nauseating. Kathy realized it as soon as I did and scurried into the bathroom where I heard water running. When she returned with a damp washcloth, her crooked clown nose had been fixed.

I strode to the front door and closed it as Holder drove off. I waved but he didn't see it. "Be like that," I said.

When I turned around, Kathy was daubing at Burton's smeared face with the washcloth. It took him a while to come down from whatever ragged cloud he was hugging and focus on Kathy.

"You . . . who? Oh, Kathy. I didn't recognize you." Holder's drubbing had swollen one lip, torn a small patch out of Burton's cheek. Holder invariably wore large rings. Nice guy.

Dressed in a pair of faded jeans and nothing else, his back against the doorjamb in the bedroom, Burton rolled his face away from Kathy's washcloth and began weeping.

"They took Angel," he sobbed. "They took my Angel.

That big"—he racked his brain for a fit word to describe Holder—"turkey."

He was talking around the puffy lip expertly now, a quick study. Perhaps he had taken pastings before.

"Why did they take your daughter?" I asked.

"It was Melissa's folks. They said I was an unfit parent. That they would get a court order."

"Fat chance," said Kathy. "Legally, it's almost impossible to take a child away from her parents. What they did, actually, was kidnap her. We're going to file a complaint right away. Don't worry, Burt, we'll get her back."

"I don't know," said Burton Nadisky, rolling his head from side to side, defeated before the battle had begun. "They said I could visit. If I got a lawyer and tried anything fancy, they said they'd skip the country with her."

"Sure. They know they're in the wrong."

"They've got an awful lot of money," conceded Burton. "I suppose they could go anywhere they wanted."

"Tip your head back," said Kathy, wiping his nose. "Thomas, this bleeding isn't going to stop. Do you know what to do?"

"No," I lied. "Why don't you take my truck? Ballard Hospital is down the street. They'll know how to stop it."

As the two of us stuffed him into a shirt and some battered hiking boots, I could see why he'd been such a pushover for Holder. Burton Nadisky was five-foot-seven, blond, fair-complexioned, and was built like a last-place marathon runner. My guess was he had been last place in everything he had ever attempted in a gym class. He wasn't fat, merely soft. And there was a certain gentleness to his manner that was evident immediately—in his eyes, even in the way he breathed and spoke. His words burbled out softly like those of a sleepy child.

"He told me to stay down," said Burton, tears runneling off his pink cheeks. "But I had to try. My Angel. He hit me and I got up. He hit me every time I got up."

"You did what you thought was proper," said Kathy. "Angel will be fine with her grandparents until we can get her back. By the way, Burt, this is Thomas Black, my landlord and my friend." I liked the way she said that.

Burton looked at me with new eyes. He poked his limp paw out to shake but withdrew it when he realized it was dappled with blood.

"I'll wait here," I said, "in case they come back."

"Sure, sure," said Burton, genially. "And make yourself at home. The TV works now. We've got eggs in the fridge. Help yourself. Whatever is mine is yours." He said it as if it were an expression he used frequently. I spied a photo of his pretty wife sitting atop the Zenith and wondered if she were the same way.

Propped up by Kathy, he hobbled away. When they got to the front door, I jangled my truck keys and tossed them to her. She caught them neatly in one fist. As a storm lumbered across the sky, they drove away slowly.

Too nice to suspect that I would plunder his house, Burton had left me in total trust. It was a trust I betrayed immediately. In order to locate his wife, it was best that I knew everything, even things he wouldn't freely divulge.

I scoured the house like a freeloading relative searching for penny rolls. He had about sixteen dollars in crumpled ones in plain sight on the dresser top. There were no penny rolls. Their checkbook had been drawn down to zero for a week or so. I scanned the list of places they had written checks to. It was easy to distinguish the different handwritings. His was large, rounded, and careless. Hers was almost neurotically cramped and precise, every loop closed. The messy house was not her doing. Not likely.

He had scrawled his last check for five dollars to the food bank. The guy couldn't afford socks, but he was tithing his money, doling it out to people who probably had more than he did. Her last check had been written eight days earlier to Tradewell. It was all pretty mundane, until I saw the fifty-dollar entry to the Hopewell Clinic. The Hopewell was a low-cost mental health center on Capitol Hill. Her handwriting. I wondered, had they gone in for marriage counseling? If so, she was probably just another routine runaway housewife.

The refrigerator harbored eight brown eggs in the door, a full jug of cultured milk, and half a slab of margarine. The rest of the shelves were bare. They didn't even own a squirt bottle of mustard. A shopping list and a booklet of food stamps sat next to the toaster. I had the feeling the kid ate and the father went without. The dishes in the sink corresponded to that. One plate. Someone had eaten an omelet and toast that morning and imbibed the last drops of orange juice.

Scattered across the kitchen table were the pages of a partially completed poem.

I sat down and studied it. It reminded me of Poe's "Annabel Lee" and was dedicated to "Melissa, my only love." I wished I could write like he did. I hadn't read such embarrassing and touching lines since school. Geez, Burton adored her. It turned a different light on him.

Outside, in the backyard, a small plot had been spaded up and was blanketed with layer upon layer of soggy leaves, probably garnered from the local park. I could envision a blonde woman and a blonde tot dragging them home in plastic garbage sacks. The flattened dregs of a pile some little feet had twittered through lay like a pyre in the center of the lawn.

In the living room, I picked up the Sears family photos off the Zenith and examined a pastel Burton and a pastel Melissa.

Once in a while I saw couples like them strolling down a shopping mall. Burton and Melissa were one of those strange twosomes who looked like brother and sister. Same bone structure. Same coloring. Same blond hair. Same bland facial expression. Usually those couples consisted of two extremely shy people who had seen nothing to fear in a near mirror image of themselves. Angel resembled a younger sibling instead of a daughter.

Melissa was a slightly built, blue-eyed blonde, wearing her long, straight hair parted in the center. If I hadn't known she was married and had a three-year-old and was missing—if I hadn't heard that she had been a tramp and didn't think there was a good chance that she was screwy—I could have fallen in love with her. Any man could have.

The brilliant macho detective tumbles for the elusive prey he stalks. Shades of *Laura*.

Bit by bit, I went through their house like a monkey combing his tail for ticks. I was shameless, snooping under their pillows to see what sort of night gear they wore, riffling through their medicine cabinet to check on contraceptives.

Geez, I love to snoop. We all do, given the right opportunity. I found no contraceptives. Perhaps she had taken them with her. Perhaps she would be needing them. Folded tidily beneath her pillow was a floor-length cotton nightgown. Her pillow smelled of wildflowers and, like all pillows, of spit.

All my hocus-pocus could draw no more of their story out of the house. It was rented and shabby. By the looks of the penciled marks on the baby's wall, charting her growth, they had lived in the house since before she could walk. The baby had few toys. The parents had fewer clothes. It was all very spartan and hip, right out of the late Sixties and early Seventies. Kerouac, e.e. cummings, and A. S. Neill dotted the bookshelf.

I had lived like that once. Now I was a full-time American. Now I cherished my La-Z-Boy and my color television, and I hoarded pennies for the copper content no matter what the treasury said.

In the living room, someone had embroidered a sampler in colored floss and hung it on the wall. It said: *Love is having a family that cares.*

Some family. The daughter kidnapped by Grandpa. The mother missing. The father at Ballard Hospital getting his nostrils cauterized. You would almost suspect they were jinxed.

The 49ers were annihilating San Diego when Kathy and Burton came through the front door.

"Good game?" asked Burton jovially, as if that were all that mattered that morning. A small Band-Aid had been pasted to his cheek and he was still limping, still anemic.

I clicked off the black-and-white Zenith and said, "I suppose Kathy told you I was a detective?"

"Why, no." Burton turned around and gave Kathy an awkward look. "She didn't. I'll bet that's interesting work." He shook my hand limply. "I'd like to sit down and talk to you about that sometime. You might have some interesting material for my novel."

"Don't be so damned complacent," I said. "Somebody

just kidnapped your daughter. Your wife is missing. A jackass spent most of the morning playing break-a-face with *your* face. Get mad!"

He did the opposite. Burton Nadisky's voice collapsed into softness. "I'm sorry if I don't live up to some expectation that you have of me." He dumped a pile of doll clothing from the end of the sofa onto the floor and offered Kathy a seat, which she accepted. "I'm not like other men, I guess. I can't get angry at any of these people. They're only doing what they think is right."

"I'll tell you what," I said. "You sit here and feel sorry for yourself and I'll go find your wife."

Burton looked like a man in a Chinese restaurant who'd just been informed that his bill was six thousand dollars, no charge for the fortune cookies. Kathy interceded.

"Burton, we want to help you. It won't cost you a thing. Today is Sunday, but tomorrow I'll get a friend of mine who owes me some favors and we'll get an injunction to get Angel back. In the meantime, Thomas can look for your wife. He's really very good. He once located a cat that had been missing for two years."

My eyes rolled involuntarily toward the ceiling.

"Gee. That's awfully nice of you to offer, Kathy. You don't know what it means to me to have a friend like you. But really . . . there's nothing to be done."

"Don't you want Angel back?" Kathy asked.

"Of course I want her back. But I'm not sure it's the right thing for her. We don't have much money. The family's kind of breaking up. Maybe she *is* better off with Nanna and Angus."

"What about your wife?" I asked, pointedly.

A muscle in his right cheek quivered. "She's . . . I'm

sure she'll come back if ... Really, I don't know what good it would do to find her."

"You know where she is then?" Kathy asked, hopefully.

"Melissa? Gosh, no. Do you?"

"How did she disappear?" I asked.

"I took Angel to the park last Sunday afternoon. When we got home, she was gone."

"Just like that?"

"Yeah. It was kind of funny. You know."

"No warning? You hadn't been quarreling? Was she worried about something?" In their financial straits it was difficult to imagine her *not* worrying.

"No. Nothing like that."

"She leave a note?"

Digging into his jeans pocket, Burton pulled out a partially shredded scrap of paper and handed it to me. He was reminiscent of a kid caught with his fingers in mama's undies drawer, as if the note were something he shouldn't have and was ashamed of being caught with. He'd obviously had it in his pocket all week. Perusing the wrinkled note over my arm, Kathy leaned in until I could smell her greasepaint.

Burty,

I have to go away. Things haven't been working out and I know they won't get better unless I leave. I am no good for you so please don't worry.

Love,
Melissa

Where she wrote "I am no good for you" there was a natural break in the continuity of the writing so that "I am no good" was almost a separate entity and not connected with "for you." As if she unconsciously wanted to make a point of the words: "I am no good." The script was less businesslike and precise than her handwriting in the checkbook.

Melissa Crowell Nadisky was a woman in trouble.

4 "SHE HAVE ANY MONEY WITH HER when she left?" I asked.

"Cripes," said Burton. "I never thought about that." I wondered what he did think about. Money was the first thing most people would have considered. "No, she didn't. A couple of bucks, maybe. And we only have the one checkbook. She left that." I knew why. "She didn't take hardly any of her clothes."

"Where do you think she went?"

Burton shrugged. "I really couldn't say."

"We're going to find her," said Kathy. "If she doesn't want to come back, fine. But we're going to locate her and talk with her."

"Sure," said Burton. We probably could have said "Let's go get your balls amputated" and he would have said "Sure." I bet the Fuller Brush men and the Avon ladies and the pixie girls selling Scout cookies loved him. For that matter, I bet his little girl loved him.

"You must have a theory," I said.

"I really don't. I just believed she would be back. And now it's been over a week. And they took Angel. I don't know what's happening. Angus said I was a Jew. Why

29

would he say that?" His voice began to grow strangled. "I'm Lutheran, just like he is."

"Would she go to her folks' house?"

"No!" said Burton emphatically. It was the largest bullet of emotion he had fired all morning. Then, in a more controlled tone, he added, "They don't get along real well. They've had a few tiffs. She's okay with her mom. But her dad and her . . ."

"Any other relatives? Or friends I might try?"

"We don't have a whole lot of close friends. I've phoned everyone here in town."

"Maybe somebody's hiding her."

"Melissa doesn't know anyone that well."

"Where else might she go?"

"There's an aunt, maybe. I understand Melissa stayed with her one summer during high school. They used to be close."

Burton staggered into the other room and returned with a Christmas card and its torn envelope which he handed over timidly.

The aunt's name was Mary Dawn Crowell. The address was in Bellingham.

"She ever run away before, Burton?"

He hesitated, but not for long. I had the feeling he would tell me anything I wanted, if I asked—even how and where they had sex, as if the rest of us had more rights to his life than he did. "She's been gone before. Never this long."

"Where did she go?"

"I never found out."

"Weren't you mildly curious?"

"I figured if she wanted to tell me, she would. I guess she never wanted to."

"When was the last time she took off?"

"About six months ago. But she only stayed overnight. I don't know, maybe she doesn't love me. I honestly want her to be happy. If she'd be happier somewhere else, I'll even help her move. She knows that." He was a real scrapper, like a worm on a sunbaked sidewalk.

When we left him, Burton was heading toward the kitchen to hack away at his poem. He had given me a photo-booth snapshot of his wife. I stuck it in my wallet. In spite of his passiveness, I liked him. He was goofy, but maybe that was what it took to be a poet. Maybe that was what it took to spill your guts across the page for the whole world to see, and maybe to laugh at.

Under a sky the color of a bad bruise, we stood together beside the truck, each wrapped in our own thoughts.

Kathy chewed on her lower lip, a habit I invariably found appealing, even in white face. Across the street from the Nadisky household stood another tumbledown bungalow, the only other run-down place on the tidy block. I'll bet the neighbors loved it.

A woman leaned over a davenport and stared at me through the window, curlers in her hair, lines from a sleepless night tweezering her eyes, heavy breasts tugging at her bathrobe. Something told me she had more interest in Nadisky's problems than just that of a snoopy neighbor. If I reached any dead ends I would double back and look her up. Sometimes the neighbors knew more than the husband. Lots of times the neighbors knew more than the husband.

Before I realized what was happening, Kathy began trembling. I reached out and held her in my arms. She was small and frail as she shivered in my grip. The woman across the way didn't take her eyes off us for one moment. Perhaps she had never seen a man hug a clown before.

"Oh hell," said Kathy. "This is the second time I've gotten the heebie-jeebies over this family."

We climbed into the truck. She had shrugged off her shivering fit and was now staring at the top hat in her hand. From it she produced three colored juggling balls and began fiddling with them. I slid the seat all the way back from where she had adjusted it to drive Nadisky to the hospital. The woman across the street had vanished from the window. I could see a football game on their color television in the background.

"What about that man? That awful guy who was beating up Burton? Who was he?"

"He works for various detective agencies. He free-lances when somebody offers him a wad of bills. He's a nice guy. He was going to give your dentist a lot of work before I grabbed you."

"He wouldn't hit a woman?"

I fired up the truck and edged into the street. Kathy had buried the tires against the curb. They made a ripping noise. "Don't bet on it. Holder'd whack himself in the head with a brick if the money was right."

"What was he doing with the Crowells?"

"My guess is Angel's grandfather brought him along as a sort of policeman, to make sure there were no hitches."

Kathy tumbled the colored juggling balls into her top hat and spoke through gritted teeth. "Oh, that gripes me. That makes me so mad how they waltzed in and beat up Burton and took his daughter."

"Burton doesn't seem as angry as you do."

"Don't let him fool you. I've seen him mad before. He's written some real angry poems. You should see them."

"I read some of them."

Kathy did a double take. "Thomas, you didn't! These are my friends. How could you do such an embarrassing thing?"

"He had a poem right out on the kitchen table in plain sight."

"Oh."

"But I snooped through their place anyway."

"Thomas!"

"You want me to find Melissa? Or would you rather I was polite?"

"Can't you do both?"

I shrugged. "I never have yet. I wouldn't know how to start."

5 BELLINGHAM IS A LONG HAUL WHEN your thoughts are dark and distant. Kathy's premonitions were beginning to worry me. I'm not easily frightened, but she was seeing something in conjunction with this family that didn't belong, something ugly, and I didn't know if I wanted to find out what it was. Years ago, I had wanted to know everything. Needed to know. Now, I realized there were some things you were better off not discovering.

North and over eighty miles distant, Bellingham was a small city, not mentioned much in Seattle. The central feature of the burg was Western Washington State College. A long time ago I had seriously contemplated enrolling there.

I could have telephoned Mary Dawn Crowell, but you never find out as much on the phone. Besides, I had nothing else to do. The drive would give me a chance to think things through.

My buggy was a six-cylinder and red-lined at seventy. I saw no reason to strain the old girl. I kept the needle a hair past the double nickels. It showered most of the way. It was pouring in Bellingham.

Mary Dawn Crowell lived near the heart of the city in

34

a condominium that had clean lines and freshly planted, plastic-looking shrubbery in front. She wasn't home. The manager, a congenial grandmother-type with gray hair and gray eyes and gray dentures, was more than helpful to the tall stranger who had motored all the way up from Seattle in the rain squalls.

She escorted me up carpeted steps to the third floor where we spoke to one of Mary Dawn Crowell's neighbors, a hunched-over gentleman named Felton who must have immigrated from Latvia or some other obscure country. He wore a shabby suit, though it was readily apparent that he hadn't gone out and wasn't planning to. He lived in suits. He probably had two of them and rotated every Tuesday. He told me Crowell had taken a Sunday drive with some oldsters and would be home in the late afternoon.

I conned her phone number out of the manager and drove around looking for someplace to wait. It was just after one o'clock.

I grabbed a hamburger at a greasy spoon opposite a shopping mall. Strolling across the street to the mall, I window-shopped and watched the young women in tight jeans. I watched the old women in tight jeans, too, and the matrons in tight jeans, but mostly the young women in tight jeans. Everyone was dressed the same. Same designer denims with the same decals on their butts, same baseball caps with the same logos on their brains, same reds and blues, same cuts and styles.

One man trundled past wearing my shoes. Another came past in my coat. In the parking lot outside, there were at least two trucks identical to mine. It made you wonder how many had your brain.

I bought a thick Sunday paper and found a movie

theater playing *Body Heat*. I'd seen the flick, but I could easily tolerate it again. After the murder, I slipped out to the lobby and phoned Mary Dawn Crowell. No reply. That particular flick always made me thirsty. I floundered back to my seat with a tall cool 7UP and evaporated into the celluloid miracle.

It was half past five before a woman who might have been Crowell parked a shiny new road-gray Buick in back of the condominium and scurried through the pattering rain to the glass doors. I allowed her enough time to get inside and take care of business before I climbed out of the truck. I stalked through the wet and thumbed the buzzer next to 304.

"Yes?"

"I'm Thomas Black, a friend of your niece, Melissa Nadisky."

"Who?"

"Melissa Crowell? Your niece. She married a fellow named Nadisky."

"Yes, of course. Is Melissa with you?"

"Not today."

"Come on up." The door buzzed and I went in. The joint smelled of new carpets.

Mary Dawn was a spicy old gal, a spinster or widow by the looks of her clothing, which was thirty years out of date. The world was full of short little mannish women like her. She had a wide, squat body and a broad face that seemed to get broader toward the chin, as if the wide jaw belonged on someone else. Brown curls lay so snug that her scalp looked bald in patches. She sized me up while I introduced myself. She spoke in bursts the way a lot of people with pent-up energy do.

Though I was an exceptional liar, I decided the direct approach would be the most efficient.

"My name is Thomas Black. I'm a detective. Some friends of your niece asked me to find her."

"I didn't realize she needed finding," said Mary Crowell, abruptly plunking into a wooden armchair smothered in cushions. The apartment was crowded with wooden furniture, all of it meticulously polished.

She motioned for me to sit opposite her on a cushioned love seat. "Would you happen to know where she might be?" I asked.

"Don't know. Haven't seen Melissa for a spell. Don't get along with her father, Angus—he's my older brother. What's the matter with that husband of hers? Doesn't he know where she is?"

I shook my head. "When was the last time you heard from her?"

"Last time I talked with Melissa was Tuesday."

"What'd she say?"

"She telephoned and asked if she could stay with me for a few days. Said something was bothering her. Something had been bothering her for a long time. Something from her childhood. I told her of course she could stay. She's been up before, don't you know."

"Has she? When was the last time?"

Mary Crowell mulled it over and her eyes grew distant. I shifted on the love seat. My trousers were wet all down the back from splashing through the rain in the parking lot.

"Maybe six months ago?" I suggested.

"Yes, about six months ago. How did you figure that?"

"She turns up missing every once in a while. Generally,

it's just a day or two at a time. I gather she was up here each of those times."

"I don't know when she was *missing*, as you call it. She's visited me a few times."

"Have you heard from her since this week's phone call?"

"No. Said she'd be up the next morning, which would have been Wednesday, but she never appeared. Greyhound, she said."

"And she didn't let on where she was phoning from?"

"Matter of fact, she did."

"Seattle?"

"Tacoma. Said she was calling from someplace in Tacoma. Why she'd be clean down there, I have no notion. Course, what do I know? I'm just old Auntie Mary. I don't rate much more than a nickel card every other year when they can afford one."

"She tell you why she wanted to stay with you?"

"Just that something from her childhood was bothering her."

"Nothing else?"

"Melissa isn't much of a conversationalist. I had the feeling somebody was waiting for her, the way she tried to rush-rush everything along. Said she'd bring Angel along. Asked would it be all right if they stayed a few days. I said it would. Even stocked some butter brickle ice cream for her. That was always her favorite when she was a little tyke. Used to come up and spend a week with me every summer. That was back when Harry was still alive . . ."

"Harry your husband?"

"Naw. Although we *were* going to get married. He was Angus's business partner, the brains of the company.

Things were swell in those days. Me and Harry. And Melissa coming up every summer." The old woman's voice grew sorrowful and her mind seemed to retreat to another dimension.

". . . till she got older," she said, snapping out of it, completing a sentence I hadn't heard the first half of. "It's still okay. You locate her, you tell her she can stay with her old aunty anytime she wants. Can bring her baby, too. I'm not anxious to have that piker husband of hers here, though."

"They tell me he's quite the poet."

"You listen to that claptrap? Poetry won't put that baby into shoes."

"I understand Melissa spent most of a summer up here while she was in high school. If she was in the habit of spending one week up here each season, why did she suddenly come up and stay most of the summer?"

"Who told you that?" she asked.

"Burton."

"Did Burton tell you *why* she spent the summer up here, Mr. Black?"

"I was hoping you would."

She glowered at me. She tapped the ends of her gnarled fingers together. It was apparent that I had wormed as much out of this old gal as she wanted me to worm.

I took a deep breath, rubbed a knuckle into my eye and said, "Angus Crowell is your older brother?" I was fishing.

She snapped up the bait. "Born ten years before I was. He left home for the navy when I was nine."

"And you don't get along."

"Never have. Don't make no bones about it. He's not

my kind of people. Neither is that wife of his," she stated, bluntly.

"In what way?"

"In every way. He was a mean kid and he turned into a shrewd, crafty adult. I don't like them kind. Used to torture little animals when we were children. Set fire to more than one cat in the neighborhood. Had a dog once almost walk away with his hand. Whatever Angus was up to, you can be sure that pooch had good cause."

"Angus took his granddaughter today. Took her by force. Kidnapped her, actually."

Mary Dawn Crowell had a tendency to tip forward when she spoke. This time she almost tumbled out of her chair. "Angel? Melissa let her father take Angel? I don't believe you."

"Melissa didn't have anything to do with it. She's still off somewhere. Angus took the baby from his son-in-law."

"I'll bet he just handed her over, too! That spineless . . ."

"Now, it wasn't Burton's fault. Your brother brought friends along. They overpowered him."

She tried to settle herself down. She was like a nervous chicken after the hound has been shooed out of the coop. "Melissa loves that child. I know that for a fact."

"I'm sure she does. Help me find her and we'll get the baby back."

Mary Dawn Crowell squirmed in her seat, crossed and uncrossed the bones she called legs and nibbled on her thin upper lip, sucking it into her mouth like a kid playing contortionist games. Finally she came to a decision.

"In her senior year of high school, Melissa came up here to have a baby. She was three months pregnant.

While she was here, she miscarried. I dunno, maybe it was the best thing. In September of that year, she enrolled at the University of Washington. She was a torn-up girl, Mr. Black. Something was awfully wrong in her life."

It was obvious from her teary eyes that she harbored a warm feeling for her niece, that she had mothered her and thought about her often.

"Do you know who the baby's father was?"

"Nary a hint."

"Burton?"

"Phooey. That was long before she met that stumble-bum. Matter of fact, I don't think she saw a lot of boys in her high school years."

"Did anybody know who the father was?"

"Nope. Melissa wasn't going to talk about it. She was so depressed and weepy that summer, I didn't dare broach the subject. Never had occasion to bring it up since."

"Why did she come up here? To you?"

"What are you getting at, Mr. Black?"

"Her parents are wealthy. I gather they could have sent her almost anywhere in the world. To a doctor in Sweden. A Swiss sanitarium. Anywhere."

Mary Crowell pursed her lips until her whole face was nothing but crow's-feet centering on her mouth. "Like a lot of other well-to-do people, Angus is a tin-plated cheapskate. Besides, Angus has developed an unbeliev-ably strict code . . . of behavior, not just for himself so much as for other people. Melissa was on the wrong side of that code. He was at the point of disowning her."

"What caused the rift between her and her father?"

"Morals. It's all morals. Melissa was a Sixties baby.

Angus is rooted in a past that we'll none of us ever see again. That's all. It's the old story. Every generation gets tangled up in the same dilemma. I remember one of my girlfriends ran off and became a flapper years ago. Her papa and brothers wanted to shoot her. Same thing."

Fooling with something inside her mouth, her tongue pushing around some unknown object, possibly dentures, Mary said, "Melissa is one of those girls who's so at odds with her folks that she lives her life with only one object in mind—to irritate them. Oh, she doesn't perceive her life that way, but that's precisely what she does.

"And the funny thing is, if you met Melissa, after a few minutes you wouldn't believe any of this. She's so quiet and shy and well-mannered. But there's an avenging angel buried somewhere deep inside, Mr. Black, trying to seize repayment for all those years of strife with her mother and father."

"She ever run away from home as a teenager?"

"Not that I know of. That wasn't her way. She was more adroit than that."

"How so?"

"She associated with the lower elements. Almost married a biker once. You know, one of those greasy chaps in leather pants on a Harvey Jonathon?"

"Harley Davidson."

"Whatever. I don't know how he did it, but Angus put the *kibosh* on that one."

"It wasn't anybody she still might be seeing?"

"Melissa is a married woman."

"Married women have been known to step out."

"I don't think so. One rumor had it that Angus paid him a small fortune to go off and join the army. Some members of the family told me he broke his neck in a helicopter accident shortly thereafter. I don't know if that's true or not."

"How old was Melissa when that happened?"

"Must have been a little past twenty."

"For two people who don't get along worth beans, their lives seem to stay intertwined."

"Kids are that way. Sometimes it seems like the more trouble a kid has with her folks the more ties she has to them," said Mary Dawn, gazing out the window at the rainy night.

"Miss Crowell?"

Slowly she came out of her rain-induced trance. "Call me Mary."

"Why don't you see your brother and urge him to give Angel back? Won't he listen to you?"

"Angus listen to me? Hmph."

I had the distinct feeling the old woman had skipped something in her tale, something vital. Mary was a raconteur, but she had been stifled by something I had said. Something I couldn't quite put my finger on. As a youth, her brother had tortured little animals. I wondered what sorts of games he had played at with little sisters.

It drizzled most of the way back to Seattle. I got stalled in a hazy mist in the U District. Forty-fifth was jammed with glowing brake lights, weary students in idling cars returning to the university after a weekend at home trying to finagle mom into doing the laundry.

He came out quickly when I pulled into the driveway, a pair of long, dark legs racing through my headlights. He sprinted across my backyard and vaulted over the tall back fence.

It was a man's stride. A tall, athletic man. I was sleepy and bushed. I had two choices. I could chase him without knowing what he had done, if anything, and without knowing whether he was armed. Or I could venture inside to see what he had been dallying at, if he'd even been inside. Perhaps I'd merely startled a casual prowler. I let him flee.

The back door stood wide open to the misty night.

In the living room, I found a picture hanging crookedly on one wall, slash marks across the face of it. He had been inside. He had begun ransacking the upstairs but hadn't completed the chore. The picture was ruined. Muddy, indistinguishable footprints were tracked across the kitchen linoleum. The door to the basement was partially open.

"Sweet Jesus, no," I said. "Kathy . . ."

6 I WAS NOT CONSCIOUS OF MOVING, BUT suddenly I was downstairs in Kathy's apartment.

Furniture was smashed and splintered, phonograph records cascaded across the floor, the contents of a closet dumped helter-skelter into the center of the room. Something thumped heavily in my throat.

For some oddball reason all four burner units on her electric range were switched on, glowing orange-hot and smelling menacingly of electricity. Picking my way through the flotsam, I clicked off the burners. Had the intruder been trying to set the house on fire?

It would take a solid week to clean up this hodgepodge. Her stereo and both speakers had been smashed to bits. Textbooks and school papers were strewn across the living room. But where was Kathy?

I booted the heaps of clothing in the center of the room, testing. No bodies. I searched the empty closet. Only a few shoes remained. There was only one other spot, the tiny bathroom.

She looked like something on the cover of *True Detective*. He had tied her hands over her head, tied them to the

45

shower rod and gagged her. She wore a leotard and tights such as a dancer would wear.

"Kathy?"

She moaned. Her eyes opened. They were frightened pools of violet. She was alive.

"It's okay," I said. "He took off across the back fence." She slumped forward like a swimmer finishing a race.

Untying her gag, I reached into the medicine cabinet and found a razor blade which I used to slash the knots at her wrists. She had been tied with her own nylons. Her arms didn't come down so much as they fell, flopped to her sides as if she'd been in that position longer than she could tolerate. After the first few moments of freedom, of shrugging and shaking to work the circulation back into her shoulders, she reached up limply to adjust the rips in her body suit. Clumsy hands had mutilated the suit in several strategic places.

I had to admit she was a cool one. I would have to add that to the list of her traits that I admired. Cool under fire.

She cleared her throat and spoke softly, too softly.

She spoke to me exactly the way she imagined an ex-cop wanted to be spoken to under these circumstances. "He had brown eyes. He wore a ski mask, so that was all I could see. He was tall, dressed all in black. A black turtleneck and black slacks. Not jeans, but slacks. He hit his head on the top of that doorway. He hit it hard. That's when he spoke. And it was the only thing he said."

Stepping into the doorway, I straightened my spine. My head just brushed the top. I was six-one.

"What did he say?" I asked.

" 'Muthefucka.' Just like that. 'Muthefucka.' I kept asking him what he wanted, but he wouldn't answer. He seemed to know exactly what he was doing."

"How long was he here?"

"It seemed like forever. What time is it?"

I glanced at my wristwatch. "Five to seven."

"I started my exercise routine at six forty-five. I was almost six minutes into it when I heard something upstairs. Gosh, I guess he was only here three or four minutes. It seemed like about a lifetime."

"It would."

"At first I thought it was you up there," Kathy said, softly. "Then there was this banging. It didn't sound quite right. And I didn't hear your truck. So I went up. I shouldn't have. He spotted me right away. I made a beeline for the basement door. I thought if I could lock it, I might be able to dive downstairs and get out the side door. But I didn't even get it locked. He grabbed me by the hair on the stairs, tied me up, and . . . oh, my God." Kathy had just stepped out of the bathroom to catch her first glimpse of the havoc.

"Looks like a giant egg beater ran amok," I said.

The cops who came to investigate and take our report were women. I didn't recognize either of them. They were sympathetic and sharp. Afterward, as they went out the front door, one of them spoke with empathy to Kathy. "Do you have a place to stay tonight?"

Kathy tilted her head up at me with only the glimmer of a smile and said, "I think so."

While the spaghetti sauce simmered, she trudged downstairs, changed her clothes, and tried to straighten up her apartment. It was funny. She had this prescience or ESP or whatever. She could see someone else's misfortune coming but not her own. I hadn't told Kathy about the business of the burners. Nor had I told the cops. I'd seen no point. One could only speculate on the reason, and speculation of that sort wasn't going to help Kathy sleep at night.

Working cops were hardened, caustic, and suspicious by nature. Elaborate theories eluded their easy grasp. If they believed me about the burners they would attribute it to something innocuous. People did not go around torturing other people. Not in Seattle. As a matter of fact, they had already chalked the whole incident up to a simple interrupted burglary. Maybe they were right. Maybe that's all there was to it.

First my dog. Then my house. But Kathy had interrupted him. The brute hadn't even been aware there was an apartment in the basement. Most people weren't. But instead of dispensing with her and going back to work on my place, which he could have easily done, he had set out to systematically decimate her apartment, too.

Late in the evening I was thinking pretty hard, visualizing those four glowing burners I'd seen on Kathy's electric range. A burner could manufacture a nasty burn. A mere touch would do it. If someone big and strong were to take a body part, someone else's body part, and force it down and hold it there, the pain would be excruciating. The injuries would be permanent, physically and mentally. Of course, it might have been intended merely as a threat, a scare tactic. Or maybe my imagination was running hog-wild. Maybe he was planning to cook four soups before he left.

"Why so glum?" said Kathy.

"Just thinking."

"Don't hurt yourself."

"It was lucky I got home when I did."

"Thomas?"

"Yeah."

"Is that a gun in your belt?"

I hoisted up my shirt tail so she could see the handle of a .45 automatic I had dug out of its hiding place. Normally, I kept all my guns concealed inside a secret compartment in a wall. I couldn't even remember the last time I'd burrowed into the cache and loaded one.

"I thought you didn't use guns anymore. I thought you had sworn them off."

There was no reply to that. I wasn't sure I could use the automatic. I wasn't even certain that I would remember the weapon in an emergency. Four years ago, I had been mustered out of the police department largely because of my antipathy toward guns. The official pension hearing had blamed it on a bum knee, but everyone knew my days as a gun toter were finished. Once, I had been as gung ho as the next rookie. I had been ranked third in the city in combat-style shooting, had practiced religiously twice a week.

When those baddies drew on me I was going to put dimes in their eyes. And then one day a baddie *did* draw on me.

He took a stolen Volvo and tried to crush me against the wall of a downtown alley with it. Geez, I was good. I nailed him in the kisser. The bullet puckered the windshield and blasted bits of glass and shredded lead into his face, wreaking incredible damage. He was fifteen.

Had he died instantly, I might not have felt it so keenly. But he didn't die instantly. He talked to me before he died. He said he was sorry. While the medic unit wailed in the distance, he wept through the blood and the glass and bits of face and told me to apologize to his mother for him: a promise I never kept, was incapable of keeping. And then he had the audacity to linger on through a seven-hour operation at Harborview, passing on only when the entire family had gathered in the hallway to confront me with their big brown, matching brother-sister-father-mother eyes.

I was exonerated. My partner and two civilians in an apartment building had all witnessed him trying to run me down. I was exonerated, but I was not guiltless. I replayed that ten-second episode a thousand times a day, calculating dozens of ways I could have stopped him without resorting to murder.

It was said that a lot of cops required counseling after a shooting. I had never reckoned myself as a candidate for a post-shooting counseling session and I shunned it. I told myself these feelings would pass in time. But they did not; they became more acute, more troublesome.

After a while, I stopped carrying the mandatory hide-out gun off-duty, but still I steered clear of the police psychologist. Then one day, on duty, I was forced to draw my pistol on a wife-beater.

It was a messy business to begin with, but it became messier when my gun arm began wagging and he could see that I was scared. And I was. Not of him. But of shooting him. I didn't ever want to shoot another human again.

Fifteen hundred hours of combat training on the police range went down the tube.

I could have let it go and pretended everything was hunky-dory, put in for a desk job or a sleepy-hollow beat, but I couldn't leave it at that. I squawked. My career was a crushed dream and I no longer wanted anything to do with it. I had to be the best or I had to be nothing at all. I squawked and they mustered me out and called the reason a bum knee. They were generous.

Now I was a PI. A peeper. Now I took pictures through windows, tailed philandering husbands who were plugging bottle-blondes, searched for runaway teenagers, and was always first to hit the dirt when the lights blinked. Who the hell wanted to be chief anyway?

Besides, I had come to like snooping on people. It was fun. Sure, I was a voyeur. So was anyone who ever watched Doris Day mug with Rock Hudson, or gawked at Bill Holden kissing Kim Novak. We're all voyeurs and life is a picnic. People have little boxes in their living rooms and they sit in front of the boxes six or eight hours a night and goggle at other people living their lives. It's called television by some. Me, I call it voyeurism.

"You were very brave tonight, Kathy," I said. "I mean that. I admired you."

She had thrown on some sort of ethnic-looking robe for supper. It extended all the way to the floor and flowed gracefully around her body. Her hair was long and loose and freshly combed. She looked good. In fact, the only physical marks left by her ordeal were a set of rather measly scrape marks on her wrists and a red cheek where he had cuffed her.

When she spoke, her voice was fogged with emotion, and I had the feeling she was about to burst into tears. "I guess the dollar damage downstairs isn't as bad as I thought at first. Under two thousand." Noticing where my eyes rested, she rubbed her cheek and avoided my gaze as she continued. "Mainly the stereo and the television. And some records. How was it up here?"

"You stopped him before he got out of first gear. He got those two pictures and the lock on the back door. And of course, the basement door. I'll fix the doors in the morning."

"Who was he? What did he want? Thomas, do you know?"

I told her I had no idea, although I had a dozen grue-some ideas. If I'd arrived twenty minutes later it would have been a different story, a story some newspaper writer would be pounding out at this very minute. *Co-ed Tortured and Killed by Intruder.*

Kathy stepped close to me, laid her head gently against my chest and clasped her arms tightly around my waist. "Can I sleep with you tonight?" She sounded desperate.

"Sure."

"No. I mean with you. In your bed."

Her strong arms pulled against me, generating an easy feel for all her contours. "I had it in mind all along."

We slept with the .45 under a book on the nightstand beside the bed. The book was a Doubleday. The gun was a Colt. Kathy was a gem.

She hauled a down comforter up from her apartment and curled into a catlike ball on top of my covers. I didn't know precisely what she had in mind, but I could sense that she was amenable to almost any move I made.

When I kissed her forehead she smiled slightly, and when I kissed her lips she kissed back for as long as I did.

But there was a certain temperance to the exchange, a certain chaste lack of absolute passion that somehow made me angry. She was using me, and maybe I was using her, and using was not what I wanted my life to be about. I decided, amenable or not, she would be better off with a comforter rather than with me on top of her.

Before she dozed off, Kathy ran a warm hand across my face and said, "You awake, chum?"

I grunted. I was more awake than her. The thought had

occurred to me that the prowler might backtrack and try to finish the job.

"I was thinking about it today. I *did* tell Angus Crowell your name. Remember when you asked me about that? I saw him Friday morning at his office in south Seattle. He works for Taltro Incorporated. He was a real peach. I only saw him for a few moments, but I do remember telling him your name. Why?"

"Let's go to sleep."

"I just want to know how you're doing on this case."

"Yeah, maybe it was important. It's possible he was so upset about somebody butting in on what he considered his own business that he came here Saturday night and killed my dog as a warning. Or had someone do it. It's possible, but it sounds goofy, even to me."

"Or he might have paid someone to break in here for the same reason. To warn you off?"

"That's what I was thinking."

"Thomas?"

"Go to sleep."

"Isn't that a little farfetched?"

"Yeah, it is."

"I think the dog and the burglar are coincidental. Sometimes these things just happen, you know?"

"I know."

"I saw a body. Some bones, that is, in a pit. And a little girl was there, crying."

"Is this your vision?"

"Yes."

"Go on."

"There was a terrified little girl. And some bones at the bottom of this pit."

"Who was the girl? Angel?"

"I don't know. Angel. Or maybe Melissa. You have to find her. There is something dangerous going on, something involving Melissa. I know it. Do you believe me, Thomas?"

"I believe you."

"What do you think it could be about?"

"Sleep. Go to sleep." Outside I could hear the wind riling up the night. We both drifted off.

I awoke bolt upright, the .45 in my fist. It was cocked and the safety had been thumbed off. I was pointing it at the window. It was a quarter to four in the morning. In my sleep, I thought I had heard something chafing the windowpane. There it was again. A bush swayed against the pane to the tune of the wind. If only it had been a face in a ski mask, I could have let fly. I could have fired. I think I could have.

My body was bathed in a cold sweat, and I knew it would be a good half hour before I would saw any more zzz's.

Quietly, I uncocked the automatic and snicked the safety on, sliding it back under the Doubleday. Outside, roly-poly clouds scudded across a low sliver of a moon. A thin chalky light fissured through the bush at the window and marbled the bedroom with light.

I brushed a hand across Kathy's hair. It was thick, almost wiry.

She was breathing heavily, her mouth slack. She stirred and one of her feet poked out from beneath her homemade comforter. She had stitched it herself. She was interested in all the old-fashioned arts, adept at most of them, and gathered new hobbies into her fold every year. She even had a loom.

For a long while I lay awake on one elbow and watched

her sleep. In the moonlight, her oval face took on an almost boyish grace, an innocence. There was a chameleon quality about her. People she knew could bump into her in the street and not recognize her. It wasn't only her costumes and lavish collection of historical clothing, it was her. It was difficult to describe. She had a smooth, oval face and she could make it up a hundred different ways. Beautiful. Silly. Plain. The vamp. She tried them all.

It took me an hour to get back to sleep. It was the second time in my life I had slept all night with Kathy. We had never made love.

7 MINDLESSLY, I MENDED THE TWO DOORS the next morning, first the back door, which had merely been rifled, and then the door which led to the basement. It had been nearly ripped off its hinges. Jagged splinters of bare wood hung from the frame and reminded me of the hideous reality of yesterday's events. When the case was finished I would replace them both.

Kathy had woken up sprawled across me, had stretched hard like a cat, grinned, and said, "You're a sweetheart."

"Oh, pooh. I thought I was macho. At least quasi-macho."

"Didn't he used to ring bells?"

"You called me Sam Spade the other day."

"That was before I found out you were a puppy-dog."

She got off to her first class in a 1930s formal gown covered with a long fur coat she'd picked up cheap at an auction. At ten, she had an appointment with one of her law professors who owed her a favor. They were going to request an immediate injunction to return Angel to her father. I wondered if Kathy was planning to change clothes before she went downtown.

In the cold light of day, the .45 looked ridiculous, resembling something archaic from a long-forgotten war, an artifact some dumbfounded farmer had plowed up and turned in to the government. Ejecting the clip, I forced out the round in the chamber and returned the whole business behind the sliding, secret panel of my closet.

I had some phone calls to make, but I didn't want to make them from my home phone. I had spotted a suspicious coffee-colored van parked across the street. Perhaps I was getting paranoid, but I strapped on a knapsack and wheeled my ten-speed out through the spongy grass in the backyard to the alley. It didn't join my front driveway, so some yokel tailing me wouldn't be expecting it.

At the alley, I stopped, cleaned out my cycling cleats using a key, then rolled away. Portions of the sky were blue, although the roads were still damp and oily. If my luck held, I wouldn't get wet.

After tooling through the neighborhood streets until I was certain nobody was trailing along behind, I pedaled a mile through the thick of the University District to a three-story white house on Fifteenth.

Smithers had mustered in with me fourteen years ago. He had always been at the bottom of the police academy class while I was at the top, but somehow we had forged a bond of friendship. A year earlier, he had divorced a woman who weighed one hundred pounds more than he did, and now he was bouncing around in a barn of a house all by himself. Doreen had taken night classes in Spanish, and the Spanish professor had taken night classes in Doreen. It seemed like every couple I knew was splitting up.

Chubby-cheeked, fat, jolly, and perfectly contented that

way, Smithers was impossible to envision in a police uniform unless you had seen it. He wore his Sam Browne belt wrenched around so that the service pistol was almost in back, as if some prankster had attached it when he wasn't looking. He worked from eight at night till four in the morning, so he was usually around when I needed him.

"Don't tell me," said Smithers, raising a pudgy pink hand as he swung the door open. "You need me to call in some numbers."

Wheeling my Miyata into his entranceway, I unlaced, then heeled off my cleated cycling shoes. "Sorry I only get over here on business. But let's be thankful for that, otherwise we might never see each other."

Smithers chuckled and closed the front door. He had been tottering around in slippers and a bathrobe, balancing a mug of coffee. It was a curious house, all hardwood floors, no rugs and little furniture. Doreen had pirated it all when she absconded with the professor.

"Coffee?"

"No thanks." I was peering out his front window at the street, one last look-see, wondering if I had been followed. Maybe I *was* getting paranoid.

"You look grim. Somebody tailing you?"

"Last night a guy busted into my place. You remember Kathy?"

"The gal who wears the funny clothes?"

"That's her. Somebody busted into my place and Kathy interrupted him. He tied her to the shower rod. She's okay, but I think he had some unwholesome plans for her."

"What scared him off?"

"I did. I got home at just the right minute and spooked him."

"You know who it was?"

"He wore a ski mask."

"How about prints or . . ."

"The guy was a pro. Or he acted like one. Dressed all in dark. Cotton work gloves. Didn't even say anything."

"But you have an idea?"

"Ever hear of a guy named Holder? A big fella? A little on the mean side?"

"Holder? Holder?" Smithers sipped steaming coffee from a mug and tapped a fingernail against his stubby front teeth. "Holder." Tap. Tap. Tap. "I know I've heard that name."

"A tall guy. Black and Mexican mixed, maybe. Or Indian. For some reason, I get the feeling he was foreign-born."

"Julius Caesar Holder!" exclaimed Smithers. Tap. Tap. Tap. "Yeah, he had some trouble with the dicks downtown a few months back. I never paid much attention to it. They weren't happy with him."

"Can you find out about him for me?"

"Yeah. Sure."

"Also, this license number. Holder was driving the car yesterday. It's probably registered to him, but I want to make certain. Then there's this phone call. I need some records from the phone company. Can you get them for me?"

"Geez, I dunno."

"It's not going to court or anything. A woman I'm tracking made a phone call to Bellingham Tuesday night around nine o'clock. I believe she phoned from Tacoma. I'd like to find out for sure."

"Don't want much, do ya?" chided Smithers.

"This is serious business," I said, grinning.

Smithers slurped coffee and sucked striped candies while he made the calls. It didn't take long. When cops start running errands for each other, things flow along pretty smoothly.

The tan sedan Holder had driven Sunday morning was leased by Penworthy Investigations, Incorporated, leased from a local car dealership. Two more calls produced this nugget: Penworthy contracted security work to Taltro Incorporated, the same company Angus Crowell worked for.

On Tuesday evening, Mary Dawn Crowell's phone number in Bellingham had indeed received an incoming call from Tacoma. Melissa had phoned collect, otherwise we never would have found out where she had been. She had the loot for a bus ticket but not for a phone call. Somebody on the other end of the line made a computer hookup and told Smithers it had originated at a pay phone on Pacific Avenue. Melissa and her aunt had gabbed a little less than one minute.

I recognized the address of the pay phone. It was a few blocks from the Greyhound station in Tacoma. Great. A pay phone and a leased car. People were covering things like cats in the garden.

While he still had them on the phone, I asked Smithers to ask his contact to trace the number in the ad Kathy had showed me. I had called the number earlier in the morning, reached a recorded message and hung up. It turned out to be a phone line in the Taltro complex in Georgetown. Everything was ending up at Taltro.

On a hunch, Smithers phoned the dicks downtown and inquired about Julius Caesar Holder. Furrows broke across the smooth lines of his brow and he grew somber, almost gloomy as he listened.

When he hung up, he swiveled toward me and said, "The guy used to be a boxer. He's trouble. He killed a guy in the ring. A private eye down in San Diego crossed swords with him a coupla years back and hasn't been heard from since. No body. No traces. No nothin'. The snooper's widow stirred some politicians up and accused Holder, but nothing ever came of it. I would stay away from that guy."

"Does he always carry a piece?"

"They didn't say anything about that."

"Get an address on him?"

"He moves around a lot. He got in an argument with some woman in Chinatown a few months back. Slapped her silly. A couple of off-duty dicks stepped in and he knocked 'em both through a plate glass window. The boys were a little on the drunk-and-rowdy side, so it was hard to build a case on Holder. I guess he's always had woman trouble. They say he's married and divorced the same woman five or six times. Cuckoo."

"That sucker is almost as mean as I am." Smithers exploded into laughter.

"Met a great gal," said Smithers, walking me to the door. "I found this place that's just incredible for meeting real women."

"A club or something?"

"It's called Overeaters Anonymous."

He was serious. I guess if he was hunting for the reincarnation of his ex-wife, that was the place to hunt. It was my turn to laugh, but I did it after Smithers had closed the door.

It took ten minutes to cycle to the Hopewell Clinic.

Burgling the Hopewell would best be done during the next nuclear war. It squatted on one of the busiest blocks on Capitol Hill. Across the street stood a gay bar, open and overflowing with noisy crowds until all hours. Behind the clinic was a well-lit parking lot, and fronting the lot, with a clear view of the backside of the clinic, stood a four-story apartment house. Cater-cornered from the clinic was a bustling all-night grocery store.

On its own, the clinic posed no problems. A converted mansion, it was splintered into offices and meeting areas. I could have jimmied a window in a minute. The hitch was, I would have to be invisible to pull it off. Perhaps if I suited up in a uniform, a police uniform . . . I'd used the ploy before, but somehow I wasn't that desperate. Not yet.

I got home at one, soaked to the skin from the rain. The coffee-colored van was still slotted across the street, but it had been moved several parking spaces farther north. It was impossible to see through the dark windshield. I dragged out a pair of battered Bushnell's, focused them, jotted down the plate number, and phoned it to Smithers. Twenty minutes later, Smithers returned my call and advised me that it belonged to one of my neighbors, a guy who lived six houses down. I wondered why I had never noticed it before.

I began simmering a stew, fooled with the weights and a jump rope in the spare bedroom for an hour, skimmed the afternoon paper and then dipped into a piping-hot tub. On cue, the back door opened. I could tell who it was by the footsteps. I had just gotten the .45 hidden under a towel when she came around the corner and sat on the throne, sorting her rain-soaked mail.

"You botched the stew," said Kathy, without looking at me. "The meat's burned."

She had changed her clothes. She wore a pantsuit, a frilly white blouse and a black string bow tie. She looked very much the way I expected a lady lawyer to look.

When I had arranged the washcloth in a satisfactory formation, I spoke. "How'd it go downtown? You guys get an injunction?"

"We didn't get anything." She looked up and frowned when she noticed the washcloth. Pulled back into a severe bun, her hair glistened like a lump of shiny wet coal.

"What do you mean?"

"Burton chickened out. He's afraid of his father-in-law. He thinks Angus will run off to Brazil and take Angel if he makes any legal moves." Kathy shook her head and scanned the rest of her mail.

"That's foolish."

"I know. But he's such a loving man, it's hard to get ticked off at him."

"There's a difference," I said, "between being loving and being a doormat."

"What'd you find out about Melissa?"

"That she phoned her aunt last Tuesday and was expecting to be in Bellingham Wednesday morning with her daughter."

"With Angel?"

"That's what she told her aunt. She phoned from Tacoma. She know anybody in Tacoma?"

Kathy hummed and thought about it. "Not that I can recall."

"She still might turn up on her own."

"I noticed tonight's paper on the table. Read it yet?"

"The reward was there again. Same wording and phone number as before."

"Maybe we should dial it and see who answers."

"It's a recording. Leave your name and number and they'll get back to you. The phone is in the Taltro building downtown."

"It must be Melissa's father."

"Yeah. I didn't see any point in leaving a number. It would be awfully hard to worm information out of someone on the phone. Besides, the guy is obviously looking for her himself."

"Oh, Thomas. I want you to talk to her father and see if you can get him to give Angel back. Would you do that for me? Burton's so pathetic without her. He's cleaned up the whole house and he's dragged out a collection of her toys and spread them across the living room as if she's been playing with them. It's pathetic."

Reviewing the one snatch I'd seen of Angus Crowell, commandeering the steering wheel of his Cadillac as if it were a chariot from hell, I deliberated. I said, "You think he'll listen to me?"

Kathy pursed her lips. "Can't you try?"

"Sure. If you bop over to the Hopewell Clinic with me."

"The what?"

"The Hopewell. On Capitol Hill. Melissa wrote a check to the joint a couple of weeks back. They do cut-rate counseling and psychiatric work for the downtrodden. I thought you and I could go in and be downtrodden."

"Us?"

"All I want is a quick peek into their files."

Kathy clucked her tongue and looked at me reprovingly. "Thomas! How can you be like that?"

"You want to find Melissa? Tell you what. I know she might be in Tacoma. What do you say we drive down and start knocking on doors with a Polaroid of her? That might take about five years, providing we start within the hour and brown-bag all our meals."

"We could tell them who we are."

"No social worker or psychologist is going to spill anything to a detective. Or to anybody."

She sighed, squinted at my carefully arranged washcloth, and chewed her lips as she decided. "Do we dress up for this?"

"I do," I said.

8 SHE DRESSED LIKE A WHORE. IT WAS
funny and ridiculous and interesting all at
the same time. She wore tall, shiny, black leather boots
and Levi's so tight I doubted she could sit in them. Over
her blouse, she wore an open, waist-length fur coat. It
had taken a passel of dead rabbits to make it. The perfect
chippy.

Oh, we were going to stop traffic tonight. Kathy's
teased hair ballooned around her head like an enormous
black helmet. She was out of makeup downstairs, she had
to be; it was all daubed onto her face. Her cheeks were
tinted ruby, scarlet, and a tinge of cinnamon, her eyelids
heavily white, spattered in indigo. Her eyelashes were
bat wings. She was simply not recognizable as Kathy
Birchfield.

I wore a T-shirt and a pair of dirty jeans reserved
exclusively for working on my truck. She made me take
a rakish-looking golf cap she had surprised me with last
Christmas. To cut the wind, I threw on a worn-out leather
air force flight jacket.

While Kathy buffed her nose and played with her hair
in the rearview mirror, I tilted the seat forward and
stashed my loaded .45 into the space between the gas

tank and the seat springs. In all probability, I would not use the pistol, but I wanted it handy.

First we drove by the Nadisky household in Ballard. Kathy wanted me to speak to Burton, talk him into standing up for his rights. The house was dark and no one answered the door. Burton was undoubtedly down at the public library brushing up on his Emily Dickinson. I said as much.

"Give the kid a break," urged Kathy, popping a wad of bubble gum. "We can't *all* be brave, hey Cisco?"

"Hey, Pancho."

The Hopewell was closing for the day when we strode up the front steps together. An old woman wearing a bitter face crossed our path in the doorway, muttering to herself. She looked at my flight jacket disgustedly and said, "You merchant marines are all alike. Sailors!"

The hallway was bare wood and gritty, grime tracked in from a day of the downtrodden. The plaster on the walls was cracked. One window was chipped and scarred.

"I'm afraid we're closing for the day," said a woman at the end of the hallway, as she stabbed a key into a door. She wore enormous tortoiseshell glasses. Her arms were burdened with files, folders, papers, and books. She maneuvered unsnapped galoshes like snowshoes.

"We sure need your help," said Kathy, enunciating around her wad of bubble gum. "My husband here don't know who he is. And when he does know who he is he thinks he's someone else, if ya know what I mean."

"We're closing for the night. I'll give you one of our cards."

"I mean, he's got like three, four, six different people inside him. Really. Right now he's a bum named Joe

Blooey. I hadda haul him away from the dumpster at
Safeway. I mean . . ." She snapped the gum deftly inside
her mouth. "Can ya help him? He thought he was a jet
pilot two days ago. They didn't stop him till he taxied a
747 right out onto the runway at Sea-Tac. I wouldn't be
so worried, but sometimes he thinks he's like that Ted
Bundy, you know, the mass murderer? Buries gals up in
the mountains? Oh, don't worry. He ain't dangerous
now. Now he's Joe Blooey. Now he's so stupid he hardly
knows what we're saying."

I grinned moronically.

The woman in the tortoiseshells squinted at me, shoved
her glasses back up onto her nose, and unlocked the door
she had just locked. Switching on the yellowish lights,
she ushered us in and bade us sit together on a ram-
shackle sofa.

"My name is Ms. Gunther," she said, primly. "I'm a
psychologist. I work here at the clinic two days a week."
She eyeballed me. I grinned my best Jack Nicholson grin,
not caring if a trail of saliva snaked down my chin.

Her gray eyes radiated visions of treatises, newspaper
articles, magazine spreads, a book, and perhaps movie
rights. Perhaps, one day, her own syndicated column.
"How do you know he has different personalities?"

"'Cause I seen him change," said Kathy. "He changes
three, four times a day. His daddy used to beat on him.
That's what started it, I guess. He used to get these
headaches. Then one day he thinks he's this Dr. Richards,
a gynecologist. I come home and he's got some woman
in these stirrup things."

Ms. Gunther frantically grabbed a stenographer's pad
and a pen out of a desk drawer. "What are your names?"

"Ixnay," said Kathy, masticating her wad of chicle loudly.

"Pardon me?"

"Ixnay on the amesnay." She jabbed her thumb in my direction. She peeled off the wrapper on another block of bubble gum and popped it into my mouth, a mother feeding her child. "Maybe we better do some of this amenay usinessbay omewhereelsesay? Huh? Some people get real upsetnay about it."

"Oh," said Ms. Gunther, eyeing me warily, as if I might metamorphose into a full-blown madman in front of her. "Sure. Where would you like to . . ."

"Maybe if we left him here and went into another room? I hate to move him once he's settled this way. Sometimes it starts him acting up."

"Acting up?"

"That Undybay person is hard to control."

"Oh."

At the door, Ms. Gunther peered back at me and paused. "It's okay," said Kathy. "Long as nothing disturbs him, he'll sit that way for hours."

"Fascinating," Ms. Gunther remarked. "Absolutely fascinating."

As far as I could ascertain, only the three of us were left in the building. Kathy's loud footsteps were clearly audible as they walked down the hallway. I was counting on those loud boots of hers to signal the alarm when they came back.

Two gray, paint-chipped file cabinets stood behind the desk in the corner. The first cabinet was unlocked and didn't contain much of interest, primarily pamphlets and magazine reprints categorized according to topics. The indexed titles read like rock albums. Grief. Weight Loss. Depression. Holiday Blues.

I wasn't much good at locks and the second cabinet was a bitch to pick. The top two drawers belonged to a Dr. Weaver. The bottom two to a number of others, including Ms. Gunther. I flipped through the folders as quickly as I could, scanning hundreds of names. "Nadisky" did not appear.

I blew almost three minutes in an adjoining room, picking the lock on a file cabinet. Nothing but financial information and bookkeeping records.

It wasn't until I had roosted on the couch again to wait for Kathy and the psychologist, that it occurred to me to riffle through the stacks of papers and files Ms. Gunther had abandoned on the desk top.

This was it. El Dorado! The third file was a manila folder labeled "Nadisky." I tried to speed-read it, but the process was aggravating. She had only sketched her thoughts. To make matters worse, Ms. Gunther's penmanship could have been improved by a bird fresh from an ink well.

I read snatches:

"Neither partner facing up to the responsibilities of their commitment. She maintains a tremendous emotional conflict with her father and father figures in general. Must resolve the paternal struggle, or her life will grind to a halt. Thought of father paralyzes her thinking and action. She must uncover the childhood trauma. Expose it to the light. Hypnosis? However, I find it difficult to believe someone could be married for forty-two months and only have had sexual relations three times. Are they fabricating?"

It took me a moment to realize I was being watched.

Ms. Gunther and Kathy stood frozen in the doorway, staring at me. I slammed the folder shut and quickly arranged it back in the stack. What was going on? Things like that rarely happened to me. I *never* got caught.

"That's Neil," said Kathy, wincing. "I told ya about him. Anything for a good time."

"Howdy, ma'am," I said, in a slow drawl. "I don't believe we've met."

Ms. Gunther glanced from Kathy to me, to the file folders, and then back to Kathy. I said, "We're goin' out dancing a little later. Care to boogy? I'm sure we can find a man for a cute little gal like you."

Ms. Gunther blushed, then gathered up her reserves and said, "What were you doing? You were reading my reports."

"No ma'am. Fact is, I can't read a lick. Left school in second grade to work on my daddy's horse ranch. Tell you the truth, I was looking for some snow. Know what I mean? I got the spoon but ain't got no sugar."

When she gave Kathy a quizzical look, Kathy nodded and smiled tightly. We were millimeters from being exposed. "I didn't think he'd change on us. Usually it takes some outside thing, you know?"

"Fascinating," said Ms. Gunther. "Why don't you both sit down? I'll get my tape recorder. We'll put some of this on tape."

"Sorry, ma'am," I said, moving to the doorway where I took Kathy's arm. "Me and this filly has got some mighty serious drinking and hoofing to do tonight. You care to come?" My eyebrows twittered and I gave her my best corn-pone leer.

After seriously considering the scientific aspects of such a liaison, the research grant, the article in *Psychology*

Today, an appearance with Merv, maybe even one with Johnny, Ms. Gunther shook her head, churning her page-boy. "I want you both to come back. Do you understand? I want you both to come back!"

"If I can get him back," said Kathy over her shoulder as I guided her down the dim corridor toward the front door. "The only time he does what I say is when he's Joe Blooey."

"Who the hell is this Joe Blooey you keep blabbing about?" I said loudly. "You been steppin' out on me?"

Ms. Gunther muttered, "Fascinating."

Outside in the truck, Kathy got snippy, a reaction from the pressure and from being forced to lie. "You find out anything, Buster?"

"Not much. Maybe we should talk to Burton. I wonder where he could be."

"Was I all right?" Kathy asked, her tone changing abruptly.

"Are you kidding me? You were fabulous. I've never seen anything like it. You're a better liar than I am."

"Thanks," she said. "I think."

"You were great."

"Now what? The Crowell place?"

"I don't know what good it will do, but here we go."

No matter how long I live in Seattle, I am constantly amazed at the variety of the city. The Crowells resided on the waterfront in West Seattle. It took five minutes and a good map to pinpoint the precise location. It took another twenty minutes of prowling around on pitch black, rain-spattered streets before we found it.

Melissa's parents lived on a numbered street smack dab on the water. The road came down off a hill, dropping a good hundred and fifty feet in elevation as it approached the select community. We descended through three-quarters of a mile of virgin woods inside the city limits before we found it. The dead-end road was narrow and pitted, mired in spots, partially blocked by small mud slides, doubling back upon itself twice.

We discovered five houses on the beach. Guard dogs yapped at our headlights. One streetlight wobbled on a pole in the wind. None of the houses looked as if they could even be discussed for less than a million.

Angus Crowell's place was a sprawling stucco ranch-style house, baroque iron grillwork barring all the street-side windows and doorways. What was he expecting? The Nez Percé had been peaceful for more than a century. The grillwork alone undoubtedly cost more than my entire house.

My best guess was that the nearest house, except for the four others on the beach, was about half a mile away, through the moss-covered trees and up the slimy hill.

The last storm off the sound had topped a maple at the end of the block. Some industrious soul had chainsawed it into pieces and carted most of it away.

"Maybe I'll just sit in the truck," volunteered Kathy, peering out at the dark house as she listened to the throaty guard dogs up the street. "Besides, I look like a strumpet."

"Yes," I said. "But your heart is pure gold."

I wheeled the truck around so that it was pointed toward civilization and parked it in front of a single-story garage sixty feet long. I could see the roofs of at least three autos inside. A Mercedes two-seater. The Cadillac we'd almost collided with on Sunday. A new Bronco.

"What do you want me to say to this bozo?"

"First of all, don't call him a bozo," warned Kathy.

"Don't antagonize the man. Remember, this is on behalf of Burton and Angel. We want them back together. Okay? Just ask him if he'll return his granddaughter. And if he won't, ask him under what circumstances he would."

"Got it."

Before I traipsed up to the front door, I went over to the windows in the long garage and peeked inside. Crowell had collected five cars, a lawn tractor, several bicycles, a row of motorcycles, and a dune buggy. The man liked his toys. Through windows on the opposite side of the garage, I could see the marbled reflections from a lighted swimming pool.

At first, I took the stooped hag who swung open the door for a servant. It was only later that I realized it must have been Mrs. Crowell. In the army, they used to say shit rolls downhill. Mrs. Crowell was at the bottom of the hill and she knew it.

She said she would fetch her husband, and then she shuffled through the living room and ragged at the little girl, warning her of the dire consequences should she happen to spill her milk. She bossed with the sad vengeance of one who is rarely allowed the privilege.

"Not again, Angie! You've made too many messes today. That's my favorite flavor," she added, as an afterthought, when she saw the scowl on my face.

I sidled around the corner and spotted Angel Nadisky sitting dejectedly at an ornate table in front of a coloring book and a tall glass of milk, too tall and bulky for her little hands. A bowl of butter brickle ice cream was melting in front of her. Any fool could see she was about as happy as a spider in a jar.

The house was dead silent. No music. No TV. Not

even a parakeet I could teach a few quick curses to. Only one lonely little blonde Angel sitting at a table too tall for her and straining dutifully to crayon in a book she could barely reach.

I had to stifle an urge to run across the room and give her a hug. I could see it wasn't the thing to do. She was terrified of me. She was terrified of everything. Her face was molded into a mask of fright. I began to scout around the living room. That was me. Snoopy.

"Ooooooh," she said. "Ooooooooooooh."

When I looked, she was staring somberly at the tipped milk glass, at the growing puddle of whiteness. "Ooooooh. I'm gonna get it. I'm gonna get it. Oooooooooh."

I went over and said. "Tell you what, sweetheart. I'll clean this up and nobody ever has to know it happened. How's that?"

Angel shied away from me, evaluated the plan, both pudgy little hands on her cheeks, and then evaluated me. I found a towel inside the door of an ornate buffet and used it to mop up the spilled milk. I polished off the table top, righted the glass, and crammed the sopping towel into my flight jacket. Then I patted Angel on the head and winked. A tiny, cautious grin spread across her face.

I was entertaining the kid when Angus Crowell came in. He wore gym shorts and a Hawaiian shirt, a patina of sweat glistening on his brow. He had enough excess beef on him that a walk from the other end of the house would make him break into a sweat, though I sensed that he had been exercising.

"Do I know you?" he asked, in a voice that was gruff and authoritarian. A look of suspicion blackened his thick features. He brooked no guff. His broken, stooped wife bespoke that.

"My name is Black."

"So?"

"I'm here to talk about your granddaughter."

Without taking his hard brown eyes off me, Angus Crowell shouted for his wife. "Muriel! Get the hell in here!"

She came higgledy-piggledy, the original Edith Bunker, a damp dishrag dangling from her hands and a look of wrinkled concern on her face. "Muriel, why the hell did you let this bum in here?"

Glancing at me in sudden coerced disapproval, she said, "He looked like a nice young man, dear." She was past fifty, but her life was not her own. She wouldn't start living until her husband's body was under six feet of sod. I bet she was counting the days, scratching a wall somewhere with a rusty nail.

"Get Angie to her room! I've had enough of this shit!"

Angus was several inches taller than I was, outweighed my one-eighty by a good sixty or seventy pounds, and had the look of a man who had put in years of hard labor in his youth.

"I keep in shape," he said. "Got my own handball court here. Unless you want to see what sort of shape, you better hustle your ass out that front door, Mr. Thomas Black."

I hadn't told him my first name. The gray and reddish hairs on his eyebrows formed an interesting weave, tufted like that of an aggressive baboon. He was in his mid-sixties, I would guess, and imbued with the kingly air of a monarch who held court daily. Behind him, Mrs. Crowell scurried away, pulling her granddaughter by her arm. The frightened tot cast a sidelong look at me and smiled conspiratorially. At least I thought it was a smile.

"I'm sure you realize that this whole deal is on shaky ground," I said. "If the police or newspapers got ahold of this, you'd be forced to give up the child."

A large, hirsute paw came up and pointed a thick finger, like a gun barrel, at my face. He sighted down it, aiming it at my nose. I noticed a series of ancient, thickened scars on his hand and remembered his sister in Bellingham saying something about a run-in he'd had with a dog in his youth.

"Somebody calls the newspapers on this and I'll hold you personally responsible, Mr. Thomas Black. Got that?"

He wouldn't have gotten sore if I hadn't struck a nerve.

A jagged scar ran down his left leg as if it had been spilled, as if one could spill hurt. Another series of smaller serrations crisscrossed his skull near one temple. He was a man who lived life hard, and yet, he still bore that aura of a commander used to making people hop.

"You know as well as I do that the child belongs with her folks," I said.

"What folks? Her father sits around on his butt a year at a time and writes poetry. You call that folks? Her mother's a slut."

For a moment, I was taken aback by his viciousness. I should have expected something along those lines, but it came as a shock.

"You know where your daughter is?"

"The bitch can be roasting in hell for all I care."

I began moving slowly toward the front door. "We saw your ad in the *Times*. You want her back. I'm looking for her, too. Why don't we get together? Pool our resources."

"Don't call me a liar," he said, threateningly.

"I'm not calling anybody anything. You're the one who's putting a tag on it. I only want to find her."

He guffawed. It was loud and brash and phoney as a three-dollar bill. It was a practiced laugh he probably used on somebody new each day.

"I traced the phone number in the ad to Taltro," I said. "It's your ad all right. A two-thousand-dollar reward."

"Now I am getting mad! Who the hell do you think you are?"

"It must be lonely for a kid, raised down in this gully."

"What the hell you doin', sneaking around my life, boy? You're going to be sorrier'n a rat's ass."

I didn't reply. Turning around, I shambled to the front door and opened it.

"Hell, boy. I could buy your life for the price of one of my wristwatches. You hear me? I've got sixteen watches. You listening careful, boy?"

"Stick it up your ass."

Voice booming, he flailed his arms, jounced the meat on his huge torso in a mad dance and pretended to chase me out the front door. I proceeded at my own pace and noticed off-handedly that he did not catch me, though he easily could have. He slammed the door like a cannon shot, warning me I would never forget this night. No wonder Melissa was screwed up.

Damn, maybe I wouldn't forget this night. When I climbed into the cab of the truck it was empty. Kathy had vanished.

9

PEERING DOWN THE DARK STREET through the drizzle, it took me a minute to spot her. She had been skulking in a flower bed alongside the Crowell house.

"You want, we can get you a PI license," I said, as she scrambled into the moving truck.

She slammed the door. "You saw her? I looked through all the windows, but I couldn't see anything."

"I thought you didn't believe in snooping."

After making sure we weren't being tailed, I dropped Kathy off at one of her friend's for safekeeping and made her promise to dig up all the information on Angus Crowell that she could the next morning. I wanted to know why he had been so antagonistic toward me with so little provocation. I wanted to know how he knew my first name.

I wheeled the Ford back to Ballard and rapped on Burton Nadisky's dark front door. No reply. Out of whimsy, I twisted the doorknob. The door popped open. I went in. Nothing much had changed in the dark house. It smelled like the inside of an old coffeepot.

Burton was in the back, in the kitchen, asleep facedown on the table, a sheaf of papers splashed out in front of him. A rhyming dictionary was splayed open, its back broken. Groggy and disoriented, he woke up when he heard my footsteps on the crinkly linoleum.

"Oh," he grunted. "You?"

"Evening, Burton. I just came back from visiting your daughter. She's not happy."

"Angel? You saw Angel?"

"Yeah. And I met your in-laws. It was about as thrilling as watching a cat dig a hole. When are you going to get her back?"

He struggled up, went to the sink, elbowed some dishes aside and splashed cold water across his face several times. It had been a while since I'd watched another man do that. He turned around without toweling the water off and looked at me, droplets running off his cheeks and nose.

"I'm afraid of what Mr. Crowell might do. That's all. I'm afraid."

"Do you have a reason to be afraid? Has he threatened you?"

"Christ!" Burton shouted. "What do you want from me? He came here and had some goonybird knock the poop out of me. He took my daughter. What more do you want?"

"Maybe you're right," I said. "He threatened me a few minutes ago. Maybe you're right. Let me tell you what I've found."

"Melissa?"

"I'm on her trail, but I'm not very warm." Briefly, I gave him a rundown on Mary Dawn Crowell, how she had sheltered Melissa so many other times, how Melissa had phoned on Tuesday but never arrived.

"Did she sound okay?" Burton asked.

"Her aunt only spoke to her a minute."

"You mean all those times Melissa disappeared on me, all that worry . . . She was at her aunt's all those times?"

"As near as I can tell."

"God," said Burton, sponging some of the water off his face using his shirt sleeve. He plunked back down into the rickety kitchen chair, offering me one with torn upholstery. I remained standing.

"What's in Tacoma?"

"Why?"

"That's where your wife phoned her aunt from."

"Nothing."

"You sure?"

"Yeah. Nothing."

Burton looked up at me, his pale blue eyes blank and unresponsive. "Geez, Mr. Black. I've had a rough couple of days here. Would you mind if I crashed now? I've gotta get to bed."

"You don't want me to find your wife?"

"Yes, find her. But I'm bushed now. I can't talk anymore."

"Sure, Burton." I went out the front door without locking it.

The house of the snoopy neighbor across the street was dark, too, but I was convinced the almost phosphorescent light seeping through a crack in the living room curtains was a television. Somebody was doping on an electronic fix.

When he answered the door, it was plain to see he was potted already, and it was only half past seven. Though he was no older than me, he already had the florid face of a drunk. Wearing threadbare socks, rumpled trousers, and a dingy T-shirt, he invited me inside. He flopped onto a couch, stretching his legs out onto an ottoman.

Balancing a can of brew on his marshmallowy beer gut, he addressed me the way an overeager salesman might. "What can I do for you?"

"You know the Nadiskys across the street?"

"By the way," he said, grinning widely and extending a hand without jiggling the Rainier can on his belly, "my name is Iddins. Sid they call me, when they ain't callin' me other things." We shook hands.

"Thomas Black."

"The blonds across the street? That's their last name? I never knew it. I seen him. Her too. Even trotted my ass across the street one afternoon and fucked her." His grin ripped wider with each word. I had to pinch myself to be sure I'd heard correctly.

"Don't shake your noodle," he said. "She's a cute little thang, so I walked over there one afternoon, palavered with her for a few minutes, then took her into the bedroom and raised her skirts. Trouble was, the wife got onto it. She put the nix on my return ticket. But once was fine. She's a sweet-looking little thang but she ain't all that warm. Matter of fact, she got downright persnickety afterwards. Tried to pretend she hadn't cottoned to it."

"Did she?"

"Well . . . I've had more cooperative women."

Melissa was a woman who may have had sexual relations a mere handful of times with her own husband. Now this buffoon wanted me to believe he had gone across the street and seduced her in a trice? No matter how promiscuous she had been at other times in her life, I found the tale Sid Iddins told highly improbable.

"Sounds almost like rape," I said, voicing my thoughts.

He laughed quietly and put his eyes on the Monday night football game.

"Rape? Hell, you don't see no bars around me, do you?"

"Your wife around?"

"Helga's at work. Downtown at the titty palace. On Second?" Sid stared at me in the dim light, trying to gauge how his words affected me.

"She takes tickets, or what?" I asked, trying to be discreet. I was wasting my time.

"Hell, no. She peels. You know, like a banana. That's where I met her. Used to spend most of my free time down there. Asked her if I could take her home one night. When we got here, I tried to smooch, but she poked a .357 in my ribs. She's *all* woman, that gal. I gotta hand her that. 'Bout a week later I took her home again." His grin grew to mythic proportions. "I ain't never left since."

"She's been dancing a long while, then?"

"Oh, yeah. She likes the atmosphere. 'Sides, she's got lots of friends down there."

"She ever talk to the people across the street?"

"The blonds, you mean? I told you she put the nix on me and blondy. She went over there one day to duke it out with her. Didn't come back for one hell of a long time. Hell of a long time. Tell you the truth, I thought she'd killed blondy and was tryin' to dispose of the body." He laughed at that, grabbing the teetering beer can on his stomach so it wouldn't topple off. "Wouldn't that be funny? Have two women fightin' over Sidney Iddins?"

"A riot. You know where blondy is?"

He shook his head and sucked on the aluminum can. "Nope. Seen the grampa come Sunday morning and take the little one away, though. Helga talked to the guy about it later. They just sashayed right in and then sashayed right out with the kid. The guy's a ding-a-ling to let 'em do it."

"You think Helga might know where the wife is?"

"Fuck, I don't know what Helga knows. I don't keep tabs on her. Why don't you mosey down there and ask her? Or you're welcome to sit here and wait. She'll be back around two-thirty or three. Sit down. Have a brew."

"Later."

When I went outside, I could see Burton had lied to me. He hadn't gone directly to bed. His living room light was on, as if he were expecting someone. I waited outside for an hour and fifteen minutes, but nobody showed. And I hadn't seen any movement inside. He was probably asleep on the kitchen table again. Or maybe he had left while I was talking to Sidney.

It cost fifteen bucks to walk through the door of the converted theater. The place was murky and smelled of cigarettes and Pine Sol and booze. I found myself checking to see if anyone I knew had seen me going in. There was a bar in back and ten or twelve tables under a stage. A reedy-looking girl, naked from the waist up except for some pasties, bobbed to an old Three Dog Night tune. It was pitiful.

Eighteen patrons watched her, displaying varying degrees of interest.

"I gotta talk to Helga," I said to the bartender. He was half bald and looked too good for the joint, as if he were moonlighting from a job in a brokerage house.

"Helga?"

"Helga Iddins. I don't know what name she dances under. It's important."

He didn't even reply, just rubbed a beer stein with a grubby towel and shook his head. I took a deep breath and slid a dollar bill across the countertop. He glanced down at it and whined, "Are you kidding me?"

I replaced the one with a five, but that was a joke, too. He shook his head patiently, a tight, grim smirk planted on his kisser. It cost a sawbuck for him to reach under the counter and press a buzzer several times in some sort of code.

When Helga swaggered through a door at the end of the bar, a young buck at one of the tables, a navy boy from the look of his haircut and ill-fitting civvies, ogled her and said, "Nice hooters, baby." His three buddies giggled and slopped beer over their wrists and avoided Helga's hard eyes.

"Drop dead, asshole!"

She wore a velour bathrobe, black net stockings and heels, and apparently nothing else. Her chest quaked when she walked, and she folded her arms across herself to hold it still. The stockbroker tipped his head at me, and she stopped and said in a smoky voice, "Well?"

"I spoke to your husband."

"Not for long, I hope," said Helga Iddins. "That sort of activity destroys brain cells."

"I'm looking for Melissa Nadisky."

"Who?" The woman onstage was grinding toward her finale. Helga watched out of dispassionate professional curiosity. The three buddies of the navy guy whistled encouragement. The one she'd rebuked glowered at us mutely.

"The blonde woman who lives across the street from you. She's missing."

"So?"

"I'm a private detective. I'm looking for her."

Helga's entire manner altered. She twisted back toward me and tried to arrange the puffball of hair on her head. It was a soft, pleasant color, like dead grass in the middle of summer. "You're a detective?"

I flopped my I.D. out of my wallet, hoping the creep at the table would spot it and think it was a badge.

"Come in the back," she said, starting toward a door behind the bar. She led me down along a dark L-shaped corridor to a cubicle directly behind the stage. The muffled sounds of Three Dog Night rattled the roomful of mirrors. A washed-out brunette was scrunched in a corner breast-feeding a baby. She read from a psychology textbook. With her free hand she puffed on a cigarette. Cute. Suckle the baby with one hand and suck a Salem with the other.

"Hey, Margaret," Helga said. "This guy's a detective."

Margaret glanced up with bored eyes, covered up her breast with her cigarette hand and yawned. I grimaced and waved. It was nice to be famous.

"I don't go on for half an hour, so we got some time," Helga said, sitting before a mirror and brushing her hair slowly. She had never been beautiful, but I could see that up until about five years ago someone might have thought her alluring. Now she was spent, slack fat dragging at her chin. Either Sidney was being pickled in alcohol or he was six or eight years younger than his better half. I preferred the pickle theory. "Now what's this about the girl across the street?"

A *Woman's Day* was folded open in front of her chair. She'd been reading a page of recipes: holiday fruitcakes.

"Melissa," I said. "She's missing."

"Missing? She probably ran away from her hubby. Nothing abnormal about that. I'd do it myself, if I had somewhere to go."

"Somebody posted a two-thousand-dollar reward for information leading to her whereabouts."

"Two thousand?" She whistled. "Too bad I don't know where she is."

"Yeah, too bad. I understand you talked to Melissa?"

"Sidney went over and tried to get what he could. I didn't know what she was like. From across the street you can't tell nothin'. So I knew Sid had seen her and I went over with the express intention of breaking her face, know what I mean? Had some trouble with a girl here about six months ago and I broke *her* face. I can break a face if I have to."

"What happened between you and Melissa?"

"I could see right away Sid had taken advantage of her. Right away she starts bawling. Said she didn't want anything to do with Sid, but he grabbed her and she didn't know how to get rid of him. It was easy to see she was telling the truth. Boy, talk about a poor self-image. She thought she was the scum of the earth, her with a little girl and a husband who writes poetry. There I was, *me*, trying to cheer her up! She musta cried an hour. I did my best, but she really needed some sort of professional help. That's what I told her. I think she got it, too."

"The Hopewell Clinic?"

"How did you know? Yeah, I told her about that place. Margaret," she said, nodding her head toward the woman breast-feeding in the corner. "Margaret works there part-time for college credits. She's always tellin' us about the crazy palookas who come in."

"What else did Melissa say? She mention Tacoma, by any chance?"

"Naw." Helga Iddins raised her arms over her head, fiddling with her hair. The movement cracked open the front of her robe, revealing an interesting wrinkled cleft between her sagging breasts. "She did tell me about some guy named Romano who seemed to be giving her a lot of trouble."

"That his last name or his first?"

"Just Romano. Kind of a Latiny-looking guy. She used to be involved with him and now he won't let her alone. Like I said, Melissa had a hard time saying no. Christ, she was messed up. Tell you the truth, I wouldn't be surprised to hear she killed herself."

"You think that's a possibility?" I jammed my hands into my pockets and got a fistful of milk-soaked towel.

Staring at her own face in the mirror as if seeing it for the first time, Helga nodded and the whole business I was watching shook.

"You've seen this Romano character?"

"Sure. From across the street. He used to show up maybe once a month, once every other month. A real creepy guy. Old enough to be her father. He'd drive over and stay a couple of hours in the afternoon, if the husband wasn't home. I wisht she'd called me. I would have busted his chops."

"What'd he drive?"

"Nothin' much. It was an old pest control van. Acme? Admiral? Something like that. I can't really remember. I guess nobody ever told poor Melissa she didn't have to lay down and spread her legs for every Tom, Dick, and

Harry who wanted to see what it was like. She's such a smart little girl, too."

"She say what this Romano guy wanted with her?"

"She didn't have to. They had an affair once years ago, maybe when she was in college. Now he shows up. What do *you* think he wants?"

I had to stop and mull it over for a few minutes. Melissa had had sex with her husband only three times in almost four years, yet the neighbor across the street wanders over and jumps on her five minutes after they meet. And then some Latin roach-killer makes regular trips to her place to get his pencil sharpened. I wondered what dear Burton would think of all this if he knew. Burton the cuckold. I wondered if he knew.

"Think you could remember the name of the company on the side of the van?"

"I only remember it was a pest control company. After I found out who he was, I kept thinking how ironic. After all, he was the pest."

"When was the last time you saw the van in front of their place?"

"He didn't always come in a van. Sometimes he showed up in a real old Cadillac, all spruced up. They used to call them pimpmobiles. That's what he had last weekend. Not this past weekend, but the week before. I think it was Sunday, but it might have been Saturday. He didn't stay very long that time."

"You see him leave?"

"Sidney and me were having a little spat."

"I was wondering if he left alone."

"You mean maybe Melissa went with him? I couldn't tell you. I only seen him pull up. But that's an idea. Don't think I seen her since. Is that when she ran off?"

"Last weekend," I said.

"Maybe she went with him. Christ, people do dumb things."

"You wouldn't remember his license plate, would you?"

"You think if I had that kind of brain I'd be working here?"

"I guess not," I said, moving to the door.

"One thing, though."

"Shoot."

"It wasn't a Seattle plate. I remember that. The first letter was a *b*."

"Tacoma, Pierce County," I said.

"Yeah. You gonna stay for the show?"

"Not tonight."

"We could, uh, maybe have a drink after."

"I've got an appointment."

"Sure." She turned to the mirror as if I had never existed.

I reached the first set of doors in the main room before the navy kid jumped me. The auditorium was dark and they were projecting blue movies onto a hoary screen behind the stage. First a movie, then a dancer, then another movie. It was an endless cycle of sterling entertainment.

Two of his friends stood off to one side. I looked around in the darkness for a bouncer. Places like this always had them, ex-football players or karate freaks.

"Think you're pretty hot stuff," said the navy kid. As soon as he spoke, I could see he'd had a snootful. "Talkin' to the strippers. Mr. Cool."

I wasn't in the mood to get bounced around by someone who wasn't even old enough to recall Adlai

Stevenson. He smirked at his two pals, as if to say, "Doin' pretty good, huh, guys?" He wasn't as stuporous as you'd hope a drunk attacking you would be.

I could see he wasn't going to stop until I hit him or the bouncer broke his arm, and I couldn't see a bouncer anywhere. Probably sipping tea in the back room with a Harlequin romance.

"Oh, geez," I said, incredulously, glancing in the direction of the screen. "I didn't think that was possible."

When the navy kid wrenched his head around, I doubled up my right fist and gave him a stiff shot directly below the belt. He folded up, making a groaning sound the way a record played too slowly does. His body slapped the hard sticky floor with a thud. It made a sweet sound like a sack of sugar tumbling out of a grocery cart.

I gave his buddies a sloppy salute and left as they both bent over, searching for him in the darkness. I wasn't much of a boxer, but I could sucker punch with the best.

10

I PICKED UP KATHY AT HER friend's apartment. On the way home she hammered me with questions about Melissa, but I found it difficult to answer them. I told her about Romano. I was struggling to form an accurate mental image of the missing woman.

Her photo told me she was pretty. Her husband told me she was sensitive. Her neighbors told me she was weak and neurotic. Yet, her father told me she was a slut. Whatever she was, I didn't feel it was my duty to besmirch her reputation any further. But so far, I hadn't discovered anything that was going to do her reputation a hell of a lot of good. When I found her, if I found her, she could speak for herself.

I felt like a fool, but before I allowed Kathy in, I hauled the heavy .45 from behind the truck seat, pointed it and searched the house, upstairs and down. Still dressed in her strumpet costume, she had scrubbed her face and combed her hair. Even so, I didn't want to see her die in those clothes. They were fine for a lark but not for dying.

"Can I stay up here again?" she asked, in a small, meek voice.

"You scared?"

"Maybe I am. I don't want to find out. Not until we learn who that was in the mask."

"Fair enough. I'll sleep on the couch this time."

"Not on your life," she said. "I'm not going to kick you out of your own bed. Besides, I like that couch. I'll take the couch."

Her violet eyes bored into mine as if she were trying to read my mind. I wondered what she hoped to see. Sometimes I had the niggling suspicion Kathy and I avoided physical intimacy because we didn't want to sully a perfect friendship.

Before I slipped under the covers, I examined the Colt again, brooded about it for a long while, then dismantled the semi-automatic and put it back into its nook inside the closet wall. I'd shot only one human in my time and I very much wished to keep the tally at one. Even now, four years later, I often woke up in the night thinking about that kid and feeling the sweat trickle down the small of my back.

If some boob stumbled into the house in the night, I guess I'd have to take him on hand-to-hand or maybe with a heavy slipper from under the bed.

After the house was still and dark and I thought she was fast asleep, Kathy called from the living room, "You awake? Thomas?"

My answer was a bovine grunt.

"Tomorrow I'll dig up everything on record about Angus Crowell."

"Good."

"What are *you* going to do tomorrow?"

"Think I'll try to find this Romano creep. Maybe get Burton squared away so you can go to a judge with him.

If everything doesn't work out right away, I'm driving back up to Bellingham."

"You think her aunt knows something?"

"I *know* she knows something. I just don't know if it'll help us. Or whether she'll tell me."

"I thought the jig was up when Ms. Gunther and I walked in on you."

"I got involved in what I was reading."

"Was it something weird?"

"It was private."

"About Burton and Melissa?"

"Yeah. I'll tell you if you want, but it was private."

She thought about it for a few moments. "Maybe I'd better not hear."

"Good night, Kathy."

"Thomas?"

"Eh, Pancho?"

"Do you think he'll come back? The man in the mask? Do you think he'll come back?"

"I have no idea."

"He had something to do with Melissa, didn't he? The burglar?"

"The way I see it we have three basic possibilities. Either Crowell did it, or orchestrated it. Maybe he doesn't want us to find Melissa, maybe he's trying to throw some stumbling blocks into our path."

"Why?"

"Who knows? Maybe Melissa stole something from him, something he doesn't want anyone else in the world to see. I don't really have a glimmer."

"What are the other two possibilities?"

"Number two: that Holder broke in on his own, without Crowell's knowledge. I told you before that

Holder would do anything for a buck. And there's a two-thousand-dollar reward for finding Melissa. It could be he just wants to derail the opposition, meaning us, only long enough so he can find her himself."

"What's the third possibility?" Kathy asked.

"That the burglary has no connection to any of this. That it was a random crime like hundreds of other random crimes across this city every day."

"Maybe Melissa's been kidnapped."

"I've thought of that. That would be a reason her father wouldn't want us messing around. Maybe he's trying to scrape together a ransom. Maybe they've threatened to kill her if he calls the police. The only trouble with that is, why would he put the ad in the newspaper?"

Tuesday, we caught Nadisky early, hauled him out of bed and began haranguing him about his daughter. It took him only a minute to acquiesce. Kathy did the talking and this time it looked like it might stick. The story about the spilled milk was what tipped it. Tears slid from his pale blue orbs. He jumped into blue jeans, a flannel shirt, and boots and was ready.

Burton was now more dignified than I had seen him. The mouse under his eye was shrinking and he looked a whole lot better without Holder standing over him slapping his brains out.

Before we left, I stopped him at the front door and put a hand on his narrow shoulder. "A couple other things, Burton."

"Sure, sure, sure," he said, nervously. He was worried about testifying before a judge. My guess was he didn't usually fare well in front of authority figures.

I signaled Kathy to vamoose. It took her a moment to

realize what I was saying with my eyebrows, but then she obediently walked into the kitchen looking a little peeved.

"You haven't heard anything from your wife, have you?"

Burton knit his wheat-colored brows together into a frown and shook his head. His body was stiff from the cold in the house and from the tension. "No, why? Have you?"

I shook my head. "She know anyone in Tacoma? Either of you know anyone in Tacoma?"

"Nobody that I can think of right off the bat. We haven't been down in a coon's age. Two years, maybe. I went to the writers' conference there."

"How about an old boyfriend? Melissa have any old boyfriends?"

"I didn't feel I had the right to question her about ex-beaux."

It was a pretty good bet Burton was the only one on the block who used the word *beaux*.

"What about the name Romano? That mean anything to you?"

Burton combed his fingers through his shock of blond hair and shook his head. I could tell by the blank television-eyes, he was telling the truth. "What's in Tacoma?" he asked. "You think Melissa went to Tacoma?"

"I told you that last night. But you must have been rummy. How about somebody in a pest control van? You ever see anybody in a pest control van?"

"A pest control van? What has that got to do with any-thing?" Burton winced like a child getting a hypodermic injection.

"You've seen one, haven't you?"

"There was a guy here visiting Melissa about a year ago. He drove a pest van. She said he was an old friend . . . of the family."

"Tell me about it."

Studying his scuffed hiking boots, Nadisky measured his breathing for a few counts, then finally spoke. "I was working at the Esso station, but I got sick, so I came home early. This man was here. A tanned fellow. Italian, he looked like. About forty-five or fifty, maybe. Melissa said he was here to see if we had mice. But she was real fidgety. He kept grinning. He wouldn't stop staring at me and he wouldn't stop grinning. It made my skin crawl."

"Did you have mice?"

"Once, yeah. But something else was going on. I never found out what. I had the feeling she knew the guy real well from before, you know? He just kept grinning."

"You didn't figure maybe he was someone she used to date?"

Dual lumps of anguish knotted Burton's cheeks and forced his mouth into a pout. "Why do you have to ask these questions? I don't want to know."

"The guy was seen here last weekend. I think Melissa went off with him."

"She wouldn't run off with that guy."

"I think she did."

"She wouldn't do that!" he shouted. His face burned a bright pink. Kathy appeared in the kitchen doorway for a moment, then disappeared. "Melissa wouldn't run off with a . . . man."

"What makes you so certain?"

Burton shrugged, embarrassed, one eyebrow quivering.

"Is it because Melissa isn't capable of enjoying sex with a man?"

"God . . ." Burton's startled eyes widened and he stared at me. "How do you . . . where . . . ?"

"Don't worry about it. I'm not blabbing it to the congregation at your church. I may not even write it on any rest room walls. You saw me send Kathy out of the room. I'm not trying to put anybody on the spot. I only want to find out anything that might help me locate your wife. Right now I'm not sure what the hell is going on. If I knew the exact reason she left I might have more clues."

"She didn't go anywhere with a man. I'm sure of that. Melissa doesn't like men. We only . . ."

"How do you know?"

His voice shrank. "She has a lot of trouble sleeping. One time, when she was a little girl, something happened in the night. Something awful. Most nights I slept in the bedroom and she slept with Angel."

"Was that what you were seeing Ms. Gunther about?"

"You've pried into everything, haven't you?" It was a statement more than an accusation. He was resigned to it.

"I'm only trying to find your wife. There's some real trouble beneath all this."

"We talked to Ms. Gunther about sex, but that wasn't why we went, not initially. Melissa has this thing about her father. They've got a real love-hate thing going. Ms. Gunther told her she was going to have to confront her father."

"How did Melissa take that?"

"Badly. Ms. Gunther told her she was going to have to tell him what she really thought of him. Ms. Gunther is a real believer in clearing the air. I suppose part of it was my fault. I'm real close to my folks, and I've always urged her to mend the fences. Melissa got a little hysterical."

"Hysterical? In what way?"

"She went flippy. It was the week before she left. She kept talking about confronting her father. She didn't want to do it, but Ms. Gunther convinced her she had to. I guess maybe it could have had something to do with her leaving."

"Did Melissa make contact with her father that week?"

"Not that I know of. But if she did . . . it was the kind of thing Melissa would have done on her own, after work or sometime. Melissa did some sneaky things where her father was concerned. I remember once, she took a bunch of money out of savings and bought him a cable-knit sweater. Didn't even ask me. A hundred bucks."

"You said something happened when she was a kid. What?"

"I don't know. She never got it clear enough in her own head to talk about."

"But it was something ugly?"

"I only know about it from the nightmares she used to have. She would cry in the night and have these ferocious nightmares."

It was a quarter after nine when I dropped off Kathy and Burton at the county courthouse where they were to meet one of Kathy's law professors. Brusquely, Kathy turned back to me at the half-open Ford window and said, "Be careful, Big Boy."

I nodded absently, my mind already light-years away.

"Hey, Cisco?"

Snapping out of it, I met her worried smile. "Hey, Pancho."

She wore a chic pantsuit. A fraction of my mind was disappointed that she had no more occasion to dress like a strumpet. In its own way, it had been interesting.

I had a hunch. A strong hunch. I didn't get them often, so when I did I rolled with the crazy things. I had awakened that morning with an urgent desire to speak to Mary Crowell again. I parked the truck, found a pay phone, and dialed her Bellingham number. It rang twelve times before she picked up the receiver and coughed into it.

When she was finished coughing, Mary Dawn Crowell spoke in a crisp, scholarly manner. She was so melancholy and yet so precise in her enunciation that I suspected she'd been tippling, was trying to camouflage signs of it.

"Mary? This is Thomas Black."

"I had an inkling it was you. I don't know why, I just did."

"Yeah, the morning is rife with hunches. I think we should talk some more, Mary."

"Yes." Her voice was drifting off. "Perhaps we should." She sounded preoccupied. "I have much to reveal, and I guess . . . I guess it's about time I opened this particular can of worms. I've held suspicions for years. It's about time somebody else heard them."

"Suspicions about what, Mary?"

"I'll tell you in person. I don't like speaking about these matters on the phone."

"What matters?"

"When you get here, I'll spill the whole can."

"I'll be up in a couple of hours."

"Come after lunch. That would be better. I have a rather unpleasant errand to run this morning."

"After lunch, then."

In the Seattle Public Library, I spent an hour and a half thumbing through phone books and looking up pest companies and citizens named Romano. One pocket sagging with quarters from a bank down the block, I started making telephone calls, explaining to the bewildered Romanos who answered that I was an attorney looking for a specific Romano in the pest control business. My story was that some eccentric old widow had kicked the bucket and willed Romano her jewels out of gratitude for what he had done to her termites. It only took twenty minutes of pushing buttons and telling lies to reach a dead end. Four numbers had not answered.

The Tacoma listings for Romano were short and sweet. Same results, with two numbers unaccounted for. Then I phoned all the pest companies in Seattle and Tacoma asking for Romano. "Romano who?" they wanted to know.

Next, I might try Federal Way, Burien, Bellevue, Mercer Island, Puyallup. If I wanted to, I could force-feed another hundred quarters into the black box. Perhaps Romano was the guy's first name instead of his last. That would be a doozy. I'd never find the bozo.

Despite what she said, I had the feeling my face was the last one in the world Mary Dawn wanted in front of her that morning. But she had something vital to tell me and the butterflies in my stomach galloped in anticipation. This case was about to break wide open. Secrets were going to spill like blood in a slaughterhouse.

Bellingham was farther away than a schoolboy's Christmas on that long gray ribbon of damp interstate. It was twelve-forty-five when I finally got there.

I parked in the lot beside Mary Crowell's condominium and thumbed her buzzer. Nobody answered. I guessed she was still off, running her unpleasant errand. If she was, she hadn't taken her car. Her road-gray Buick was parked in the same stall it had occupied on Sunday.

A whistling florist bustled downstairs and opened the main doors from inside. Feigning an attempt to find my keys, I scampered in as he went out. On the third floor, I thumbed Mary's doorbell. Her front door was slightly ajar and I could hear the chimes inside playing a snatch of something classical. Tchaikovsky. Nobody else was in the hallway. I was discreet. I rang twice before I shoved the door open with my foot. I was like that. It was part of being a private eye.

"Mary?"

Her apartment was as unsullied and pristine as the first time I'd been there, except now there were empty glasses scattered throughout the rooms, and two bottles of sherry, one in the kitchen and another snuggled beside her favorite wooden rocker. She had been tippling. A game show bludgeoned me from the television set. I switched off the sound and blessed the room with peace.

A half gallon of butter brickle ice cream sat melting on the dinette, a warm pool of goop swimming across the table top. Two small, unused bowls sat in the creamy puddle. She had told me herself butter brickle was exclusively for Melissa.

I found the old woman's body under the table, daubs of ice cream splotching her printed dress. It looked as if she'd been sitting in a chair at the table spooning out a snack when the blow felled her.

It hadn't even made much of a mess. Not really. Someone had merely grabbed an economy-size ketchup bottle out of the refrigerator and brained Mary Dawn Crowell. Brained her good. Most of the left side of her skull was caved in. I didn't want to check her carotid artery, but I did anyway. No pulse. She was dead as a doornail. And as warm as the cat.

11 I STOOD UP AND PEERED AROUND, feeling a little wobbly, but not because of the corpse. I had handled plenty of corpses. I was worried about the implications for my case. I had genuinely been looking forward to this discussion with Mary. She had wanted to bend my ear and we both had realized it was going to be important.

After stashing the sodden butter brickle container in the freezer, I scouted around the condo.

In the living room beside the visitor's chair, I located the papers, a sheaf of poems stapled together, all authored by Burton Nadisky. The first poem was a completed version of the ode to Melissa he had been hacking away at Sunday morning. It was still beautiful. It still made me wish I could write like that. Even if it was a murder clue.

Had he mailed the packet? I didn't see any discarded envelopes kicking about. The condo was not equipped with a fireplace. Inspecting the wastebaskets and the kitchen trash, I found nothing. No, somebody had hand-carried the poems to Mary.

If it had been Burton, he had been there sometime between nine, when I had dropped him off at the county courthouse, and twelve-forty-five, when I arrived. It was a two-hour drive, so even if he had a car and had dashed out of the courthouse immediately, he wouldn't have arrived until eleven or so. I must have just missed him. I suppose he could have hitchhiked up last night or yesterday afternoon, but that wasn't likely. Perhaps he was the visitor she had been expecting that day. The unpleasant errand?

Or maybe somebody else had brought the poems. But for what purpose? To implicate Burton in a killing? If that were the case, someone had come here with the explicit intention of murdering Mary Dawn Crowell and pinning it on Burton. Who? And why?

And the butter brickle ... Mary had told me it was Melissa's favorite flavor and that she had purchased it especially for her niece. Would Mary have been apt to have squandered this on just *any* visitor. I checked the freezer. There were two other quart containers of ice cream. Two different flavors. Supposing Melissa had been there?

But why would anyone bludgeon poor Mary Dawn Crowell? What could she ever do to harm anyone? It would be interesting to see what the Bellingham cops dredged up.

The plainclothes detective in charge was a black man named Herman Percy. He was dapper and slight and he dressed as if he thought he was a ladies' man. He wore a tiny sliver of a mustache like something left over from dinner. His gold bracelet and matching gold tie on an off-white shirt must have cost most of a two-week check. Everything was prim and tidy except his loafers, which were badly scuffed around the toes.

Four uniformed police had beat Percy through the front door, arriving in staggered sequence. They filled him in on what I had said and on what they had seen, which wasn't any different than what Percy now saw. Nothing had been altered. I did notice some new footprints dappling the shiny linoleum kitchen floor. Cop prints.

Percy sauntered over to the window where I was watching a small crowd outside milling around the police cruisers amidst a light rain. "You find the body? You her son, or what?"

I didn't answer the detective, I was so startled at what I saw below in the parking lot. Holder was speaking with one or two elderly onlookers. Where the hell had Holder come from? And how long had he been in Bellingham? Long enough for some ice cream to melt?

"Guess I should repeat myself," said Herman Percy, displaying a burnished badge in a leather case. "You the one found the body?"

"Excuse me," I replied, turning from the window and wondering how many times he had tried to flag my attention. "There's a man down in the parking lot who might be connected to this."

"There's a man right *here* who might be connected to this," Percy said.

"There's another one in the lot. And he might get away. *I* won't."

Percy shot me an exasperated look. I said, "Yeah, I'm the one who found the body. The only thing I did in here was toss the ice cream back into the freezer. I'm a private investigator from Seattle. I came here to talk to this woman about some family matters. The man down in the parking lot is mixed up in some of those matters."

"What family matters?"

"He's going to get away."

Herman Percy stared at me.

"He's got a history of violence. Sunday morning he slapped the hell out of this lady's nephew."

"Okay," conceded Percy, sliding toward the window. "Which man?"

I pointed Holder out to him and waited for a reaction. After all, here I was a white, accusing a black to another black. Percy's only reaction was to instruct two of the uniformed officers to run downstairs and take a statement from Holder. Perhaps it was my imagination, but he seemed more officious when he turned back to me.

"Okay," said the police detective, flopping out a small spiral-binder note pad. "Let's have it."

I dished out all the information he wanted. The other cops in the room strutted about, taking it all in, sneaking wary looks at me, pacing back and forth as if they actually had duties to attend to in the room. They were gawkers the same way the crowd of senior citizens outside were gawkers. There was nothing for any of them to do except stand by and rubberneck, and now twelve or fifteen of them were doing just that.

I kept answering Percy's questions until he asked what my case was about, why I had come. "Can't tell you," I said.

"Why not?"

"You know I can't."

"Come on, Black. You been watching too many Rockford reruns. This is real life and I got a murder here. Cough it up."

"I wish I could."

"You'll wish even harder after a couple of days in the slammer."

"Huh-uh," I said, not sure who I was protecting or why. Something in the back of my mind told me to get my hands on Melissa Nadisky before I spilled my guts to the cops.

"Did you kill the old girl?" Herman Percy asked.

He was on a fishing expedition and I told him so. Undaunted, he continued, "Sure. You came here to put some sort of squeeze on the old dame. Information or money? I don't know what you wanted. She wouldn't satisfy you, so you got a little rough on her. Then a little too rough. You knew people had seen you entering the premises so you pretended you found her this way. She's still warm. You know that? I'm willing to gamble she was alive two hours ago."

"So am I. But that doesn't mean I killed her."

"I'm going to look into your record very thoroughly."

I tried not to sound nervous. The last thing I needed was two or three days in the jug while they decided they had the wrong number. And I wasn't sure about Percy yet. He might actually believe some of what he was saying.

"Nice theory," I said. "But nobody saw me come in here. I could have flown the coop easy enough instead of calling you, and nobody would be the wiser. You'll be better off talking to Holder." I gestured toward the window. Together we glanced outside and watched two uniformed officers interrogating the giant.

"He doesn't look like he just bashed in some dame's head," said Herman Percy.

"Neither do I," I said.

Percy gave me an odd look. He cocked his thumb at the window. "Why is he here?"

I shrugged. "Might have followed me up from Seattle."

"Why would he do that?"

"Ask him."

"Let's not get cute."

"You want some help? Those poems in the living room. I don't think they were here Sunday when I visited. They belong to a man named Burton Nadisky. It's a baffling case and I'm not sure I understand half of it yet, myself. When I find out anything pertinent to your investigation, I'll let you know."

"What makes you think you'll be finding anything out at all? I could hold you as a material witness. Or as a suspect."

I took out a pad and a pen and scribbled a name and a number. "Captain Henderson. Seattle Police Department," I said. "He'll vouch for me. I think."

"Don't you know?" Percy went across the room, picked up Mary's phone and dialed Henderson. When he made contact, he spoke so low I couldn't catch any of it. He looked at me differently after he hung up.

"Black, I'm giving you the benefit of the doubt," he said, snatching up Burton's sheaf of poems gingerly so as not to smudge any of the prints. "You think this guy was here today?"

"It's a possibility."

"What's he look like?"

I gave a detailed description of Burton Nadisky, feeling vaguely guilty as I did it. Percy wrote it all down in his notebook. At least I was keeping the possibility that Melissa had been here a secret. Sure, I could keep some things to myself. I wasn't blabbing everything.

"He's probably hitchhiking," I added.

Percy ambled across the room and spoke to a sergeant. Then he stooped down and meticulously examined Mary Crowell's body. It wasn't until the police photographer came in and began snapping photos that he moved away, sorting through the notes by the phone, opening drawers and poking through anything else he saw. I could have saved him the trouble of checking the notes by the phone. There was nothing except a number for the television repairman.

Downstairs, the two uniformed officers who had been grilling Holder finally let him go, after inspecting his I.D. and writing some numbers onto their note pads. Holder strolled away at a leisurely pace, stopping once to turn back and eye the two cops.

After Percy had hunkered on Mary's wooden rocker for ten minutes scrawling notes, he stood up, stretched, cracked his knuckles ritualistically, and strode over to me.

"You acquainted with this gal's relatives, you might do us a favor and stick around. Maybe make a few phone calls, have somebody come up and make the funeral arrangements. The manager's out and none of the neighbors here want to have anything to do with a murder. You know how that goes." Captain Henderson had told him I had been a cop, bragged me up good. I could feel it. We were brothers now.

"Sure," I said. "I'd kind of like to see how the relatives react."

Percy looked at me as if I were a ghoul.

"For the case," I added hastily, but I didn't dislodge the morbid impression I'd given him. "One last thing, Percy."

"Yeah?" He regarded me without compassion. I had

some sick instincts and he was going to keep his eye on me.

"I was going to meet Mary today. She had something she wanted to tell me. She never said what it was. But she did mention that she had an unpleasant errand to run first."

Percy scratched his mustache with a long polished fingernail. "What sort of unpleasant errand?"

"I have no idea what it was. You might check to see if her car's been driven today."

"I've already thought of that, thank you. You can use this phone. We'll have the body downtown. Just get somebody up here to make a positive I.D. and arrange the services."

"Sure."

The people at Taltro wouldn't put me through to Angus Crowell. "His sister was murdered this morning," I said, nonchalantly. "Does that make a difference?"

"Oh, my God," gasped a startled secretary. Ordinarily I wouldn't have bestowed that sort of news through a third party, but Crowell did not have my total sympathy.

Her official mien punctured, the secretary said, "Mr. Crowell has been out of the office all morning. I don't know when to expect him back."

From the long distance operator, I obtained Crowell's home phone number, surprised that it was listed. A maid answered. I asked for either the lady or the gent of the house.

"Who may I say is calling?" the maid asked, with a strong Mexican accent.

"A representative of Mr. Crowell's sister in Bellingham."

It was a while before Muriel Crowell came on the line. She was businesslike and taciturn. "Who is this?"

"The name is Thomas Black, Mrs. Crowell. You met me last night under rather unfortunate circumstances. It's about your sister-in-law in Bellingham, Mrs. Crowell. Mary Dawn is dead."

The line was silent for ten counts. "I'm afraid I don't believe you."

"It's true. I found the body. If you want to confirm this, phone the Bellingham police and ask for Detective Herman Percy. He's in charge of the investigation."

"What do you mean, you found her? What investigation?"

"Your sister-in-law was slugged in the head with a bottle."

"You mean Mary really is dead?" Her voice rose in pitch, the truth slamming home at last.

"That's what I've been telling you."

"How did it happen?"

"I wish we knew. Somebody apparently bashed her on the side of the head with a bottle of ketchup."

"Ketchup?" Her voice was strained, disbelieving.

"It's too awful for me to have made up, Mrs. Crowell. I was wondering when you or your husband might be able to come up here and make . . . a positive identification. And some funeral arrangements. I'm assuming you are her next of kin. She never married, did she?"

"No, she never married."

"When can you get up here?"

The line was silent for almost thirty seconds.

"Mrs. Crowell? Are you all right?"

"You've got a lot of nerve!"

"Mrs. Crowell?"

"First you poke your nose into our personal family affairs and now you expect me to come up and identify *that* woman? I simply am not going to do it. She was a spiteful woman. Mentally unbalanced. She was under the care of a psychiatrist. Some of the lies she spread . . . No, Mr. Black. You arrange a burial yourself." The line went dead.

"Mrs. Crowell?"

Herman Percy strode into the apartment again, looked at me and said, "You get ahold of anyone yet?"

"Almost," I said, grinning weakly.

"I want you downtown when you get done. You'll have to make a statement."

"Sure thing."

"By the way," said Percy, smiling like a man who had just won a coveted trophy, "we nailed the nephew. A prowl car nabbed him trying to thumb a ride off the freeway."

"What'd he say?"

"Don't know yet. But he tried to take a swing at one of the officers who picked him up. I'm going down to interrogate him now. It doesn't look good."

It took me a long while and a lot of imagination before I could conjure a picture of Burton taking a poke at *anyone*, much less a city cop with a pistol strapped to his hip.

**12** Sheets of rain spattered the condominium windows noisily. I pored through Mary Dawn Crowell's small personal phone directory twice before discovering the notation on the inside cover, feeling like an absolute fool for not looking there first. It said:

To whom it may concern:
Should anything happen to me, please contact my brothers:

> Stephen J. Crowell
> Shady Lane Rest Home
> Sedalia, Missouri

> or

> Edward and Clarice Crowell
> 1-213-555-4358
> 29 Beach Rd.
> Malibu, California

So, she had at least two additional brothers besides Angus. That made sense. Families were larger sixty or seventy years ago. I dialed the number in Malibu. An old man who had a very slow and very deep voice answered on the first ring, as if he were sitting next to the telephone.

"Edward Crowell?"

"This is Ed Crowell speaking."

"My name is Thomas Black. I'm calling about your sister, Mary Dawn Crowell."

"Yes, of course. What is it? Is it her heart?" He spoke slowly and lugubriously.

"I'm afraid she passed away this morning."

He paused, and then said, "Are you the manager of her condominium?"

"No, sir. I'm a private detective. I came up here early this afternoon to speak to your sister and found her dead."

"Had she been ill? We hadn't heard anything."

"I'm afraid someone murdered her."

"Murder?"

"That's right."

"A detective? Why on earth would a detective want to speak to Mary?"

"It's rather complicated, but I assure you Mary had done nothing wrong."

"My God. My God. Murder? Who? A cat burglar? A rapist? Some young thug?"

"Good questions, Mr. Crowell. Nobody seems to know anything right now. Can you fly up here today and take care of . . ."

"On my way. I'm on my way. Let me call the airport and make arrangements. I'll phone you back in a few minutes so you'll know when to expect me."

I told him where I was and we hung up. For ten minutes, I watched a couple of sleepy-eyed bumblers trying to shove Mary Dawn into a large plastic body bag. The bag was too big, the men were in too much of a hurry, and they zippered a lock of the corpse's thin, graying hair grotesquely outside the bag. A Filipino officer dusting for fingerprints shuffled over and asked me what I had handled in the apartment besides the phone, which he had already checked. I told him.

The phone rang. "Black here."

"Ed Crowell. Clarice and I will be in Washington in about three hours. I've a lodge brother who flies and he's bringing us up. I'll lease a car at the airport."

"The body will be downtown, Mr. Crowell. It won't be pretty."

"Don't fret about me. I was a funeral director for thirty-five years. Now, who should we speak to when we get to Bellingham?"

"A detective named Herman Percy is in charge. I'd like to speak to you also, if that's all right."

"By all means. Where do we get in touch?"

"I'll wait for you downtown."

I liked his no-nonsense approach to life. Or to death.

Percy sent me to a vacant office for an hour where I dictated my statement to a bespectacled police officer who was straining to grow a mustache. Percy came in, coatless, perused the statement, had me sign it, and then asked, "How well do you know this nephew, Nadisky?"

"Not well. I've been around him. We haven't cut our thumbs or anything."

"You want to see him for a few moments?"

"Is that kosher?"

"Not usually. Me, I get creative once in a while. He

seems to have a grudge against you. I was thinking if he came face to face with you, he might blurt out something stupid."

"Like a confession?"

"Or a motive."

"I doubt if he did it."

"You let me worry about that."

Burton was ensconced in another office similar to the one I had been in. The only furnishings were file cabinets, a coffee machine, which wasn't percolating anything, and a desk buried in papers. A small mirror was bracketed in the wall. It was obviously a one-way window connected to the next office. Dectectives would observe from behind it.

When Percy and I walked into the room, Burton leaped up and tried to take a poke at me, both his hands cuffed in front. A burly uniformed officer restrained him, shoving him back down into his chair with one thick hand.

"You prick!" Burton bellowed.

"Burton," I said.

"You prick. You squealed on me the first chance you got."

"What's the matter? You get into the catnip?"

"You ask me what's the matter? You people think you're all one cut above someone just because you have more money than they do. That's it. Judge everyone by their income. That makes Al Capone upper class and Carl Sandburg lower class. That makes Herod upper class and Christ lower class. Good way to do things. It never occurs to you that some people may have different values. You think because I write poems and don't have a master's degree in business administration that I'm some sort of slime that crawled out from under a sidewalk. I'll tell you something. You people are wigged out. You don't know what life is all about. None of you."

Percy looked at me and spoke calmly, in stark contrast to Burton's shrillness. He had seen it all too many times and he was tired of waiting for the second-act curtain.

"Claims he didn't kill her. Claims the old lady was going to meet someone else. That he was only there for a few minutes and she shooed him out the door because she had a visitor coming." Percy looked away from the huffing, wild-eyed Burton distastefully. Nobody liked a killer. "Well, I'll leave you two here with Simmons. I've got some business to take on."

"Are you holding him?" I asked, more so that Burton could hear the answer than anything else. If they were true to form, they had left him up in the air over his fate.

Percy stared down at Burton for a moment and surveyed the prisoner almost sympathetically. Almost. "Him? You bet."

I walked over behind the desk so that Simmons was between myself and Burton, glancing out a dirty window at the rain and the dingy buildings across the street. Simmons didn't seem to give a hoot what happened. He pawed through a *Sports Illustrated*, twisted his hips and farted loudly. I hoped they were getting all this on tape.

Glowering like a cat that had just been de-balled with a pair of rusty shears, Burton's face reddened even more, the veins bubbled out on his neck, and he tried hard to think of something vicious to say to me.

"Jesus, you're a sneaky bastard," he said.

A mouse under his eye, his lip split, wearing faded jeans—he did not look like much. Except for his baby face, he looked like one of the thugs on the local news being led, shackled, down a dark hallway, a gang of cameramen tagging along. He fit the mold. Sullen. Indigent. Unshaved. Belligerent. Disrespectful.

"Did you kill her?"

"Sneakiest sonofabitch I ever ran across."

"I don't know why you're ticked off at me. All I did was tell the cops those were your poems in the living room. They would have found out anyway. Your name was on them. You must have left prints all over the place. They were going to pick you up sooner or later. Why all the pandemonium?"

"But you had to help them along."

"A guy gets mad this way, Burton, especially a mild-mannered guy like you, and it makes people suspect he's trying to hide something."

Burton glared at me and mulled it over for a few minutes. "Eat shit," he said, finally.

"Flowery words won't turn my head."

Suddenly Burton's face collapsed. He slammed his forehead onto his folded hands on the desk.

"You okay, guy?"

"What do you care?" he asked, bitterly, his lips an inch off the desk top.

"I want to see you and your wife and your little girl back together. That's all I'm in this for."

Burton swiveled his head up at me, his pale blue eyes trying to discern whether or not I was conning him.

"Have you seen Melissa?" he asked, a trace of hope lacing his voice.

"Nope. You?"

He shook his head despondently. "Gawd. What's happening to me?" he said, with a hiccuppy sigh. "What the hell's happening?"

"It's just pressure, kid. It downs all of us. Don't let it depress you."

"What can I do?" he whined.

"Tell me what happened this morning."

"I hitched up to talk to Aunt Mary. You said she knew where Melissa was."

"I said she got a call from Melissa."

"Yeah. That's what she told me, too. She got a call. She never did like me much. She couldn't believe the way Melissa and I were living." A touch of pride infected his voice, as if the way he and Melissa were living was something they had worked very hard to achieve.

"I guess that was part of the whole trouble. Melissa's parents didn't approve of the way we were living either."

"The evidence doesn't suggest Melissa was too keen on things herself."

Burton looked at me for a moment, ice in his eyes. Although he was acting like a three-year-old, he had more strength of character than I'd given him credit for.

He inhaled deeply and said, "Maybe you're right. I just want to find her. I *need* her." He stared down at some obscene graffiti on the desk, his strength dissolving suddenly. I feared he was going to start crying.

"Melissa was supposed to marry a doctor. That's what her folks wanted. Especially her mother. Or an executive. Someone with money. Me . . . my folks wanted me to be an architect. Then Dad decided I should be an accountant because I got A's in math. All I ever wanted to do was write poems. You should have seen the cop's face downstairs when he asked my occupation. You should have seen it!"

I said, "It's not very practical."

"You too? I knew it. You're cold. People are cold. You

should have seen all the stiff faces on the freeway. They won't give rides easy. I heard one of the cops mention a private dick from Seattle and right away I knew it was you. I'm sorry for what I called you. You're right. They would have pinched me anyway. I guess I must look guilty as hell."

In the other room, Percy summed it up. Burton had come to Bellingham angry, demented, looking for his wife. When Mary Crowell wouldn't tell him where Melissa was, he flew into a rage and clubbed her. In his haste to escape, he forgot his poems. Plain and simple.

"Nice theory," I said. "But anyone who knows Burton will tell you it isn't possible. He's not the violent type."

Percy laughed. "Not the violent type? He tried to hit you. He took a swing at my two officers when they arrested him . . ."

"He's scared. He's almost paranoid of cops. He'd never hit an old lady. His lawyer will get a couple hundred people on the stand to testify to that."

"We'll see," said Percy.

"Besides," I said, "she had an appointment this morning. She told me that. She told him that. I didn't prompt him. He brought it up himself."

Percy said, "I doubt if this phantom appointment showed. And if they did, Mary didn't answer her door because she was already in never-never land."

"What about Holder?"

Percy gave me a look of incomprehension.

"The guy outside in the parking lot," I said, refreshing his memory.

"He was tailing you. He admitted that."

"And?"

"What you want me to do? Arrest him? No law against tailing somebody."

After the dust settled and they had led Burton away to a cell, I sat down and tried to clear my mind. Someone had killed my dog. A woman was missing. Someone had attacked Kathy and ransacked her apartment. Someone had murdered Aunt Mary. I could assume all these events were related in one manner or another. Maybe they were. Maybe they weren't.

I went outside and trundled two blocks through a light rain until I found a pay phone booth that smelled like a wet poodle. It was two-thirty. Kathy answered on the third ring.

"June . . . I'm home," I said.

"Ward?"

"You're early."

"I cut class."

"How're things?"

"Oh, miserable," said Kathy. "Professor Creighton and Burton and I all went before a judge this morning, but Crowell has a lawyer and he's really good. He said Melissa was hiding from Burton because Burton beat her and the reason they snatched the little girl was because they were afraid Burton would run off with her and abuse her too. They claimed they had Melissa's permission to get Angel. He twisted it all until everyone there was confused. He knows how to muddle anything. The judge was so messed up it wasn't even funny. Now he wants more information before he'll do anything."

"So some pineapple abducts his granddaughter, and the judge says fine?"

"Temporarily. We could have asked to have her put into a home, put her on neutral turf, but Burton figures

Angel's had enough upset. We tried to talk Burton out of it—after all, it's not a strategically smart move—to let his father-in-law keep Angel—but he wouldn't budge. Unless we can find Melissa and straighten out this mess, Crowell's likely to keep control of his granddaughter for a long while. That lawyer is smooth, Thomas. Real smooth. I thought Processor Creighton was pretty slick, but I guess he's a little rusty. But we'll work it out. Where are you phoning from?"

"Bellingham."

"Did you talk with Melissa's aunt again?"

"I drove up to see her, but she was dead when I got here."

"Cisco?"

"Pancho . . ."

"Did you say . . ."

"Somebody beaned her with a bottle of Heinz ketchup."

"Cisco?"

"That's what I said. They yanked it out of the refrigerator and clubbed her over the head with it. It was a Heinz economy size."

13

WHILE WAITING FOR ANGUS Crowell's mortician brother, I made arrangements with Kathy for her to stay with a friend until I got back into town. I saw no point in taking chances. Maybe the burglary wasn't related to any of this, but some peabrain with a penchant for mayhem was still loose and I didn't want him stalking Kathy.

Edward and Clarice Crowell arrived within fifteen minutes of when they had promised.

After he had identified his sister's remains, discussed matters with the cops, driven behind me in their rented Subaru to Mary's condo, and pawed lackadaisically through some of her things, Edward was ready to talk.

We ended up at the International House of Pancakes. Slow of foot and slow of mouth, Ed Crowell was tall, taller than me. He was somewhere in his late sixties. A certain timbre infused his voice, a timbre that undoubtedly had a soothing effect on the bereaved. I imagined he had been more than adept at his chosen profession. A cluster of diamonds on his pinky attested to his prosperity. He resembled his brother Angus, but he was without that definite sense of power. He was not, however, without a secure and implacable sense of his own grandioseness.

I sensed a gulf between the couple. Clarice was almost twenty-five years younger than Ed, had a Silly Putty shine on her face, and looked at me in a way that wasn't good, caught herself at it, and then, as if one of us merited punishment, virtually ignored my presence.

A waitress came to the booth. The mortician and his wife ordered coffee. I asked for hot chocolate. I hadn't eaten a thing all day, but I wasn't hungry yet. It was five-thirty and the place was beginning to fill up with the dinner crowd. Clarice ignited a Pall Mall and blew a lungful of smoke into my face. If I had to guess, I would have figured it was some sort of naughty signal.

"Now," said Edward Crowell, speaking in his inimitable slow drawl, "what did you want to speak to us about?"

"Just some background information. That's what I need, mainly."

"I'm still not sure what your job is," said Clarice Crowell, glancing around the bustling restaurant. "Do you work for the police?"

"I'm private. I was hired to find Melissa Nadisky."

"Melissa?" Crowell tapped his fingertips together and focused his empty gray eyes on my face. "Melissa's husband was the bastard who killed Mary, wasn't he?"

"He's the bastard the cops think killed Mary," I replied. "I doubt if he did. Your sister had made plans to meet someone else this morning."

"But they arrested him," said Ed Crowell, as if that clinched it. "They arrested the little rat."

"I was a cop for ten years. Cops arrest a lot of people. They make boo-boos just like you and me."

Our coffee and hot chocolate arrived. Ed Crowell spent a few moments watching the waitress's rump as she walked away. Clarice watched her husband's eyes as he watched the rump, and I thought I noticed a trace of lingering resentment in the way her lips twisted around the cigarette. Without thinking about it real hard, she blew another cloud of smoke into my face.

"And you believe this someone else killed Mary, whoever this was who had an appointment with her?"

"I have no idea. But I don't think Burton had a motive."

"Why would the police arrest him?" Clarice asked, sipping coffee. I noticed ashes from her Pall Mall floating on the surface of her java.

"The police arrest a lot of people," I repeated, trying not to grow impatient with their blind trust in authority. "Some of them turn out to be guilty, some just turn out to be convenient."

"You never did tell us what you were here to see Mary about," said Ed Crowell. "I presume it concerned Melissa?"

"I spoke with your sister Sunday. She agreed to meet me again. She also stated there was something important she had to tell me. But she wouldn't give me any hint of it over the phone. You wouldn't happen to have any idea what it was, would you?"

"Us?" said Clarice, startled that I would even ask.

Ed Crowell eyeballed a boisterous group of teenagers waiting to be led to a table. I could tell by the dour look on his face he hoped they wouldn't be seated anywhere near us.

"We only saw Mary once a year. We'd motor up for a weekend every autumn and take in the North Cascades Highway together. All the autumn foliage. Sometimes we'd take in a musical comedy in Seattle. Since I've retired, I've begun enjoying life more thoroughly. I've taken up photography. Bought myself a Nikon system."

His wife was bored with his discourse. Her foot bumped mine under the table.

"Were you in touch with her?"

"Certainly," said Ed Crowell. "We phoned."

"But not since a month or so," added Clarice. "Maybe even longer. I think it might even have been Labor Day . . . the last time we spoke to Mary."

"It was Labor Day," concurred Ed, stroking his chin with a large, hirsute hand. "She had dinner with some friends of hers. Some people from her office. We called, and I remember telling her to buy gold. But she refused. She was like that."

"Where did she work?"

"Masdan Insurance."

"That's a big outfit."

"Been there since 1953. She was thinking about retirement. I had her almost talked into it. I've got her into some smart investment programs. I even had her buy into some real estate."

"What sort of real estate?"

"Nothing important. She's got some land near Sultan."

Catching my eye with her dark brown raisinlike pupils, Clarice said, "You're trying to find Melissa? Where do you think she is?"

"I wish I knew. She called Mary last week and wanted to come up here and visit. But she never showed up."

"How long has she been gone?" Ed asked.

"A little over a week."

"It's been so long since we've seen little Melissa," mused Clarice. "We might not even recognize her."

"You might not."

"Oh, it hasn't been all that long," contradicted her husband.

"Sure it has," said Clarice. "I don't think we've seen little Melissa since she was in high school. That was at least eight years ago. It was right after Herb died. Remember?"

"Oh, it wasn't that long ago. More like four years."

"I'm more interested in some of your family history, Mr. Crowell. I found out today you have another brother besides Angus."

"Two others. Stephen and Charlie. Chuck lives in Minnesota with his wife. Grace isn't well. Steve is in Missouri in a rest home. He had a stroke, oh, about a year back. He can talk now, but he doesn't get around much."

"Four children in all?"

"Our family? No, there were five." He stirred his coffee, banging his spoon on the sides of the cup so hard I thought he might crack the glass.

Clarice explained. "A younger sister died right after she was born. That's when your mother passed away too, wasn't it, honey?" Crowell grunted, as if being reminded of it still hurt, even after all these years. He clearly didn't appreciate the direction our conversation was heading. But Clarice loved gossip and ancient history, and she loved to prattle. There was no stopping her.

"It really was sort of a tragic upbringing," continued Clarice. "I don't know how you all turned out so well. Mary in insurance. An executive, two lawyers, and a mortician."

"A funeral director," said Ed, correcting his wife.

"But, honey, how did you all turn out so normal? Look, your father committing suicide and all that? Your mother dying. I guess poor Mary had the worst of it. She was the youngest, wasn't she, honey?"

"Angus was the youngest boy, and Mary was ten years younger than him. We were mostly grown up when it all happened."

"But it was such a tragedy. Your mother dying like that. And Angus had some sort of beef with your father, didn't he?"

"Father was from the old school. We all had trouble with him from time to time." Ed was doing his best to play down the dramatic aspects of the family history just as surely as his wife wanted to relive them.

"Trouble?" said Clarice. "He used to whip all of you boys. I thought you said he almost killed Angus once, right before he ran off and joined the navy. He whipped him until he almost died."

"I actually don't recall."

It seemed to me an event like that would be hard to forget.

Clarice looked at me conspiratorially and spoke in a lower tone. Edward winced. This particular act had been played out before in their lives. "Their father committed suicide only a week after Angus left for the navy. Isn't that strange?"

We all chewed that one over for a moment or two.

I said, "Is there any particular reason Angus and his sister weren't on speaking terms?"

The couple exchanged glances. This was a new one for both of them. Clarice said, "Muriel had some sort of spat with Mary, but Angus spoke to Mary. Of course, while Muriel and Mary were on the outs they couldn't have any family get-togethers or anything like that, but for goodness' sake, they were brother and sister. Of course they spoke to each other."

"I understood they hadn't spoken to each other in years."

"That's wrong," said Clarice. "A brother and a sister? Of course they spoke. They were close."

Edward Crowell stood up, jangled some coins in his trousers pocket, glanced around the room with the pretension of idleness, and said, "I'll pay." The conversation was at an end as far as he was concerned.

Clarice and I walked into the foyer together while Edward paid the tab, a peeved look on his face. The timid girl at the cash register was frightened of him. Our words had disturbed him. Raking up the family skeletons wasn't his idea of muskrat heaven. I continued pumping Clarice, who took it all very personally, simpering and batting her false eyelashes at me. We might as well have been playing footsie at the beach.

"Did Mary have any sort of drinking problem?"

"How did you know about that? She was a practicing alcoholic most of her life. She'd been out to the farm to dry out two or three times. Two years ago when we came up she was stoned day and night."

"She never had any men around?"

"Mary was a confirmed old maid. Poor dear. Mary never wanted to have anything to do with the opposite sex. Not her."

"What about Harry?"

"Yes. There was Harry. But that didn't amount to much."

In the back of my mind I wondered if perhaps Mary and Melissa had some sort of sexual relationship. I wanted to ask her if Mary ever revealed any lesbian tendencies, but I suspected Clarice wouldn't take it well. It would shatter our delicate courtship, I with the solicitous inquiries, she with the fawning replies.

Surreptitiously, I handed her my card and told her to give me a ring if her husband decided he wanted to fill me in on the family history. She said she would try to talk him into loosening up. She said it as if she had been trying for years. When Ed Crowell sauntered into the foyer, we said our good-byes and thanked each other as if we meant it.

Clarice kept her raisin eyes on me as I trotted through the rainy parking lot to my truck. She observed me with extreme care while she waited for her husband to fetch their car.

I drove home in the splashing rush-hour traffic, mesmerized by the headlights knifing through the raindrops.

Some pundits claimed the weather was growing worse each year, that we were plummeting into another ice age. It did seem to be colder and wetter than last year. Maybe another ice age was possible. Maybe things *were* going from bad to worse. I knew one thing. We were all involved in an intricate pattern of violence that was slowly escalating, just like the winters.

14

THE MORNING SKY WAS LIT UP IN the east like a house on fire. The weather people had assured us it was only a temporary lull in the rains, that the clouds would move in and drench our fair city by noon.

She lived in a basement apartment, almost a nook, in the back of a large sprawling complex of stucco apartments on Capitol Hill. It was early, before seven-thirty, when I tramped through the tall, wet lawn and knocked, catching her as she was getting ready to leave.

Her front door was in a well, all the windows barred with wrought iron. It was the least accessible and most isolated apartment in the complex, the only one that had iron bars across the windows.

Jerking open a small peekaboo window in the door, she rose up on tiptoe and peered at me.

"Ms. Gunther?"

"You?"

"I need to speak to you about Melissa Nadisky. I believe you treated her at the clinic."

The woman behind the door thought that over for a long while. "Is that what that fiasco was all about the other night? That sham?"

"I'm a private detective. I'm looking for Melissa. She's been missing for over a week."

"Go to hell." She slammed the peekaboo window. It made a tinny thud. I thumbed her doorbell and held it. After thirty seconds, the peekaboo window screaked open again.

"You're no detective," she said.

I passed a photostat of my license through the five-inch window. She grabbed it, read it, tore it into quarters, and stuffed the pieces through the hole.

"I'm sorry about the other night," I said. "But Melissa's been missing for over a week, her daughter has been kidnapped, and her husband is in the clink in Bellingham."

"Burton?"

"The police have him."

"What for?"

"Murder."

Ms. Gunther closed the small window and latched it. Then she opened her front door as far as a fragile burglar chain would allow. She stood warily in the crack, one gray eye exposed, watching me pick up the scraps of my photostat. "It really is important," I said.

"You said her daughter's been kidnapped?"

"That's what I said."

"Why wasn't it in the papers?"

"Melissa's father kidnapped her."

"I don't want to get messed up in any family squabbles."

"Could I come in for a few moments?"

Gunther looked me over again, then unchained the door and sidestepped the doorway. I wiped my sopping shoes carefully on her jute doormat. She watched, as if she wanted to inspect the job I'd done.

She wore a jumper, black stockings, and a pair of clunky boots. She moved stiffly across the room, turned, tilted against a wall, and folded her arms self-consciously across her breasts. She still didn't know quite what to make of me.

"I'm on my way to work," she said. "You've got about two minutes of my time. After that, it's *hasta la vista, muchacho.*"

The apartment was pleasant, prim, and spotless, an array of yellows and pinks. It was a single woman's abode that might have been a model for *House Beautiful.* I was accustomed to Kathy's place, its busy clutter and the invariable project arrayed in the center of the living room rug. If Gunther was in the midst of any projects, they were carefully concealed.

"I'm really sorry about the other night. We shouldn't have done it."

"No, but you had a damned good time, didn't you? All at my expense. I may be more gullible than some, but I'm not a moron. I figured it out later."

"I've apologized twice now."

Gunther reached over to a table and picked up her enormous tortoiseshell glasses, donning them fastidiously. I sensed that she didn't need glasses to see, that she wore them to place a barrier, however small, between herself and me.

"Melissa's been gone since a week ago Sunday."

She adjusted the glasses using the middle fingers of both her hands. "I wondered. They missed an appointment."

"I need your help."

"Go to the police."

"The police aren't going to look for someone who's

been missing a week, especially when she's got a history of taking off."

"I can't help you."

"You mean you won't help me."

"I do not betray confidences," she said, imperiously. "We have a code of ethics in our profession."

"I need to know some things about Melissa."

"Obviously, you found out some things. My personal files on the Nadiskys had been tampered with. You did it while your girlfriend lied to me out in the hall."

Our charade had been a formal assault on her self-image. I could see it in her cloudy gray eyes. Maybe people had been telling her she was gullible all her life and she had been telling them she wasn't. Maybe down deep she had been a little unsure about it. Now there was no disputing it. She was a chump.

"Sunday, a week ago, Melissa disappeared without a trace. She didn't say good-bye to her husband, to her little girl, she just walked out the door. Do you have any idea where she might be?"

Ms. Gunther shook her head, her thick, evenly cut pageboy flopping against her face. "If I did, I wouldn't tell you."

"I thought it was your job to help people. Your clients are in serious trouble and you don't give a hoot."

"I do!" she protested. "I do. But we have rules. Don't you understand?"

"I wonder if *you* understand, Ms. Gunther. Rules are supposed to protect innocent people, not endanger them."

"What do you mean endanger?"

I plopped down onto a plaid cloth couch, leaned back, crossed my legs, and surveyed the place.

"What do you mean endanger?" she repeated.

"What do your friends call you?"

Bashfully, she tightened her forearms on her chest and said, "Helen."

"Helen, I began looking for Melissa as a favor for a friend. Since then, the friend has been tied up and was probably about to be tortured before I accidentally walked in. Melissa's daughter was kidnapped by her grandfather. And last week, Melissa phoned her aunt. She wanted to go up there and stay for a while. But she never showed. Yesterday, her aunt was murdered. The police in Bellingham think Burton did it."

"Oh, Judas Priest," said Helen Gunther, stumbling across the room to sit on the arm of an overstuffed chair opposite me. Using the middle finger of her hand, she shoved her glasses back up onto her nose. Her fingernails were painted fuchsia, matching the slash of color on her full lips.

"Did Melissa have any lesbian tendencies?"

"I can't tell you that," she snapped. But she did tell me. From the look on her face, I judged it was something that had never occurred to her in relation to Melissa.

"How about old boyfriends? Her neighbors tell me there was an old boyfriend hanging around."

"Really, Mr. Black. Maybe you are a private detective. But I can't tell you these things. I really can't. It's against . . . I don't know." She peeled off her glasses and rubbed her eyes with a pale hand. "You fooled me once before. How do I know this isn't all some ruse?"

"Helen," I said. "We think Melissa's in Tacoma somewhere. Was there an old boyfriend down there? From the look on your face, I'm thinking there was."

Helen Gunther sighed and snagged her glasses back

around either ear. "You'll have to leave now. I need to be at the clinic in fifteen minutes."

"Call Bellingham," I said. "Ask the police if they're holding Burton. I'll be back this afternoon."

"I won't be here, Mr. Black."

"Call me Thomas. This evening, then."

"Mr. Black, I've already spoken too long. This is just one of those things. I'm sorry, but I cannot reveal confidences."

"If somebody's life was at stake, could you?"

"Whose life would that be?"

"How about Melissa's? Whoever murdered her aunt might go after her next. Maybe she's dead now."

Helen Gunther shuddered but then shook her head stubbornly. "I'm not telling you or anyone else secrets my clients have disclosed. That's just the way things are. Good-bye."

"What about Melissa and her father? What was the problem?"

Helen Gunther got up and opened the front door, staring at the floor. Reluctantly, I left. Ten minutes later when she came out, I tailed her. She clambered into a dented MG and drove to a lot near the Hopewell Clinic. She ate four frosted donuts at a shop across the street, quaffed a coffee, and then ducked into the Hopewell.

I went back home, exercised, ate, and moped around the house the rest of the morning, fretting about Kathy. Though it was a million-to-one shot, I kept imagining some ogre would snatch her off the street. Some ogre with a penchant for electric ranges.

Without gaining an ounce of good for my troubles, I telephoned all the remaining phone numbers on my list.

Nobody in any of the pest companies I contacted admitted to knowing a Romano. None of the Romanos I got in touch with admitted to knowing a pest company. Life was just peachy keen. Mother had been right. Everything just dropped into your lap if you were a good boy.

Shortly after noon the phone jangled. I knew exactly who it was because I was naked in the tub. "Kathy?"

"You must have been sitting on the phone."

"No, I'm re-reading Shakespeare. I'm into the last act of *Henry VIII*. Lord Chamberlain has just come in. The phone happened to be next to the book here."

"Very funny."

"You sound tired."

"I've been in the stacks for hours. Pick me up at the library?"

"At the U?"

"Ride your bike down here and we'll walk back. We'll talk then."

"I'll be down in a few minutes." I toweled off, dressed, and coasted down through the campus.

I spotted Kathy sitting demurely on some brick steps in the quadrangle beside the library. I freewheeled across the bumpy brick wall and called out, "Hey, little girl. Want some candy?"

A passing undergraduate lacking a sense of humor gawked at me and frowned. Kathy egged the undergraduate on. "Geez, mister. After what I had to go through last week to get those Mountain bars ... I dunno." The undergraduate eyeballed us from a distance, adjusting his load of books and keeping careful tabs on my movements.

"What are you doing down here?"

"Looking up Angus Crowell."

"What did you find?"

"Talk about making your mark in the world. He's the president of the Coalition for Better Universities. He's the chairman of the local Boy Scout Council. He was even a state representative for four years way back in the fifties. He founded his church. He spearheaded a drive to sponsor Cambodian refugees in the state. I made a list of some other groups he's either president or chairman of. It goes on and on. How could one man possibly do justice to that many activities?"

"Organizations feel the need to plaster a big name across the top of their roster, someone to boast about. The more things a fellow belongs to, the bigger his name. There's a hardworking housewife somewhere transacting the real business in each of those groups."

"You think so? Let's go this way."

Kathy guided me toward the Ave. The street signs called it University Way N.E. but students had been calling it the Ave for eons. It was on our way, a visual treat, and generally it attracted quite a hodgepodge of people to its myriad shops and stores. We ambled up the sidewalk, me wheeling my Miyata and Kathy riffling through her notes on Angus Crowell.

"Really, Thomas. The more I tell you about Crowell, the more you'll have to respect the man."

"Let's start respecting."

"He's been written up in hundreds of different articles. Some of them decades old. Some of them as recent as this month. It's my feeling that he really thinks what he's doing is the right thing. Taking his granddaughter. He's just too much of a VIP to break the law like this without good reason."

"What else did you dig up?"

She gave me a disgruntled look. "At twenty, he was decorated by the navy. Their ship had a fire and he managed to drag somebody out of it. Eleven others died. He went to school right here, at the U. In the Second World War, he went to work at Boeing. He stayed more than ten years. When he left, he had worked all the way up from a riveter to one of the top management positions. He joined an investment company for a few years, then he was a state representative, and then in the fifties he founded Taltro Incorporated with some other man. He's been there ever since. He's the president."

"How long has he been the president?"

"Twelve years. The other guy's name was Harold Stubbins. The co-founder. He committed suicide. Jumped off the Aurora Bridge. They never did find the body. It was kind of a weird deal. He had been on the verge of buying out Angus. Then he killed himself and left the whole schmear to Crowell."

"Harold Stubbins? A guy like that might be nicknamed Harry, eh?"

"Sure. Why?"

"Nothing. What does Taltro do?"

"They manufacture outdoor clothing and sports equipment. Lately, they've gotten into running clothes and cycling stuff."

"Why is it I've never heard of them?"

"Their gear is all marketed under house names. Only rarely do they use their brand name. And it's not Taltro. It's Corona."

"Yeah, I've heard of Corona."

"What are you thinking, Thomas?"

"About his private life. What else did you find out?"

"He supports the symphony, the opera, attends all the

major city functions. He's been to the mayor's for supper. I'm sure he knows the police chief."

"I'm sure he's best friends with the police chief."

"What does that mean?"

"Nothing. It just fits the rest of the pattern. What about his personal investments? You find out anything?"

"Investments? The only thing I know about is this property he owns. I guess he's a sucker for gold mines. He owns a whole passel of burnt-out mines. Some in Eastern Washington. Some in Idaho. Some up north."

"Where?"

"I don't know. You want me to go back and find out?"

"I doubt if you'd get any addresses anyway. How about Romano? Did that name crop up anywhere in your reading?"

"I don't think so. Romano? He's the one who might have been seeing Melissa on the sly?"

"He's the one."

"I didn't see it. Thomas, do you have any idea where she is yet?"

"I have a vague suspicion of *why* she went. That's as far as I've gotten."

"Why did she go?"

"Just a hunch. It's a little sordid. When I know for certain, I'll explain."

"What do you mean, *sordid*?" We exchanged looks. Kathy had had some sort of evil premonition regarding the little girl, Angel Nadisky, or her mother, or both, and I could see it wafting through her dark thoughts again.

"You'll find out."

"I had Professor Creighton phone Bellingham and volunteer to represent Burton, but Burton wouldn't have anything to do with it. He got a court-appointed attorney.

Creighton talked to him for a minute. He said he sounded real depressed."

Kathy stopped in front of a jeweler's window to stuff her notes back into her bag. When she started to walk again, she caught my eye and halted. Inside the jeweler's window, a young woman with the biggest breasts I had ever seen was leaning over a display case. Actually, she wasn't leaning. More like tipping. She wore a maroon sweater, an exquisitely snug maroon sweater.

"Eat your heart out," said Kathy, snidely.

"I am."

"They're not real, you realize."

"They look real enough to me," I said, grinning, but only enough to irk Kathy.

"But they're not real."

"I've never heard such a case of sour grapes."

"I'd bet on it."

"Okay," I challenged. "Let's make a wager and go find out."

"Who's going to find out?"

"I volunteer."

"I just bet you do."

The woman in the jewelry shop looked up and saw my awed and admiring eyes. Kathy stood to my left and slightly behind, so she couldn't see the current of electricity that passed between myself and the busty woman. A guy like me ran into that sort of thing from time to time.

The woman smiled a twinkly smile and waved, using the smallest three fingers of her right hand. I waved back, grinning wickedly. It wasn't until I cocked my head to one side to comprehend the full dizzying impression I was making upon Kathy that I realized Kathy was waving, too. Kathy trundled past me into the shop. She knew the clerk. That much was obvious. Kathy had set me up. Again.

Inside, they greeted each other with hugs and chattering and more hugs. It was plain that I had made a fool of myself. She had been waving to Kathy, not me.

After the women had gabbed excitedly for a few moments, Kathy squinted at me and motioned me in. I shook my head. She waved again. I shrugged, leaned my ten-speed against their outer window, and shambled through the doorway, my head hung low. The last time anything this lousy had happened to me had been in junior high school.

Kathy introduced me to the clerk, Barb Fensterspinner. Barb beamed, acknowledging my chagrin, and her own amusement at it. Kathy explained, "Barb and I knew each other in college."

"Oh," I said, grinning as if witless.

"I brought you this way purposely," Kathy said. "Barb went out with some of Melissa's old boyfriends. She once told me some mildly hair-raising stories about Melissa."

"Oh," said Barb. Now she was the embarrassed party. "I hate to repeat anything I heard through a third party. I really do."

"It's not a question of spreading gossip," said Kathy, her eyes mesmerized temporarily by Barb's unbelievable bosom. "Melissa may be in trouble. Thomas thinks it may have something to do with her past. There was an old boyfriend the neighbors said used to come around when her husband was gone. We *have* to find her."

"All I know is a few things Hank told me. He's really the one you should be talking to."

"Didn't you say something about a motorcycle gang?"

"I really don't recall, Kathy. It's been so long. Hank and I were more friends than anything else. He was into that leather shop on Brooklyn Avenue and then they moved over to the Fremont District. I haven't seen him in years, but I'm sure you could find him in the phone book. Unless he took off to Walla Walla and started that vegetarian commune he was always talking about."

"What's his last name?" I asked.

"Waterman. Henry Waterman."

"They're not real," Kathy assured me as we left. "The boss never hires anyone who isn't built that way. Barb knew that and stuffed some laundry into her blouse when she went in for the interview. She's been like that ever since. Kind of a funny deal, huh?"

"Hilarious."

"You're just miffed 'cause you made a fool of yourself."

"Waterman," I said. "Henry Waterman."

"You're just miffed."

"I don't get miffed. You know that."

"Ho ho. He doesn't get miffed. Take me, Lord, now I've heard everything."

"I really don't get miffed."

15

BARB WITH THE LAUNDRY BOSOM was right. We stopped at a pay phone and I found Henry Waterman in the Seattle directory. A young-sounding woman answered the phone in a wheezy, high-pitched voice. She told me her name was Judy. I had not asked, but she told me anyway, as if it were habitually the first thing she announced.

"Hello. This is Judy."

"I'm looking for a Henry Waterman."

"Hank's at work right now. Could I have him call you?"

"I need to see him today. Is he still working in a leather shop?"

"Oh, Jesus no. Hank gave that crap up years ago. That whole hippy gig went right out the window when Hank stopped doing acid, you know. No, he's working at a tire re-capping plant in South Park. After hours, he plays softball for them. Pitches. You want the address?"

It was a twenty-minute drive. I pedaled the bike home ahead of Kathy, hopped into the truck, and headed for South Park. It was a grimy industrial area in the city's south end, and the roads were blanketed in mud the color of weak tea.

144

Parking in four inches of ooze, I picked my way through a fenced yard piled high with stacks of worn, shabby tires. A spindly boy who looked too young to be working legally was crouched on the roof of the building shoveling a gritty, black substance into buckets.

Hank Waterman was operating a machine in the back room, a grinder. He switched it off, and we both waited for it to stop screaming so we could hear each other.

Long, stringy hair dangling just over his shoulders, stubble on his chin, the inevitable baseball cap, tattered jeans, and a plaid workshirt from Sears that might have last seen the inside of a washing machine in 1975—Hank Waterman had conscientiously cultivated slob-chic. Who said America had no peasant class? And who said they didn't wear a national uniform?

"You used to know Barb Fensterspinner?" I asked. Waterman nodded. "I spoke to her half an hour ago. She said you dated Melissa Nadisky."

Hank Waterman scratched his grimy forehead with a black thumbnail and gave me a blank look. "Melissa Nadisky?"

"You knew her as Melissa Crowell."

The light bulb lit up. "Melissa? Sure. How the hell is she?"

"That's why I'm here, Hank. She's missing. Her husband is in big trouble and we have to find her. Nobody seems to know where she might have gone."

"Geez, she's married? Somebody said she was married but I didn't believe it. What kind of jam is her old man in? Dope? Dealin' dope?"

"It's a lot worse than that, pal. Murder."

"Heavy, man. Shit, I haven't seen her in years. Honest to God, Buddy. Ask Judy. I'm living with Judy. I been

with her . . . oh, about three years. We even got a Saint
Bernard."

"I'm trying to track down some of her old friends,
that's all. I thought you might know some of them. You
see, we think she might have run off with an old
boyfriend, or somebody she knew about the time she
knew you."

"What are you? A cop?"

"A private detective. I'm working for friends of the
family."

Hank Waterman inhaled deeply and weighed what I
had told him. A man with short hair, conspicuously
dressed much better than everyone else in the place,
peeked through the open concrete doorway and presented
Hank with a stony look.

"Hey, man," said Hank, using a practiced tone of
servitude. It had been a while since I'd punched a company time clock. I had forgotten what it was like. "Think
I could take my fifteen now and work through at two?
This dude needs to rap."

The man in the doorway shot me a surly look, scanning me for traces of seediness. He nodded and made a
point of studying his watch before exiting.

"Nice guy," I said, facetiously.

"He put an egg timer next to the shitter once. We were
supposed to use it to time ourselves. Everybody used to
pee on it."

Waterman fired up a cigarette and waited for me to
continue. When I didn't, he said, "Who'd Melissa's old
man waste?"

"It's rather involved. Think you can remember much
about Melissa in the old days?"

"Man, she was wild. What do you want to know?"

"Barb, or somebody, said something about a motor-cycle gang. You ever hear anything about that?"

Waterman was nonplussed. He whisked off his base-ball cap and grinned crookedly. "Man, she told you about *that*?"

"One of her friends heard the story from her, years ago."

"Oh man," said Waterman, shielding his face with the back of his cigarette hand. "I don't want anyone running to Meliss and sayin' 'I heard Hank Waterman says you went to the beach and got gangbanged by the Skeletons,' ya know."

The Skeletons were a Northwest motorcycle club that had disbanded a few years back. Once in a while you'd still see a rider wearing their colors.

"Is that what happened?"

"You ain't tellin' anyone, are you?"

"I'm trying to find Melissa. Anything I find out on the way is between you and me and the fence post."

" 'Cause, man, I mean like, Meliss told me not to ever tell another soul, you know. And what do I do, first thing? I spill it all to Barb. And now I find out Barb was blabbing it all over town."

"I doubt if it went any further than me. Besides, I don't even know what the story is."

"Melissa used to tag along with this biker. It pissed her dad off royal. I think that's maybe why she did it. I mean the guy was a real toad. You'd get warts if you touched him. He was just a toad. But Melissa kept going back to him. He was some Harley freak she'd known since high school. The guy was twenty or twenty-five years older than us. I think he was maybe in his forties when she first ran into him."

"You ever hear a name?"

"The Harley freak? Naw. See, I didn't go with Melissa that long. We didn't even have sex much. It was mostly tripping out on grass, ya know. We used to get into these long confession jags. That's where I found out about this biker.

"It seems like the guy was almost straight when she first met him, was doing some sort of extermination work for Melissa's father at their house . . ."

It was my turn for the light bulb. Extermination work? According to the neighbors, Melissa's unwanted suitor drove a pest control van.

"Melissa wanted to get the toad out of her life, but he was the kind of jingo who didn't really have anything better going for him and never would, so he kept popping up."

"Tell me about her father. You said the biker was working for her father?"

"I can't remember the whole deal. Ya wanta know how they met? The dude was out working in her dad's yard and she invited him into her bedroom through the window. She was seventeen."

"That's hard to imagine."

"Melissa was an incredible person. She was so screwed up, it was hard to believe sometimes."

"You sure about this story?"

"I wouldn't swear to it. I was stoned, ya know, when she told me."

"Melissa ever tell you anything about getting pregnant in high school?"

"Naw. Did she?"

"How about this biker? I heard something about her father paying him off, paying him off so he'd join the army. Somebody thought he might have broken his neck."

"He was still around when I knew Melissa. At least that's the impression I got."

"What sort of relationship did Melissa have with this biker?"

"Bad, man. I mean real bad. See, Melissa's one of those chicks who don't feel right unless they got some man givin' 'em shit, know what I mean?"

"I've seen it."

"Geez, there was this guy, this little guy used to write poetry. He would have eaten a mile of her shit just to kiss her ass, but she wouldn't have anything to do with him. He made one bad mistake. He treated her like a queen. You had to treat Melissa like shit or she didn't know where you were comin' from, man."

"Is that how you treated her?"

"Well, yeah, I guess. I used to be into the acid gig, you know. Like, I had this little leather shop in the U District, and all these teenybopper chicks who didn't know their twat from a hole in the ground would come in, you know. It wasn't hard to nail 'em. Yeah, I was into bein' kind of a creep. Judy says I'm shaping up now. It takes a whole long time to raise your consciousness."

"What about the biker?"

"I guess he took her to the ocean on his Harley once. He took her down to Illwaco and she was thinking they were going to camp out and do a joint or two, you know. Well, this toad met a bunch of his biker buddies, Skeletons, and in order to impress them all, he sorta passed her around."

"What do you mean?"

"Meliss told me the story maybe three times, and each

time it got a bit hazier. But I had the impression that they had a good old-fashioned gangbang, you know. It haunted her. It really did. But ya know what, man? After we broke up, I saw her with this guy again. At least he was some sort of biker. It must have been him. He was a toad. In Tacoma, down on Pacific Avenue. I was in a car with some other people comin' home from a Dead concert."

"What'd the guy look like?"

"He was fairly short, and looked Oriental, maybe South American, ya know. Only he wasn't. He just looked that way like some dudes do. And he was old. They were going to a movie down there, *Bonnie and Clyde*. But the thing was, I had the feeling they had just come from this run-down old hotel right next door. And you know, she said something about this guy bein' from Tacoma. I remember now, 'cause I'm from Tacoma, and I wondered if I'd ever met him."

"Had you?"

"What, man?"

"Had you ever met him?"

"You know those bikers. That hair and those mirror sunglasses. You coulda dressed him up in a suit and a tie ten minutes after I saw him and I wouldn't'a recognized the guy. But it was kind of a weird experience. When I knew Meliss, she was real free and easy. She slept with quite a few guys, but she never took any of it seriously. And she had this little punk who wanted to marry her, this poet."

"They got married."

"Did they? Wow!"

"Did Melissa ever tell you anything about her father?"

"Man, talk about rolling in it. We went down there to

their house once and jumped in their pool naked. Some of the neighbors called the cops and they came down and hassled us."

"You had a lot of good times, didn't you?" I said, a touch of irony in my voice that he didn't quite catch.

"Yeah, man. But everybody's doing something else now. You know? Meliss got married. Jon and Paul are both dead. Jon got it in Nam, and Paul fell asleep on some railroad tracks somewhere and got cut in half. All the others are straight now, you know, working at Boeing or back in school. Fred got his law degree. Believe that? He's working for the city. There's nobody left, ya know. Just me and Judy and my dog."

Before I left, I had Waterman give me a better description of the movie theater and the hotel in Tacoma. He wasn't positive Melissa and the biker had been coming out of the hotel, but it was the only lead I had. As Waterman escorted me to the main entrance of the building, glancing nervously around for his boss, I measured his height against mine. Our burglar had been taller than me, tall enough to thunk his head on the top of the door frame. Hank towered a good five inches over me.

Outside, it was coming down in large drops the size of penny gum balls. I drove four blocks through the muddy side streets of South Park before I remembered Taltro's headquarters was nearby, directly across the river in Georgetown. What the hell? Maybe the old man knew where his daughter was by now. Maybe he would listen to reason. Maybe he wouldn't fly off the handle this time. Maybe they sold Nutty Buddies in Hades, too.

16

TALTRO WAS LOCATED IN A MOD-
ern complex of buildings, the barn-
like offices in front, and several tin-walled warehouses
and manufacturing buildings spaced out behind.

The receptionist at the main door was in her forties and
wore enough lipstick for three pairs of lips. When I asked
for Angus Crowell, her face grew dark, and I realized she
must have been the woman I had spoken to yesterday
about Crowell's dead sister.

"It's personal," I said. "Angus Crowell?"

She must have recognized my voice from the telephone. "Is it about his family problem?"

"You bet."

I passed a lot of people wearing important looks on
their faces, in important clothes, doing important jobs
before I found Crowell. Surprisingly, his secretary didn't
look too important, said I was expected and told me to go
right in. She closed his door behind me as if it were a
trap. His office was empty.

Water sloshed in a sink. "Be right with you," Crowell
said in a booming voice.

He was bent over in a washroom behind a door, scrubbing, his shirt sleeves rolled up past his elbows, a lather

of soap creeping up his forearms. I could see a slice of him through a crack at the hinge. His hands made squeaky sounds against the suds.

I sat down. He washed for a long while. Some people almost made a religious experience out of being clean. When he came out, he walked around behind his desk, unrolling his shirt sleeves, fastening one cuff button before reaching across to shake my hand. It wasn't what I had been expecting.

"Sorry about the last time we met," said Crowell, making an uncharacteristic face. "Things like that don't happen to me much anymore."

He plunked down into his swivel chair, cocked it around and glanced out the window at the steel-gray skies. "Not since the girl left home for college." He cocked back around to face me, tilting the chair backward and rocking it. "I suppose this family is beginning to look pretty bad to you?"

"The thought had occurred to me," I said, watching him carefully. He was so different from the last time we had met, I had to marvel at it.

"I've been under a lot of pressure. And I understand you tried to get hold of me yesterday about my sister?"

"I did."

"My wife and my sister have been feuding for years. I don't even recall what initiated it. If I had known about Mary yesterday, I would have driven up and taken care of the arrangements."

"Do you know where your daughter is?"

He squinted at me like a gunfighter about to draw, then relaxed. "No, I don't. Do you?"

"No, but I'll find her. That's what I've been hired to do and that's what I'll do."

"May I ask who hired you?" I had the feeling his curiosity was much more intense and all-inclusive than he wanted to let on.

I ignored his query. He already knew who hired me. Kathy had told him last Friday when she spoke to him. I said, "I have reason to believe you want her found also."

"I placed the ad in the paper. Sure I did. Two thousand dollars is not much when your daughter has vanished."

"Funny. I thought you had different feelings toward Melissa."

"She's my daughter, damn it. Nothing can change that fact. And I . . . I love her. No matter what she does . . . I love her."

The scene was almost touching. It wasn't every day you saw a gruff old guy on the verge of tears, talking about love.

"Why is she so frightened of you?"

"I wasn't aware that she was."

"She is."

Angus looked up, waiting for me to divulge the family secrets I had unearthed. As he played his thick hands about the desk top, I watched the scars on the back of one hand, the scars Mary Dawn had told me about Sunday. She claimed a dog had done it. A dog will do a lot of things if you corner it.

"Look, Mr. Black. I wish you would forget everything I said the other night. I'm not especially proud of my performance. I guess I was . . . I guess I was out of my head. We only have the one girl and she turned out so bad. She's . . . well, she's had psychological problems since she was a pre-teen."

"And now?"

"We're not sure. She's stunned us so many times.

From time to time, Melissa makes . . . weird allegations. If you get to her before I do, I hope you'll take her mental state into consideration."

"I try to take everyone's mental state into consideration."

"Good." He watched me carefully, trying to see whether I was mocking him. Finally he decided I wasn't.

"You have a man following me, don't you, Mr. Crowell?"

His brown eyes suddenly turned hard. I was glad I didn't have regular business dealings with him. I'd lose my pants.

He was striving to be mellow and relaxed when he replied, "We have security problems in this industry. It looks like small potatoes, but we've got almost five thousand people working for us in five plants on the West Coast. Now we're trying to expand to the Midwest. We've had industrial espionage problems. Unexplained fires. Mangled machinery. The lead supervisor in this particular plant was almost killed in a freak auto accident last month.

"You see, Mr. Black, when my daughter disappeared, everything I knew warranted that it had something to do with my business interests. That's why it was so important that we had Angel in our custody. But you could never explain a thing like that to the scatterbrain." We both knew which scatterbrain he was referring to.

"Are you saying Melissa's disappearance was caused by some of your business rivals?"

"That's the hypothesis we've been working under."

"And your sister's murder? Was that related also?"

"Burton did that. The Bellingham police have him in custody."

"So you do have a man following me?"

"That's not what I said." He was irked, but he remained civil. "I said I have every reason to believe Melissa's present problems, whatever they are, are related in some way to this business I'm trying to run. We've hired a security firm to look into it. It was only this morning that I discovered that, among other things, the security people had been following you. I want you to know right now that I had nothing to do with it, and the moment I found out I had it stopped. Sometimes these security outfits get a little overeager."

"Then we're both after the same thing? We both want to find Melissa?"

He nodded. "My reward stands. If you bring her to me before my security people do, the two thousand is yours."

"I'll be in touch."

"I don't know how much you're being paid or who's paying you, but I can up that reward. Five thousand? How does that sound?"

"That sounds higher."

"You want more?"

"I don't want anything from you, Mr. Crowell, except to know why your daughter is afraid of you. From what I've uncovered so far, a lot of the reason she left had to do with avoiding a confrontation with you."

Angus Crowell's eyes narrowed and the caterpillar eyebrows knit together. "What sort of confrontation?"

"Nobody seems to know that except your daughter."

"Well, bring her here, boy, and we'll work things out together."

I got up to leave.

"You don't trust me," he stated flatly. "Is it because of the way I handled Burton last Sunday? Look at what he did! My judgment of that boy has been vindicated! He's everything I said he was and worse!"

"Good day, Mr. Crowell."

"Black?" He got up and limped around his desk like an old grizzly. An affectation. He hadn't limped earlier. He dropped a heavy arm around my shoulders and said, "When you find her, be gentle. She's a troubled girl. She needs more understanding than anybody can know about. Be gentle and try not to judge her."

Outside in the parking lot, I knelt and ran my fingers under the sidewalls and bumpers of the truck. My palms were black by the time I discovered the transmitter under the rear bumper. It was no larger than a crab apple. That was why I hadn't spotted anybody tailing me. Using a transmitter, a tail could afford to lose visual contact almost whenever he wished, knowing that he could be reasonably assured of picking me up again on the signal. I placed the electronic device back where I found it.

It was turning into a long day. On a hunch, I bucked the first trickles of rush-hour traffic and drove back to Helen Gunther's apartment.

Four blue-and-whites and two unmarked city cars were parked in the street. I should have known while I was still outside. I walked around the apartment complex, through the wet grass to her basement unit. A uniformed policeman in her doorway grabbed me by the arm and held me.

Before he could grill me, I peeked over his shoulder and saw a part of her body sprawled on the bed, the rest of her obscured by dark blue uniforms.

"Is she dead?"

"What's your name, Bub?"

"She's dead, isn't she?"

"Give me your name."

"What is it, Hal?" A plainclothesman drifted to the door. He recognized me, but I could see by the puzzlement on his face that he could not recall exactly where he knew me from.

I volunteered the information. "I used to shoot on the team. I worked the north end."

The plainclothesman had been in uniform the last time I'd seen him. He'd obviously risen in rank and responsibility. It didn't seem to weigh heavily on him. He went about his job with a casual, confident air. It was the sort of personality you liked to see in a cop. It was the way I hoped I had been.

"You retired a few years back?"

"Thomas Black. It was a bum knee." The uniformed cop stopped scowling and let go of me.

"You know her?" he asked, nodding toward the woman on the bed.

"Not really. I spoke to her this morning. She dead?"

"They don't come any deader."

17

Two murders in two days.

Sprawled on the bed, she had been bludgeoned and probably violated. It looked like a man's crime. Her skull was dented and bloody. Her jumper had been ripped off. The skin of her chest was pale and bloodless. Her chalky white brassiere had been twisted and knotted around her neck. Her face was a purplish black. In death, her large head appeared even larger, much too big for her sleek torso.

The place was packed with uniforms. One could hardly move. The air was fetid. I found an empty chair and sat heavily, balancing my head in my hands. From the moment I confirmed that she was dead, I knew I was gong to have to make a decision. Would I tell them about the murder in Bellingham, or would I keep my trap shut? Coming here had been a mistake. I would have much rather read about it in the tabloids.

I had Hank Waterman's insistence that he'd once seen Melissa and her biker friend in Tacoma on Pacific Avenue near a hotel. A week ago, Melissa had phoned her aunt from a pay phone on Pacific Avenue. I had the phone number and address of the booth.

With a little footwork, I was reasonably assured of

finding her. If nothing else, I could stake out the phone booth. She had used it once. She would probably use it again.

I was sure the cops storming about Helen Gunther's tiny apartment had heard of the killing in Bellingham, but I was just as sure that it would take them weeks to link Mary Dawn Crowell's murder to Helen Gunther's. On the other hand, blurting out a few well-chosen words, I could connect the two murders and become the center of attention, the bull's-eye on a municipal dart board.

The plainclothesman who had let me in was named Gayden. After a few minutes on the phone, he came over, knelt in front of my chair and said, "You just met her, you say?"

"Twice. I saw her the other day for a few minutes and then this morning."

"You date her, or what?"

"She was a friend of a friend."

"You trying to be coy?"

I looked at him. "Am I a suspect?"

"At this point, everybody's a suspect. When it comes to killing a woman, everybody's a suspect."

"I'm a private detective now. She's a psychologist. One of her clients is missing. Ran away from her husband. That's how I met her. I thought she might be able to point me in the right direction."

"Did she?"

"Not a peep. I was going to give her one last try before I tracked down some other leads."

Gayden nodded, then held up a plastic evidence bag, a pair of crushed tortoiseshell glasses suspended inside. "You ever see these before?"

"She was wearing them this morning."

"We found them outside the door. It looks like she had quite a struggle. She's a pretty big girl. He must have been a bruiser."

"Or somebody with a lot of practice," I said.

Gayden stared at me. "You ever miss the job?"

"I feel bad about it. I don't miss it. But I feel bad about it. This stuff I'm doing now . . . it has its moments."

"Why do you do it?"

"It's what I know."

Gayden snorted. "Yeah, that's how I feel a lot of the time. It's what I know. Can you guess how we found out about this?" He gestured toward the dead woman on the bed. "A neighbor upstairs heard a commotion about an hour and a half ago. He didn't want to get involved in it, so he turned his stereo up. He heard screaming and doors slamming. He could have come down here and saved her."

"So he called you?"

"After it was quiet for fifteen minutes he got curious. He found these outside." Gayden displayed the bag with the glasses. "The door was partially open. He could see the body from where he stood. You can see where he tossed his cookies in the garden."

"That's your only lead?" I asked, debating whether or not to tell them about Mary Dawn.

"So far."

I could always plead ignorance. After all, the Bellingham police had a suspect in custody. A reasonable man had no cause to assume the two murders were connected. No cause at all. Except that both women were going to hand over information on Melissa Nadisky. Both women lived alone. Both women had been brutally murdered, probably by the same person. Not Burton. Not likely. I had never figured him for the Bellingham killing, and it would have been impossible for him to have done this from a jail cell eighty miles away.

"Want to tell me the name of this woman you're looking for?"

Suddenly I was overflowing with information and goodwill. "Name is Melissa Nadisky. A blonde. Mid-twenties. Slender. Pretty."

It did not mean beans to Gayden. He stood up and straightened his trousers. "You know who might have done this?"

"I haven't the foggiest," I said, truthfully.

Gayden speculated aloud. "A psychologist. She treats people off the street, I'll bet. Who knows what sort of flakes she's been involved with in the last six months."

"Was she sexually assaulted?"

The room had cleared out except for two uniformed cops. Gayden paced as he replied.

"Can't tell yet. Near as we can figure, somebody came to the door, forced it, argued with her for some time, then whacked her around. The guy upstairs said the yelling seemed to go on for a while. He thought for sure it was some sort of domestic dispute. Apparently she almost broke free once, because we found these outside." Gayden dangled the plastic bag containing the shattered glasses. He shook his head, stared at the corpse, and said, "Poor kid. She looked like a real nice one. Was she?"

I was wrapped up in my own thoughts. "Pardon?"

"Was she a nice one?"

"One of the nicest," I said, recalling that she had been a bit of a dope.

"I just hope we nail this yo-yo," said Gayden, staring at Helen Gunther's awkward corpse.

"Did she have any papers?" I asked. "Some folders, notes?"

"We haven't spotted anything."

"There should be a folder around somewhere. As far as I know she was in the habit of taking it home with her."

"Nothing here."

"You sure?"

"Yeah. I just hope we nail this yo-yo."

Kathy wasn't in, but she had left a note for me on the kitchen table under a nutcracker.

> Ward, honey,
> Wally and I are shopping for a surprise for the Beav.
> Back around five.
> June

She came in while I was fixing a snack, garbed in a long black coat and witch boots. Her eye shadow was dark and overdone and she wore a tall beryl-blue wool cap. Her hair was hidden, her face long and lean. Nobody in Tacoma would recognize her. She looked like a vamp from a D. W. Griffith flick.

"Let's go," I said. "I've got a hot lead on Melissa. In Tacoma."

"Can't I eat first?"

"Not this time, kiddo."

"Do I have to come along?"

"I thought you liked this detective business."

"I've got exams at the end of the week."

"Remember Ms. Gunther?"

"At the Hopewell? How could I forget? I'm going to

call her up and apologize for what we did. I don't care what you say."

"You won't reach her."

Kathy's violet eyes fixed on mine for two long beats. "Why not?"

"Somebody killed her about two hours ago."

Kathy plunked down into one of my kitchen chairs so hard it shrieked in protest. "Do you think it has anything to do with . . ."

"I think it has everything to do with . . ."

"That's why you want me to go with you?"

"I don't want you here alone."

"Oh, dear," said Kathy, tears of sympathy and grief beading up in her eyes. "Could we have . . . ?"

"There was nothing anyone could have done. Who could predict a thing like that? Besides, there's a remote possibility it doesn't have anything to do with Melissa."

"Very remote," said Kathy. "Of course it has something to do with Melissa. First Melissa's aunt, who was going to talk to you. And now Melissa's counselor. How did you find out?"

"I saw her this morning. I told her I was coming back. When I went back, the joint was buzzing with cops."

Even as I spoke, I thought about the bug under my rear bumper. Someone from Taltro's security staff might have followed me that morning, the same way Holder had followed me to Bellingham. Sure, they had tailed me. It was probably Julius Caesar Holder himself. But Holder hadn't done anything in Bellingham. He had showed up after the body had been discovered. Had he killed Mary Dawn Crowell, it was highly unlikely he would have loitered around in the parking lot afterward rubbernecking with the old folks.

Certainly Holder and the Taltro security people were implicated, but I doubted if they were running around killing people. On the other hand, Holder was just the sort of guy to free-lance a bit, wander off on his own and stir up trouble. Whoever had committed the two murders was more dangerous than anyone I had tangled with in quite a while.

Kathy climbed into the truck while I went around to the back and removed the bug from under the bumper. Fetching a large, sturdy rat trap from the garage, I wired the bug onto the spring mechanism of the trap, then vaulted my neighbor's fence, and scooted down onto the wet pavement under the rear of his Buick. Horace would never know what happened.

Whoever had set the bug would follow Horace, realize their mistake, and try to recover the tracking device when he parked. They were going to get a quick, hard lesson in retrieving things when they slid their fingers into the trigger of the rat trap. It took five minutes to tape it up and activate it satisfactorily. My jacket and trousers were wet when I jumped into the truck. I switched on the heater to dry them out.

"Whatever were you doing, Thomas?"

"Just a prank."

"It didn't look like a prank. That trap'll break somebody's fingers."

"Think so?"

"If Horace ever finds out, he'll go bananas."

"Horace is already bananas. Besides, he won't. That type of transmitter is expensive. Whoever set it will want it back. By the way, what'd you get the Beav?"

It took Kathy a few moments to figure out what I was

talking about. "Oh, the Beav. Wally and I got him a Vivaldi album."

Tacoma was as gray and smelly as I remembered it. The early winter darkness shrouded the city as we pulled onto Pacific Avenue, a main drag running along the underbelly of the burg. We bumbled through the rush-hour traffic until we found the approximate location Hank Waterman had described to me. We parked in a lot for two bucks.

An old theater had been renovated and converted into a savings-and-loan. Two doors away stood the entrance to a sleazy hotel, a pair of aging drunks in baggy plaid trousers panhandling outside.

A rheumy-eyed news vendor wearing fingerless work gloves confirmed that the savings-and-loan had once been a theater. We showed him the photo of Melissa, but he drew a blank. Across the street beside the hotel stood a plant store which looked as if it might have been a tavern at one time. The vendor confirmed that too. It had been called Joe's. Now the section of street matched Waterman's description to a tee.

We found the phone booth up the street. Some wino had relieved himself on the floor recently. The number was the one Smithers had obtained from the phone company for me. Melissa had telephoned her aunt from that booth last Tuesday night. I was as close to her as I had ever been. Kathy and I looked around the street as if we might spot Melissa after only a cursory search. Not a chance.

The hotel was called The Last Inn and it reeked. It was the sort of broken-down hovel pensioners and welfare drunks resided in, and transients died in so they could be discovered days later and their mattresses fumigated with a can of Lysol.

"Is this where you think she is?" Kathy asked.

"Waterman thinks he saw her coming out of this place a few years back. The phone she used last Tuesday night is right down the street. I can't think of a better place to start looking."

In the lobby, two obese Indian women were hunched on a pair of dingy davenports watching a flickery black-and-white Magnavox. Reruns of *I Love Lucy* that were almost as old as I was mesmerized the women.

A dried-up gentleman with a long, sepia face leaned on the counter, perusing a *Reader's Digest*.

"You ever see this woman?" I asked, pushing the photo of Melissa Crowell Nadisky under his nose.

He took his time turning away from the *Reader's Digest*. It was a back issue from 1942. He scrutinized the tiny photo for a few moments, then gave me a bleary look.

"You a copper?"

"Private," I said.

"Gettin' paid pretty good, are ya?"

I slapped a five-dollar bill down and watched it disappear into his liver-spotted fist. "Sure, I seen somebody sorta looks like her. They call her the Blue Diamond."

"You're kidding."

"That's what they call her."

"She been around long?"

"A week maybe."

"Know where I can find her?"

He raised his eyes toward the ceiling. "Up there. 301. But she ain't in."

"Know where I can get hold of her? Right now?"

He picked up the photo and examined it again. " 'Course, she don't look exactly like this. The Diamond is all gussied up, you know. This looks like maybe her younger sister."

"You sure it's the same one?"

"Not really," he said, clicking his dentures. "But it looks like her."

Kathy had moved to the other side of the lounge, chunked a quarter into a newspaper vending machine and was scanning the front page.

"What's she like?" I asked.

"Ain't never had a date with her." He was patronizing me now. He had the bone and I was the slobbering puppy.

"When was the last time you saw her?"

Slowly, he glanced up over the doorway at a clock that had a broken cover. " 'Bout two hours ago."

"Here?"

"I ain't left the place all day."

"She live upstairs?"

He nodded toward the two Indian women on the sofas. "They live here. The Blue Diamond just works here."

"She hooking?"

"She don't do no work, but she makes plenty of dough."

"She hooks."

He nodded.

"She have a boyfriend?"

"You might call him that."

"Name?"

"Couldn't tell you that. He's a mean one. I could get my head knocked off talking 'bout him."

I sandpapered a ten-dollar bill across the counter. It

disappeared into his wrinkled fist with the five. "Name's Solomon. Least that's what he calls himself. He'll stick ya if you let him."

"He carries a knife?"

"Nobody's gonna stick ya with a wad of gum, mister." He had me on that.

"She come in every night?"

"Some nights. Some days."

"Think she'll be back tonight?"

"I ain't no mind reader. She comes in when she's a mind to, or when she's got a john."

"If I wanted to find her right now, where might I try?"

Rubbing his whiskered chin with his dirty fingers, he said, "Braverman's, up the hill 'bout two blocks." We stood looking at each other for a moment, the impatient private eye and the old codger. Finally he said, "He's short and he's got snake eyes. Real mean. He kinda likes to see people hurt. His trick is he sticks without any warning. Once he gets his ire up he'll stick ya anytime. In the back. In the brain. I seen him stick a woman in the cheek once."

"Can you describe him a little better?"

"He's a pimp."

"Black or white?"

"Hard to tell. He's kinda old for the game." He picked up the *Reader's Digest* and tried to find his place.

Kathy and I left by the back door so that I could reconnoiter all the exits. It was an old battle habit. Kathy, who had been skimming through the *Tacoma News Tribune*, said, "I found nothing in the paper about Ms. Gunther." Breathing heavily as she skipped along trying to keep to my pace, Kathy said, "Where are we going?"

"We're looking for a cut-rate pimp."

"Melissa's not . . ."

"That's what they tell me."

"She's not!"

"I think she is."

"Where?"

"Right up there." I could see the cheap neon sign advertising Braverman's from the mouth of the alley behind The Last Inn. Braverman's was a small, windowless cocktail lounge.

A Pontiac with serious ring problems was doubleparked in front of Braverman's, puking smoke into the city evening. Kathy started into Braverman's, but I grasped her arm and pulled her back.

"Wait here a minute," I said.

"You know that guy in the car?"

"He lives in Ballard."

"So?"

"Across the street from Melissa and Burton."

"Oh."

Sidney Iddins grinned idiotically as I walked around the car into the street next to the driver's door. The grin looked more foxlike when I spotted the .357 magnum tucked snugly between his fat thighs.

18 IT WAS A DEBATE WHETHER TO hightail it or to coldcock Sidney through the open window of the Pontiac before he could train the gun on me. I did neither, and to my surprise he left the gun where it was—between his legs.

"Hey, guy," Sidney said, flashing a toothy grin, doing a Groucho with his eyebrows. "Who's that cunt? Pretty nice."

"She's a woman cop," I lied. "She'd just as soon castrate you as look at you."

The grin melted off his face. "Well, she ain't got no cause to be gunnin' after me."

"If she heard what you just called her she'd cut you off at the knees."

"What? What'd I call her?"

"Never mind. What are you doing here?"

"Helga got a call from Blondy. Wants a ride home, I guess. She's inside talking to somebody now. I brought Myrtle along for comfort." He took two fingers and patted the .357 between his thighs.

"Is Melissa Nadisky inside?"

"Ain't been in. Don't know. She said on the phone

171

she'd meet Helga here. I guess she figured good old Helgy could get her out of any fix."

"How long has your wife been inside?"

He glanced at his watch. " 'Bout five minutes."

Escorting Kathy through the front door into the dark lounge, I said, "Keep cool, Kathy. Stay by the door and pretend you're not with me. Just in case."

"Just in case what?"

"Let's hope we don't find out what."

I spotted Helga Iddins strutting from the rear of the lounge, indignation reflected in her walk, but still conscious of the male eyes on her.

She didn't recognize me until I blocked her path. Halting, slamming her fists onto her hips, she searched my face.

"You? Well, you've almost found her. She's sitting back there." Helga gestured toward the rear of the cocktail lounge with a toss of her long brown hair. I couldn't see Melissa or anyone who looked like a pimp, but there were booths around a corner.

"Your husband said she called you."

"This afternoon. Shit. And I have to work tonight. I should be there right now. She calls me up, whines about being scared to leave without a friend along, then when I get here she won't budge."

"She give a reason?"

"Reason? Hell, she won't even talk. Not a squeak."

"Is *he* back there?"

"Yeah, but he left. How 'bout that reward? Can I get it now?"

"You'll find a number in last night's paper. Call it."

"Shit. She could have scrammed with me. I told her

Sidney was outside with a gun. We could have gotten her home. Shit. Shit." She stormed off toward the exit.

As I followed Helga's backside, Kathy locked eyes with me across the smoky room and shot me a scathing look. For a split second I grinned wickedly.

I located Melissa in the last booth, her back to the wall, as if afraid to let anybody or anything sneak up behind her. She was slouched over a cup of coffee, fanning the lazy snakes of her own cigarette smoke out of her eyes with a cheap mimeographed menu. She held her cigarette the way a new smoker does. I recalled no ashtrays at the Nadisky house. She had adopted the habit within the last ten days, along with some other habits. I had to wonder how it would feel to be sitting across the table from her haggling over prices and contemplating what she was going to do upstairs at The Last Inn.

"Melissa?"

Her pale blue eyes seemed to sink back into her brain. I sat down across from her in the booth, wishing my back wasn't exposed to the open room. Somewhere nearby was a gentleman who liked to stick people.

In hushed tones she said, "You must be looking for someone else. My name is Blue."

"Sure it is," I said, flopping the photograph I'd been carrying for three days onto the tabletop. She peered at it, pretending not to be startled.

"Blue," I said. "Melissa Crowell Nadisky Blue. You've got a little girl who needs you badly."

Melissa picked up a tarnished spoon and dunked it into her coffee cup, watching the swirls of steam rise off the surface of the liquid. She wore a shiny black blouse.

"I'm a detective, Melissa. You don't have to worry

about escaping from whoever you're with. I can get you away. Your friend hired me to find you."

"Friend?" She glanced around the lounge. It smelled of popcorn and booze and stale cigarette smoke. It smelled like a stall in purgatory. Striving to look as bored as humanly possible, she said, "I don't have any friends."

"Kathy Birchfield is your friend. She hired me. She's at the front door right now."

The look of contained boredom vanished for a moment. "Kathy?"

"You going back with us?"

"God, no! Just go away. All of you go away. Before you get into trouble."

"You called Helga and then when she got here you didn't want to leave. Why?"

"She brought her . . ."

"Because she brought her husband along? I don't blame you. He's a bum."

"You a cop?" Her voice was small and faded and almost as delicate as the alabaster skin of her face and neck. My indictment of Sidney Iddins had won her over. Except for the gaudy makeup, the blue eyeliner and the painted cheeks, she looked enough like Burton to be his sister. Somehow Kathy executed the whore makeup routine better.

"I was a cop. Now I'm a private detective. I'm a friend of Kathy's. She asked me to find you."

"Why?"

"She was worried about your little girl."

"Angel? How is Angel?"

"She needs you."

The entire conversation was moving along without any eye contact. I was speaking to a sad young woman, but the sad young woman was speaking to the spoon in her fingers.

"Nobody needs me. Nobody at all." She stubbed out her cigarette and watched the tiny orange glow die out as if she had a bet on how long it would take.

"Angel needs you. She needs you to get her away from your father."

"My father?" Animation infused her eyes for the first time since we'd met. "My father? What does my father have to do with anything?"

"He spirited Angel away from Burton this past Sunday. He feels he is better qualified to raise her than Burton, especially since you've split the family up. He also thinks she might be in danger because of his business rivals."

Her hand darted across the table, upsetting the coffee mug and flinging hot coffee across the tabletop in a screwball arc. She ignored the spreading puddle, grabbed me, and dug fingernails like talons into the back of my hand.

"Tell me you're lying, God damn it. Tell me you're lying. He wouldn't dare take her!"

She had the eyes of a three-week-old kitten being flushed down the toilet.

"There's only one way to get her back," I said. "You and Burton have to appear together in court. Burton already tried it alone. Your father's lawyer bamboozled the court, said they took her on your say-so."

When she finally set my hand free I discovered four bloody bird tracks across the back of it. I pulled a clean handkerchief out of my coat and wound it around the hand.

"Melissa?" I said. "Are you coming back to Seattle with us?"

Her brain tried to focus, but her eyes remained blurry, transfixed mindlessly on the spill. Melissa blurted, "I'm scared of what he'll do. He fools everyone. He's devious."

"I've seen it all, Melissa. I'm devious too."

Without focusing, Melissa slid toward the aisle and began to rise, dragging her purse and coat along. Nothing had been promised, but physically and psychically we had decided to leave together.

As we rose, a small man dressed in a white pin-striped suit bounded up to us. He was small and mean-looking and compact enough to be quicker than me. He kept one hand in his coat pocket, as if caressing a talisman of some sort. Or a switchblade. He was swarthy, appeared to be of Mediterranean stock, in his late forties or early fifties. His face needed a shave, and specks of lint festooned his shiny black hair.

"You goin' somewheres, baby?"

Melissa looked up at me as if seeing me for the first time and said, "He'll do somethin' terrible. I know he will."

"You must be Romano Solomon," I said, extending a hand. He didn't take it. His fist stayed in his coat pocket, the fist that may or may not have been wrapped around some tempered steel.

"Bledsoe," he said. "Romano Bledsoe. Some folks calls me Solomon but that's jus' a nickname." He reached across to pull Melissa to him, but before he could, I took her by the shoulders and swung her behind me.

"It's all over, Bledsoe. Melissa's going home now."

Running his free hand through greasy hair, dislodging

one or two particles of lint, Bledsoe tried to see over my shoulder to Melissa. I purposely blocked his vision with my shoulder. He had a tough decision, whether or not to make a scene. Whether or not to risk pushing and maybe yelling and maybe spilling some blood on all that white he was wearing. He looked me over carefully and then opted for discretion.

"See ya later, Toots," he said, plopping down awkwardly in the booth where Melissa had been sitting. I watched him dunk the elbows of his white suit into the spilled coffee without seeming to notice.

At the door, Kathy took Melissa by the arm, helped her slip on her coat, and guided her out into the cold Tacoma night. I was surprised to find that Kathy was embarrassed by the situation, didn't know quite what to say.

Wordlessly we walked to the parking lot, got into the truck, and drove out of the city. It was beginning to mist.

"Maybe you would feel better staying with me," said Kathy, after half an hour of driving. We were crossing the Duwamish River. "Your place might be kind of lonely."

"I should see Burton," she said, resolutely. "I should see him tonight."

Kathy, who was sitting by the window, peered around Melissa and caught my eye. I shook my head almost imperceptibly, indicating that I hadn't told her about Burton's incarceration.

Kathy said, "I have some clothes you could wear."

Melissa glanced down at herself. "Oh," she said. "That's an idea. Thanks. I'll change first."

Kathy gave me a meaningful look. We both knew after Melissa heard the whole story she wouldn't have the heart to spend the night alone at their rented house.

* * *

She took it well, or seemed to. Kathy helped her change clothes and wash her face, after which they both came back up to my kitchen. We all sat around the kitchen table munching on a batch of freshly made popcorn.

We explained to Melissa exactly what had been happening in her absence. At first, she didn't utter a word. Then she asked a couple of questions, but they seemed almost perfunctory, as though she were asking things she thought we would want to hear her ask.

I should have known. The wordless, stunned reaction of Melissa to her husband's plight, her aunt's demise, her father's actions, her daughter's kidnapping, her counselor's murder—it had all been too calm, too mannered. They went downstairs and prepared for bed, and I should have known.

Switching off the lights, I drifted around in the dark, watching the rain patter on the kitchen windows, checking the street in front for unfamiliar vehicles, locking up, and skimming the evening paper. There was no mention of Helen Gunther's death in the *Times*.

It was three in the morning when I heard bare feet padding up from the basement and into my bedroom.

"Thomas?" It was Kathy. "She's gone."

"How long ago?"

"I don't know."

"When did you wake up?"

"Just a minute ago."

Flinging the covers off, I said, "I bet you heard the door closing. She's probably still within the block!"

"Think we can find her?"

Scrambling into a pair of faded jeans that had been draped across the back of a chair, I said, "The door closing is what always wakes me up. I bet she's not even two hundred yards away from the house."

Without asking, Kathy groped in my closet and selected a Navy pea coat, donning it over her nightgown. "I didn't realize you had so much experience being walked out on," she said, her face a stunning deadpan.

I interrupted my scramble long enough to bestow a long, laborious look upon her. The corners of her mouth wrinkled upward impishly and we both marched out through the kitchen.

19

IT WAS THREE-THIRTY WHEN WE started the truck. The streets were wet and slick and deserted. We looped around the block, then headed for the nearest bus stops. Half an hour into our search we drove to Ballard. The Nadisky house was dark and empty, the grass tall and damp, the rusty wheelbarrow still canted against the front porch. Across the street, Sidney Iddins was anchored in front of the boob tube gorging on beer. I had always thought the TV stations closed down before three.

I went in and searched the Nadisky place. It was still unlocked. It was empty. Thoroughly empty and cold. The family that lived there might never come back.

We paraded around the city, growing more and more discouraged, growing desperate enough to cruise past the Crowell mansion in the dark. Nothing. We checked the Greyhound bus depot and the train station and found only stranded travelers, soldiers, and bag ladies. Melissa had vanished into thin air.

"Maybe she went to a friend's?" Kathy suggested.

"Who should we try first?"

"I don't know."

"She told me she had no friends."

"That's probably true. She didn't even seem friendly toward me anymore. It was like she'd just spent ten years in another country."

When we got back to the house, it was five A.M. I heated up two cups of Swiss Miss and we sat across from each other at the kitchen table staring bleary-eyed at the walls. Finally, I broke the silence. "Which set of clothes did she wear?"

It took a few seconds for the implications of my query to sink in. When they did, Kathy sprang up, scurried to the basement door, and burst down the stairs. Thirty seconds later, she staggered back into the kitchen, visibly upset.

"She wore her old clothes, the black blouse with one button and the skirt slit up to her gizzard. Why, Thomas?"

"Don't know. I guess it was all too much for her to handle."

"You don't think she went back to . . . Tacoma?"

"She may have. I really don't know."

"Would it do any good to go fetch her again?"

"You tell me. What did you two talk about down there? I heard you talking before I dozed off."

"Melissa hardly said a thing. She asked about the burglar. She saw some of the broken stuff and asked me about it."

"Did you give her the whole skinny, about being tied up, too?"

Nodding, Kathy said, "Maybe I shouldn't have gone into all the gory details?" Her voice became small and withdrawn.

"You have any more visions? Anything to add to what you told me the other night?"

Kathy averted her eyes. "I don't want to say it."

"I think you'd better. Talking about it isn't apt to make it happen, you know. Talking about it may even help stop it."

"It's about the little girl. It's awful." Kathy folded the borrowed pea coat over a kitchen chair and walked to the stairs. She didn't finish replying until she was in the stairwell, out of sight, her voice barely discernible. I knew enough to trust her intuitions. Her hunches were right more often than they were wrong.

"Kathy?" I was afraid she would go downstairs without telling me.

"I just have a mental picture of this little girl with a man. The man is . . ."

"What?"

"I think he's going to kill her."

"Who do you see with her?"

"Nobody. I mean, it's nobody I can recognize, just a man, a grown man. Only I have a feeling it's worse than just that."

"What could be worse than that?"

"I see a girl in a deep pit. It's dark. And there is something else in the pit with her. A body. Or bones. Maybe both."

I brooded over that for a few seconds. Kathy generally had a difficult time talking about her visions, and I could tell this one was harder for her to talk about than anything she'd ever told me. "Who's the little girl?"

"It's . . ." She trailed off and I wondered whether she even knew the answer to that question.

"Is it Angel?"

"It's Angel and isn't Angel. It's Angel and Melissa both combined. I'm not sure who it is, I just know I had the strongest premonition I've had in a long while when I found out Melissa was missing. Thomas, you have to do something. We can't let anything happen."

"Did you tell any of this to Melissa?"

"Certainly not. No."

"Are you sure you can't tell me who the man is?"

"I don't know who he is. I've said too much already." She fled down the stairs. Leaving me in limbo. If Kathy was right, all my thinking on the case so far was cockeyed, for I had believed Angus Crowell when he told me business rivals were after him. And I did not see how bones in a pit could possibly have anything to do with my theories. A body in a pit, yes, but not bones. It took years for a body to become a pile of bones. That meant all this was connected to something that had happened long ago.

The jangling phone woke me at ten. A scratchy voice prodded me awake.

"Mr. Black? Mr. Black? Clarice here. You gave me your card? Remember? I found out some things I'm sure you'll want to hear about. It's just horrid all the secrets this family has. It really is. Mary Dawn was seeing a psychiatrist. Had been for years."

"Where are you?"

"Did I waken you? I'm sorry if I did. It never occurred to me a private detective would be sleeping late. In Malibu, we rise at five-thirty and take the dogs for a walk on the beach. The dogs love it."

"I wish I was a dog."

"I *did* waken you!"

"I was out late chasing bad guys. What else did you find out?"

"Oh, I've got a whole assortment of things to tell you. But I'd better see you. Don't you think? This is really such a personal matter." Her tone portended trouble.

"Are you here in town?"

They were staying with her husband's brother. When I gave her directions, she promised she would be out in twenty minutes. Before I could ask her to delay that for an hour, she banged the receiver down.

A dirty yellow cab disgorged her onto my front doorstep sixteen minutes later. Horace, my retired neighbor, was out front in an Air Force parka and hip waders, proudly sponging the flanks of his Buick, when Clarice arrived. Quickly, she paid the driver and shooed him off. Horace gave her the once-over, obviously disapproving. Horace disapproved of everything that happened on my side of the fence. I could be certain the word *gigolo* would crop up in his conversation sometime during the next week. Watching him swish the sponge across his chrome, I wondered if the rat trap was still intact under his bumper.

"Goodness," Clarice Crowell said, negotiating my front steps on a pair of rickety high heels, as if she had never been up steps before, "you're not even dressed yet."

She blitzed through my living room, toured the kitchen, peered into both bedrooms, and then looked at me. I was aghast.

"You have such nice shoulders. No, don't cover them up. I love to see a man dress. You're a bachelor, aren't you?"

I wore jeans, Pumas, and a sleeveless undershirt. I went into the bedroom, made a point of shutting the door, and selected a shirt from the closet. When I emerged,

Clarice was in the kitchen, the knob to the downstairs door held fast in her grubby little nicotine-yellow knuckles.

"You have a basement too? This little shanty is larger than it looks from outside. What's down there?" She made a move to descend the stairs.

"The old slave quarters. Don't go. I keep women down there." Clarice Crowell stared at me. In her circles people did not joke like that. "Little women. Little teeny hunchbacked women."

She didn't bat an eye. She merely went into the living room and picked a comfy spot on my couch. I followed her and offered her things to eat, but that wasn't what she had in mind. She spanked a cushion close beside her hips and motioned me to sit down on it.

"Have to stand," I said. "It's an old war wound. It flares up from time to time."

"Goodness," she said, concern gracing her hoarse voice.

"Those dirty Huns," I grumbled.

She'd been playing eye games from the moment she crossed the threshold, the kind of games you learn all about at your first pre-teen dance.

"Your husband didn't come."

"No. No." She patted her hairdo. It had cost some poor sap of a hairdresser a pair of faded blue hands and some blistered eardrums. "Edward is very upset. I'm most certain he would not want me divulging any of this."

"But you're going to anyway," I said.

"You're a detective. You have your job to do just like the rest of us." She was right. I located missing wives. Edward Crowell buried bodies and no doubt fleeced the relatives. God had given us all our own little missions.

Clarice Crowell spent her spare time trying to get laid by younger men.

Without asking permission, Clarice fumbled with a package of Pall Malls, ignited one with a gold-plated lighter, and began producing smoke. With each puff she exhaled in a different direction, making certain every corner of my house was permeated with the stench. It took a while for her to notice the absence of ashtrays. When she did, she stubbed the butt out in a planter and lit another.

"So what did you find out?"

"Oh, tons. Absolutely tons." She crossed her legs and began playing with her knee, as if to attract my attention to the knobby thing. And then it all gushed out of her. Holding in gossip even that long had been an unnatural torment. Her eyes turned from raisins to prunes.

"Ed's father committed suicide years ago. Blew his head right off with a gun. It all had something to do with Angus. Ed won't tell me exactly what happened, but it had something to do with Angus. And Angus never even showed up at the funeral."

"When was all this?"

"Their papa got so mad at Angus that he dragged him down in the cellar and nearly whipped him to death. He used to use an old buggy whip, Ed says. Right after that, Angus ran away to join the navy. Now, don't tell me you see nothing queer in that."

"If he joined the navy, he must have been close to being an adult, if he wasn't one already," I said.

"Ed says he thinks he must have been about seventeen."

"He thinks? Can't he remember? Or figure it out?"

"Don't bark at me, Tom. You should be thanking me. It took me practically all night to wheedle this out of Ed.

Ed doesn't like to talk about his family. I heard more the other night than I've heard in the last ten years. You really should be thanking me."

"Thank you, Clarice."

She simpered. "You're welcome."

"You say he almost whipped Angus to death?"

"The neighbors had to go down to the cellar and stop it. If they hadn't stepped in, he might have killed Angus. The boys said he was in a blind rage that night. Of course, Angus, with his hot temper, swore revenge. He ran off and joined the navy. A week later their father put a gun in his mouth and pulled the trigger. Ed said there was a long letter, but the pastor came and read it and took it."

"Does somebody still have the letter?"

"Nobody in the family has ever seen it, as far as Ed knows. At least, he's never seen it."

"How old was Mary Dawn when this happened?"

"Oh, she was only a baby. Eight years old. She didn't have anything to do with it all. As a matter of fact, with her father dead and her mother long since passed away, she went to live with the pastor's family. I do know this about Mary Dawn, though. She was seeing a shrink." Clarice said it the way she would have said Mary Dawn had syphilis.

"Are you certain?"

"Ed found some papers and bills and whatnot when we were going through her apartment. I wrote down the name. He's right here in Seattle. He used to be in Bellingham but he moved. Muriel knew all about him. She was a physical therapist. Still got some friends in the medical community. She is one strong woman. I've seen her pick up a couch all by herself."

She fished a Dentyne wrapper out of her purse and handed it to me. The psychiatrist's name was scrawled on the back in tiny script. Dr. Elliot Courtland. The address was in a plush district on the other side of the Arboretum near Lake Washington.

I went to the phone, looked up his number in the white pages, and dialed.

Clarice spoke musically. "I guess she'd been seeing this head doctor for years and years. That's what Ed thought . . . from the papers he found."

When the doctor came on the line, I fudged the truth a bit and told him I was a detective working on the Mary Dawn Crowell case. On the assumption that I was a cop, he made an appointment to see me at his office in thirty minutes.

Grabbing a jacket, I rushed out the back door. Clarice puttered after me with tiny mincing steps. Women like her mocked femininity. She stood on the back porch and sang out, "Tom. Oh, Tom? Are we finished? Tom?"

"Call a cab and lock up when you leave," I said. As I started to step up into the Ford, I noticed a smattering of white crystals on the side of the pickup. I found more crystals on the ground beside the pickup door. Still more of the white stuff clung to the gasoline intake spout. Kneeling, I licked a finger, pressed it to the substance, and tasted.

Somebody had poured sugar into my gas tank. If they hadn't been so sloppy, I would have driven it and destroyed the engine. Up until two weeks ago, I'd had a locking gas cap, but I'd lost it and replaced it with a standard cap. Damn.

I went back into the house, changed into cycling shoes, dug my .45 out of the closet, inserted a clip, checked the tire pressure on my Miyata, and carried it to the back porch.

Clarice Crowell still hadn't given up hope. "Tom. Tom? I may have more information. Can I call?"

"Sure," I said, making certain the .45 was well hidden under my windbreaker.

"Ed's real mad today. He found out from that Negro detective in Bellingham they're going to let Burton out."

I looked up at her. "When did they decide this?"

"Some stupid neighbor up there claims she saw him leaving almost an hour before Mary died. Some poops will say anything. And they seem to be having a problem trying to match the fingerprints they found to Burton. It's all been bungled."

"Great," I said, leaping onto the bicycle saddle and launching down the alley. "Call if you get more information. I'd appreciate it."

A block later, it became readily apparent that someone was following me.

20

HE WAS IN A SHARK-GRAY Dodge, and he was good. He intentionally lagged far enough behind so that I wouldn't recognize him.

He followed and I let it ride. I let him tail me down Seventeenth N.E. right through the University of Washington campus and out the other side by the football stadium, although I could have foiled his plans at any point. I knew a dozen choice footpaths I could have detoured onto. By the time I crossed the Montlake Bridge, I knew who he was and I had a good idea what he wanted.

When I zigzagged through some residential streets, I lost him momentarily, but he picked me up again after the industrial museum, just shy of the Arboretum. The Arboretum road was over a mile long, narrow and twisty. The area spawned a lot of crime. Pedestrians were rare and houses were nonexistent. Today, there was little traffic.

Pedaling against a moist southerly wind, I wasn't making very good time. The Dodge paced me. Twice, he crept closer, gunning the engine once, as if to make a move, but at each attempt, a car approached us from the other direction, putting a temporary halt to his plans.

190

It was Holder, Julius Caesar Holder, and I would have bet my life that his game was bump and run. He knew if he sabotaged the truck I'd eventually ride the bike. And he also knew how vulnerable a man on a bicycle was. He figured he could bounce me into the ditch and motor away, nobody the wiser. It was a neat ploy.

He made his move in front of the Japanese tea gardens, and strangely enough, he missed on his first pass. He wasn't trying to kill me. He could have easily run right over me. Instead, he tried to sideswipe my bicycle and knock me for a loop. He must have figured that wouldn't be murder. He was in trouble now. He wasn't just one motorist trying something funny. He was the culmination of hundreds of sloppy, thoughtless motorists that I had run up against in the last few years. It was rare that you caught one. It was even rarer to have a gun on you when you did. My temper got the better of me.

Suddenly, I felt the cold metal of his car brushing my hip. I had been waiting for it. I slammed the caliper brakes on. The Dodge catapulted in front of me as I decelerated.

Slowing down so that he could attempt it a second time was his big blunder.

Instead of pedaling by on the passenger side the way he expected, I swung behind the Dodge and pulled around into the oncoming lane. Sitting up and steering with one hand, I dragged the .45 out from under my windbreaker.

I took careful aim, placing a slug through his side window, as close to his face as I could manage without actually hitting him.

Tires screeched like dying animals, brakes squealed, and the Dodge veered right, bounding up over the high curb and scraping the underbelly with shrill metallic yowls.

I didn't even get off the bicycle. Riding up to the glassless window, I rammed the muzzle of the .45 into Holder's face.

I spoke evenly. "Say your prayers, bastard."

Holder was frantically trying to rub particles of glass out of his face. When he cleared his eyes well enough to see, he gaped at me. "What the . . ."

I noticed two of his fingers were bandaged and splinted. That explained a lot. He'd gone to retrieve the transmitter, met my foul play, and decided to seek revenge. First the sugar in the gas tank. Now this.

A BMW whooshed past from the other direction without slowing or seeming to notice what we were up to.

"Come on now. You know there's no cause for that. If I'd wanted to kill you I would have done it."

"How about if you'd wanted to tie up my friend Kathy. How about if you'd wanted to trash my place and you got interrupted by a cute little button you thought could provide some sport. How about that?"

"I don't know what you talkin' 'bout, man."

"You followed me. You had a bug under my rear bumper."

"I cain't deny that." He looked at me squarely, flecks of blood on his cheeks where the flying glass had punctured him.

"You broke into my house."

"No."

"You tied up my friend, and you killed my dog."

It was almost impossible to read his face. Deadpan was his specialty and he was playing his specialty to the hilt.

"I know nothin' 'bout no dog. And I 'specially know nothin' 'bout dis bitch you talkin' 'bout."

"There's no need to lie," I said. "I'm going to kill you anyway. I just want to know why you did it."

"Kill me! Man, you crazy!" He scooted across the seat until his back was wedged up against the passenger door on the other side of the car. I had no intention of actually killing him, but I liked the look it put on his face.

"Listen, you bastard," I said, as another car whirred past without stopping. "You killed my dog. You terrorized my friend. You followed me, and who knows what else you did. For all I know, you bashed Mary Dawn Crowell."

"Who's 'at?"

"The lady in Bellingham."

"Her? I din't have nothin' to do with that." His voice was evolving into a high whine. "Man, I'm jus' tailin' you."

"And you're working for Angus Crowell, aren't you?"

He mulled that over. If I could come after him with a gun, I could go after Crowell with a gun. The repercussions might be devastating.

"I work for who I work for. Ain't nobody's business but mine."

A semi-automatic pistol re-cocks itself each time it is fired, so the .45 only needed one thing. I squeezed the trigger and watched Holder's body jump. He went high enough to smack his head on the roof. The roar inside the car was numbing. The opposite window cracked and shattered. I had deliberately missed his face by ten inches. We listened together, our ears ringing as the last few bits of broken glass fell out of the frame and clinked on the metal sill.

Clearing his ears by jamming his index fingers in and
screwing them around, he said, "Okay. What you want to
know? I'll tell you. Jus' don' shoot no more. Jus' don'
fire that thing at me *noooo* more."

"What's his name?"

"I been runnin' errands for this Crowell dude."

"Angus Crowell?"

"That's the one."

Pointing the muzzle at his forehead, I said, "You bur-
gled my house, didn't you?"

"Man I swear I din' have nothin' to do with it. I swear.
What's your problem?"

"Start from the beginning. What have you been doing
for Crowell?"

"You know I can't tell you."

I cut loose another .45 slug. It smashed the door frame
to the right of his skull. Holder didn't jump nearly as
high this time. He cursed and flung his palms up in front
of the gun as if to fend off more bullets. Then he shook
his head, glanced sideways as if he were muttering to an
invisible third party in the back seat, and said, "Crazy!
Crazy!"

"You bet your ass," I said. "Whoever broke into my
house was about six-three or four and had brown eyes.
Sound familiar?"

"Lot a people *my* height got brown eyes. Streets full of
'em. You ever play pickup basketball, man?"

"You're right," I said, grudgingly. A Peugeot stopped
behind me and a woman in a business suit leaned over,
cranking down the passenger-side window.

"You gentlemen have an accident?"

"Yes, ma'am," I said, flopping my wrist with the pistol
limply down below the inside lip of Holder's car win-

dow. "But we've already got it taken care of. Thanks for stopping."

"Anybody hurt?"

"Naw." I turned back to Holder. She drove off and I raised the pistol back up. "Not yet," I said.

"You crazy."

"Nice to know people still care, eh?"

"He wanted me to follow you," Holder blurted. "Crowell wants me to tell him everythin' you do."

"But he called you off this afternoon, didn't he?"

"Called me off? Hell, no. Ain't nobody called me off."

"And what have you told him so far?"

"I tailed you to Bellingham. I told him about that bitch you visited. The one works at da nut house."

"At the Hopewell?"

"Yeah, that's the one."

"You follow me last night?"

"I started to, but I lost you in the District. I thought my set was screwed up, and then I found the box under your neighbor's car. It wasn't my set at all. You moved the transmitter. Nice booby trap. You like to took this here finger off at the joint."

"So you poured sugar in my gas tank."

He held up his bandaged and splinted fingers. "I rigged your truck. Yeah, I rigged your truck. You're lucky that's all I rigged."

"You threatening me?"

"Take it any way you want."

"Takes some balls to threaten a man who's aiming a gun at your guts."

He wadded up his cheek muscles in mock imitation of a terrified elf, then winced at the unexpected pain of his facial wounds.

"When did you tell Crowell about my visit to Helen Gunther?"

Holder didn't know what I was talking about. I explained, "The woman who worked at the Hopewell Clinic? When did you tell Crowell about my visit?"

"An hour later, maybe. You went home, then you got on your bicycle and I lost you. Man, them things are hard to tail."

"You ever try to follow a fast runner?" I asked. "I tailed a guy who ran five-minute miles once."

"Hell, I tried to track some dude in a canoe last year. I a'most drowned." We stared at each other for a long moment.

"What was Crowell's reaction when you told him about me and the woman from the Hopewell Clinic?"

" 'Get back on it.' That's what he always says. 'Get back on it.' "

"What'd you see last night?"

"This a test or something? I tried to follow you, but I lost you in the District. So I went back and staked out your crib. You came back late with Crowell's daughter and some other bitch."

"How did you know she was Crowell's daughter?"

"What you mean, how'd I know? Crowell's had the whole staff at Penworthy after her two weeks. We all got pictures of her. It was her. Wasn't it?"

"Maybe."

"Sure it was. You run into that little dude she was with? I seen him once 'bout four or five days ago. I missed her but I seen him. You ask me, he's the one iced her aunt. I bet Crowell's daughter wanted to leave him and go with the aunt. I bet that's why he killed her. Wouldn't be surprised if he killed dis other bitch, either."

"Helen Gunther?"

"That's the one. I wouldn't be surprised if he killed her, too."

I scanned his face for a few seconds, trying to decide the best way to ride off into the sunset without taking a slug in my spine.

"What kind of orders did Crowell give you when you went to take the little girl last Sunday?"

"Orders? He din' give me no orders. He jus' said, come on."

"Who told you to slap Burton around like that?"

"Burton the little girl's father?"

"Yeah."

"I warned him. He was mouthing off. Said he was gonna kill Crowell."

"You sure?"

"I was there. He said he was gonna kill the old man."

Holder knew what I was thinking about. Talk of killing had brought us around in a full circle.

"Come on," he said, watching my eyes apprehensively. "You and me's both pros. This ain't nothin' to be killin' over. You leave me alone an' I'll leave you alone. Word of honor."

"What about your money? What about your boss?"

"I'll give him some jive an' keep right on cashing his checks. He won't know no difference. I done it before."

If I set him loose, it would be his style to come right back after me, and the next ambush might be more lethal than this one. I could shoot him and endure sleepless nights and bad dreams for another five or ten years. No, that wasn't worthy of me. I could wing him, but that was assault and battery. I would end up in the slammer for that. This business I could probably get away with. I doubted if Holder would prefer charges.

Letting down the hammer of the .45, I snubbed the safety catch on and tucked the pistol into my belt. The air of relief inside the car was almost palpable.

"I wouldn't'a blamed ya if you'd wasted me," said Holder, as I slid onto the bike saddle and began pumping. I could tell from the way he said it, that he was resigned to the fact that I was meaner than he was. Maybe that was a good thing

It took sixty seconds before I was certain he wasn't going to renege on our deal and put a bullet in my spine. It was funny, but after that sixty seconds, I trusted the guy implicitly.

Dr. Elliot Courtland's office was in a one-story stucco building he shared with two dentists and an optometrist. Courtland's entranceway led through a covered patio festooned with lush ivy.

He saw me in his office. He had to boot out a patient to do it, but he sat me down and hunkered on the edge of an enormous desk, kicking one short leg nervously. He had long, gray hair, wore thick glasses and sported a neatly trimmed beard. He was trying his best to look the part of a doctor of psychiatry. You wondered about someone who had to try that hard.

"So you're working on Mary Crowell's murder case?" he said, stroking his beard with a pudgy hand and swinging his leg. I didn't know how much of the leg business I could stomach. He discovered a pipe in his blazer pocket and began tamping tobacco into the bowl.

"I'm working on it," I said. "And also on the Helen

Gunther case. I have reason to think they may be connected."

"Oh, God," he said, but his voice was still mellow and smooth. He was good with his eyes, too, as good as anyone I'd ever seen. Even when he wasn't thinking grandiose thoughts, his eyes behaved as if he were. He stared at me, squinted at the wall, and then raised his dim gray eyes toward the ceiling. I was willing to bet his patients thought he was God.

"Helen Gunther was one of my students. I knew her only marginally, however. In what way could the two murders conceivably be connected?"

"It's a rather long story, Dr. Courtland. What I need to know is what you were treating Mary Dawn Crowell for."

"You'll have to let me see some identification before I answer that."

The jig was up. I had had a suspicion I wasn't going to get very far here.

 **21** AT TIMES, I CARRIED PHONY I.D., but I figured Dr. Courtland would never get sucked in by a ruse that blatant. I dug out my wallet and flipped it open, revealing my driver's license.

He gave me an acerbic look, one he saved for gas jockeys and miscreants, and said, pointedly, "I was under the impression you worked for the Seattle Police Department."

"I worked for the police department for ten years. I'm private now."

He pursed his lips and waved the pipe like a pointer. "Then I assume you have some sort of license."

"I had a photostat. Helen Gunther shredded it yesterday."

"Ohhh." He said it as if he were trying to make a sound on a piccolo.

"You want a connection between the two murders?" I asked. "The connection is this: a young woman is missing. I was enlisted to find her. The young woman was being treated by Helen Gunther. Coincidentally, she happened to be the niece of Mary Crowell."

"The niece?" Courtland brooded over that for a moment, fondling first his pipe bowl and then his whiskers, his fingers lingering as if stroking a kitten.

"Does that mean anything to you, Dr. Courtland?"

200

"The newspapers led me to believe Helen's death was some sort of random sex killing."

"That's always a possibility. Or it's also possible some lunatic connected to my missing persons case is running around bumping off anybody who might be able to tell me something."

His leg began swinging wildly. "Are you suggesting *I* might be next?"

"I wouldn't know. I keep trying to get closer but nobody will talk. It seems more convenient to get murdered than to talk."

I got up to leave. His leg pendulumed crazily, and I could tell from the way his teeth gnashed the pipe stem that his brain was blazing away in overdrive.

"That sounds like a threat."

"No threat. It's just the way things have been."

"Just a minute. Mr. Black? What is it exactly that you need to know? Mary's dead now. She had no immediate family. I suppose I can operate under the assumption it would do little if any harm if some of her background came out. After all, this is a rather special circumstance."

"Why was she seeing you?"

Some of the anxiety drained from his tense limbs, but his face was as stiff as a turkey in a freezer. Now Elliot Courtland had the opportunity to submerge himself in his own element. He petted the pipe bowl and puffed and mulled over the question.

"Why was she seeing me?" he asked, buying time to compose a sufficiently sophisticated reply.

"Yeah."

"Mary had a whole host of problems. She'd been visiting my office for almost ten years. If you wanted to get to the crux of the matter, you'd have to go back to her childhood."

"Go on." I had an eerie feeling that I already knew what he was going to say.

"Her father committed suicide."

"That's what I understood."

"She was raised by another family from the age of eight, and it was only there that her conscious memory began. Though she never lost her curiosity about it, nobody would tell her anything concrete about her father's death. About three years ago, she went through some papers left by the family who had taken her in.

"That was when the truth came out. It seemed one of her brothers had had a serious run-in with her father. At the time of her father's demise, the authorities suspected foul play."

"You mean her father may not have committed suicide, he may have been murdered?"

"Nothing ever came of it. It haunted Mary. She began making some rather feebleminded connections between her father's death and her fiancé's suicide several years ago."

"Which brother had the run-in with the father?"

"I was never concerned with that. Don't you see? For my purposes, it clearly made no difference."

"I was wondering if it could have been the father of the niece I was looking for?"

"I have no idea."

"Supposing it was," I said. "Just for the sake of discussion. Supposing a murder had been committed fifty some odd years ago. And supposing one of her brothers did do it. Is a thing like that likely to come out later in life? Or do you believe it was just something an immature kid might get caught up in?"

"You mean, might we expect this person to commit other murders? Or to be capable of committing other murders?"

"Yeah."

Courtland lapsed into his act—puffing, producing the small noises a baby makes sucking on his foot, squinting, his eyes wandering to the ceiling, finally alighting on an ornamental fig tree in the corner.

"A boy in his teens or late teens who displays a predisposition toward this pattern of behavior is apt to maintain the predisposition throughout life—that is, unless he is treated for it. Mind you, nothing was ever proved. We have only Mary's conjectures. I wouldn't even mention it except for the fact that other . . . murders have been committed."

"Why did the authorities feel there had been foul play?"

"I couldn't tell you. We never delved that deeply into the contents of the letter. I was more interested in Mary's reactions than in what caused them."

"Are you saying one of Mary's brothers may have murdered their father and you didn't care who it was?"

"I suppose I am. Yes."

"And Mary never told you who the brother was?"

"She told me several times, though not recently. It's merely that I paid little attention."

"Do you keep tapes of your conversations, Doctor?"

"I don't operate that way."

"Did he live around here? In town?"

"I really couldn't tell you."

"What did this all mean to Mary?"

"In general, a person's problems are not linked to any one event in their lives, but to an entire pattern of events and thinking. Mary was withdrawn, asocial. She found it extremely difficult to form any attachment to persons of the opposite sex. In layman's terms, she thought very little of herself."

"An inferiority complex?"

"That is an overworked phrase, but in this instance, it fits rather remarkably well. She had other problems as well. As I said before, she entertained the odd notion that somehow her father's suicide was related to her fiancé's death."

"And what do you know about his death? Her fiancé?"

"I believe that, too, was a suicide. Yes, I recall now. He jumped off the Aurora Bridge. They never found the body. He just left some clothes and a typewritten note back at his office. That was one of the elements that disturbed Mary. The typewritten note. She claimed her fiancé didn't type. And the note wasn't signed."

"Had Mary or you ever discussed the possibility of her acting on her suspicions?"

"Mary constantly harped about her sneaky brother. That's what she invariably called him. Her sneaky brother. It's one of the reasons I cannot recall his name. She very keenly felt he was solely responsible for the death of her fiancé."

"He wouldn't be some bird named Harry, would he? Her fiancé?"

"As a matter of fact, I believe Harry was his name. That was when she first began seeing a professional counselor."

"So it was a number of years ago? When her fiancé died?"

"I believe so."

"Do you know how many?"

"Not sure. Twenty, maybe. Yes. It must be about twenty."

Twenty years ago, Melissa had been three or four, the same age her daughter was now. I contemplated Melissa's life. For years, she had been sinking into an emotional and psychological bog. I wondered if her problems might not have issued from the same source Mary Dawn's had, if she might not have been living a rerun of her aunt Mary's life. If that were true, Angel might be sinking into the same morass. For some reason, I found it all very hard to accept. I had to be on the wrong track.

 IT BEGAN RAINING ON THE
way back to my place. The
Miyata threw up tall sprays of water from its fenderless
wheels. I was soaked to the skin by the time I wheeled
the bicycle through the back door.

Kathy was loitering in my kitchen. She had been
hypnotically rearranging my spice rack.

"Where have you been?" Kathy blurted. "Your truck
was here but you were gone."

"I thought I told you to leave that rack alone."

"Some awful woman was here when I came back. She
was poured into this yucky pantsuit. She had these little
tiny buggy eyes and I think her face was coated with
some sort of Teflon."

"Have you heard from Melissa?"

"Who was the woman?"

"You haven't heard from Melissa?"

"I was just going to ask if you had."

"Nothing. I'm heading for Tacoma after I make a few
calls."

"Why? What have you found out?"

"I understand Burton got sprung from jail. I'll call
Bellingham in a minute and get the scoop."

"You think Melissa went back to that crummy pimp?"

"Yes, I think she did."

"But why would a girl like Melissa go back to him?"

"Why would a girl like Melissa be with him in the first place?"

Kathy shrugged and frowned. I had a point, and it caused us both to stop and think. I picked up the phone and dialed Smithers. He snapped it up on the third ring. Since his marriage had disintegrated, he answered the phone a lot quicker.

"Smitty? Thomas here. I've got a name for the boys downtown. He's flirting at being a small-time procurer in Tacoma. Somebody told me he was a biker years ago in the Seattle area."

"Sure thing, Thomas. You got any club colors or anything?"

"He might have been with the Skeletons."

"A bad crowd. Not many of them left. What's his name?"

"Romano Bledsoe. If nothing comes out, you might try those two names in combination with Solomon. He uses Solomon as an alias."

"I'll call you right back."

I carried a change of dry clothes into the bathroom and locked the door in Kathy's face. Disgruntled, she stood outside and spoke through it.

"Who was that hoity-toity Teflon woman, Thomas?"

"A blind date."

It was quiet outside the door. "You're kidding."

"I'm going out with her older sister next week."

Silence reigned for a few long moments. "Very funny, Thomas."

"She's one of Melissa's aunts. She and her husband flew up to make funeral arrangements for Mary Dawn."

"Oh," said Kathy.

"Her older sister's supposed to be a whiz at racquetball."

She ignored my jesting. "If they're setting Burton free, they must have found the real killer, don't you think?"

Rubbing my damp hair dry with a towel, I trudged into the living room, plopped into a chair, and picked up the phone. "I don't know. I'll call Percy now and find out."

"Thomas? I want you to promise me one thing."

Placing the receiver back into the cradle, I said, "Sure." Her tone had stopped me dead.

"Promise me that those things I told you about, my premonitions . . . promise me they won't go any further than you. Promise me you won't drag them out into the open."

"You mean about the girl in the pit? The bones?"

"Precisely. I just don't want everyone knowing about this psychic thing I have."

"Why not?"

"It's kind of embarrassing."

Kathy chewed her lower lip when she got nervous and she was gnashing it now. "I promise."

"Thank you."

"By the way, I just came back from an interview with Mary Dawn's psychiatrist."

Kathy nodded somberly.

"I'll fill you in later."

I dialed the Bellingham police. I was connected to Detective Herman Percy almost immediately. He was cordial, more cordial than I had expected.

"You were right on the button," he said. "We've got witnesses who place Nadisky leaving the building while the woman was still alive. One of the neighbors heard her open her door and let somebody in later. But nobody saw anything. Typical. And we've got the report on the fingerprints. They aren't Nadisky's. The only good thing about the case is the murder weapon. That bottle of ketchup takes a good print. We've got several good ones. Now if we could only find a suspect to match them to."

"Crowell's niece was seeing a psychologist by the name of Helen Gunther here in Seattle," I said. "Somebody strangled her two days ago."

The line went silent for ten seconds. "That's the murder on Capitol Hill? What are you saying? You don't think the two killings are coincidental? You think maybe this missing niece is running around knocking people off?"

"I couldn't say. I thought I'd mention it. You might want to contact the boys on the Seattle case. Compare notes."

"Thanks for the tip."

"You might mention my name. I should have said something to them earlier but it slipped my mind."

"I'll bet."

Smithers rang me as soon as I hung up. "Not a thing, Thomas. Must not be his real name. We tried every combination. Bledsoe. Solomon. Romano. Chuck couldn't put word-one on the screen downtown. If this cat's got a record, it's not in Seattle."

"Thanks anyway, Smitty."

I borrowed Kathy's rattly '66 Volkswagen bug, tanked it up with Texaco's finest, and swung onto I-5 southbound. Tacoma was a forty-five-minute drive. Kathy was going back to campus to try to catch up on some of her studies, so I wasn't anxious about her. On campus she was lost to the world. Holder might pop up again, but I would have to handle that when and if it occurred.

What worried me more than anything was Melissa. I wasn't certain what her reaction would be to my second appearance. Last night, we had dragged her back to Seattle more because we caught her by surprise than anything else. Today might be a different matter. Today, she might put up a struggle. Today, she might sic Bledsoe on me. She might even holler for the cops.

Tacoma was cloudy and dingy, but the streets were dry. I double-parked and checked Braverman's first. It was overstocked with weary businessmen from the lower echelons of the corporate ladder. Polyester suits and Kmart ties, trousers baggy in the butts. I spotted no pimps and only two women who looked like part-time hookers. They were probably housewives on a toot. Neither was blonde.

I drove down the hill and coasted into the alley behind The Last Inn. The buzzard was still perched behind the counter, leaning on both sharp elbows, perusing a dog-eared copy of the December 1961 *Playboy*. He slid his tongue into his cheek and tried to decide how much he was going to take me for this time.

"You again," he said.

Flashing the photo of Melissa Nadisky, I said, "You see her today?"

"How much it worth to ya?"

"You got any big friends?"

He eased up off his bony elbows and spoke warily. "A couple. Why?"

"Bigger than me?"

"She's upstairs. 301." I headed for the staircase and the old coot added, "Her man friend is with her." Considering what had recently transpired between us, he was more than generous with his information. I suppose he didn't relish the idea of scrubbing blood out of the carpets. Maybe he was running low on Lysol.

Vintage thirty-year-old jazz oozed out of 301. I rapped on the door and waited. I rapped again.

Eventually a thickened voice slurred, "What you want?"

I couldn't tell if it was Bledsoe. I tried the doorknob. The door swung open, the bottom edge rasping on the thick multiple layers of carpeting.

Bare legs crossed, Melissa hunkered in a corner, smoking hash from a long, slender, imitation corncob pipe. She wore a skimpy pair of black bikini briefs and nothing else.

Judging from the glazed look in her pale blue orbs, she had more than just hash racing through her veins. Romano Bledsoe squatted on the bed. He wore a misshapen sleeveless T-shirt and white trousers that belonged to the suit I'd seen him in yesterday. The suit jacket was slung over a chair, the elbows still discolored by coffee. His Pat Boone whites were lined up on the dresser as though his mother might have done it. I didn't see his mother anywhere.

Bledsoe pawed through an assortment of fuzzy Polaroids spread across the sheet. The blankets and bedspread had been ripped off the bed and flung against the wall. It only took a pinch of imagination to guess what had been transpiring.

"Get the hell out of here!" snarled Bledsoe.

I closed the door behind myself and spoke evenly. "Put your clothes on, Melissa."

Dropping the pipe, she covered her breasts and looked

at me, wide-eyed—wide-eyed but not innocent. Smoldering particles of hashish splashed onto the carpet and glowed like cats' eyes in the night.

Scuttling down the length of the bed on his knees, Bledsoe tumbled off the end and sprang toward me, a six-inch knife clutched in his fist.

The blade looked wicked and sharp, as if he honed it every hour on the hour. One of the Polaroids got sideswiped off the bed and landed next to his skinny, stockinged foot. It was a shadowy photo of Melissa having sex with a middle-aged fat man. The picture was made more than obscene by the fact that the fat man had doffed all of his clothes except his long black socks and his hat.

It wasn't hard to figure. Distraught and confused, Melissa had run back to Bledsoe. Seizing upon his opportunity, the scumbag doped her, gave her to the first wino he found sober enough to handle it, and froze the whole nauseating affair on film. Now she was his. If she wanted to leave, he could flash the photos around. If she got a job he could flash them in front of her boss. Her mother. Father. Even her kid. They would be a hell of a lever.

He came at me like a snake, weaving from side to side, the knife flicking from left to right. It was a steel tongue and I was a tidbit to sample.

"Out," he whispered. "Out. Get the goddamn fucking hell out of here. This ain't no goddamned business of yours. This is strictly private. The little lady and I are going into business fucking full-time, and no smart-mouth like you can do a thing to stop it."

Years ago, my first instinct would have been to pull

out the .45 and drill a slug through his foot, or maybe his brain, but I left the pistol where it was.

"Melissa," I said. "Burton's out of jail. He's coming home and he needs your help to get Angel back."

Her voice drifted from the corner like a wisp of fog. "Angel?"

"Your daughter. Remember her? You want her to live with your father for the next fifteen years?"

"Me and the little lady's got a deal," Bledsoe said, moving in on me, blade first. "A real deal."

I could hear choking and sobbing in the corner. "Angel?"

He locked his angled brown eyes onto mine, and I wondered if he were to pull a ski mask on, whether Kathy might not recognize him. He wasn't tall enough to thump his head on the top of a doorway, but Kathy had been frightened. She could have transposed some of the details. Or maybe he had been wearing platform shoes. The burglar had been a sadist. The man in front of me was a sadist.

I decided to worry him a bit. I lifted my jacket and displayed the butt of the .45. He grinned. He grinned as if we were two buddies swapping nasty stories over a pitcher of suds. He straightened up and dropped his knife-hand down to his side, as if he would not be needing it now that he had seen the gun. I knew what he was plotting. He was plotting to catch me off guard, then lunge forward, sticking and slashing. Blood would fly.

I gave no warning. I caught him cold. Before he could make a move, I kicked him in the testicles. He doubled over like a spring-loaded machine and I quickly booted him in the face twice before he could roll out of range.

Sure, it was a dirty move, but we had no referee and

someone had forgotten to deliver my copy of the rule book. I didn't wish to let Melissa out of my grasp again. Nor did I want my face butchered.

When I was done kicking him, he spraddled out against the dresser and slid to the floor. I had to admit he was game. Aching and bloodied, nose broken, he managed to scrabble to his hands and knees, still clutching the knife. He started to crawl across the obscene Polaroids toward me. I stepped on his knife-hand and heard the loud sound of fingers snapping.

Removing my foot from his broken hand, I scuffed the knife across the floor, and said, "How many pictures of her do you have?"

He was breathing the way a very sick animal might. I kneed him in the ribs.

"Pictures? I ain't got no pictures."

"Sure you do. How many?"

"You're hurting him," said the dazed woman in the corner, clutching her small breasts to herself like a pair of newborn puppies.

"Look here, dog breath," I said. "I'm going to take your little meal ticket back home and I don't want any bad pennies turning up. I don't want any funny photos getting stuffed under her door in the middle of the night.

"I ain't got no *steeeenking* pictures!"

I kicked him in the ribs. Hard. He spun around, one arm veed down between his thighs. He was hurting all over. I kicked him in the shoulder, the back, the thigh. He retracted into the corner between the dresser and the wall, a snail being chased with salt.

Reaching down, I picked him up by the belt. I slammed him into the wall. A burnt-orange painting of a sunset fell off the wall, hit the dresser, bounced off his Pat Boones, and landed on the floor.

Twice, I cocked my arm back, fist closed, and slugged his face. Then I let him slump down into a cringing heap.

"Where are the rest of the *steeeenking* pictures?" I asked.

He peered at me, slowly raising his head, squinting through a swollen, half-closed eye.

Without warning, he sprang forward, grabbed my leg and sank his teeth into my thigh, clinging like an over-sized leech. Involuntarily, I screamed, then reached down and tried to pry him off. I dug my fingers into his neck as deeply as I dared, gouging as deeply as I could without killing him. He wouldn't release my thigh. He actually seemed to bite harder.

I couldn't believe it. He was a wild animal.

I karate-chopped the back of his neck, once, twice, then three, four, five, six times. He flopped backward, eyes rolling toward the ceiling as though drunk, blood spilling from his mouth, trickling down his cheek. My blood.

Limping across the room, I picked up his knife using three fingers, hobbled back over to him, and buried it in his right leg, almost to the hilt. He shrieked like a man caught in a machine, regained consciousness completely, and tried to claw the whalebone handle out with his one good hand. I pinned his good shoulder to the wall with my good foot.

"Leave it alone until you find a sawbones," I said. "You'll bleed to death if you yank it out."

"She ain't worth all the trouble you're in now, you bastard," Bledsoe seethed, through tightly clenched, bloodstained teeth.

"That's where you're wrong," I said. "She's worth every bit of it."

"She's just a tramp."

Applying pressure to his shoulder with my shoe, I said, "How many pictures did you take?"

"They're all over there, man. Lay off. They're all over there."

I kept an eye on him as I pulled Melissa to her feet and shrouded her in a dress. He was twisted into a grotesque pretzel. She seemed to be transfixed by all the bright, shiny blood and the sight of the whalebone handle protruding from Bledsoe's thigh like a holiday ornament.

First Holder and now Bledsoe. Maybe they could organize a club. The let's-nail-Thomas-Black club. A simple missing persons case had turned into a real mishmash.

 I COULD HAVE DONE ANYTHING
with her. She didn't resist. What-
ever chemicals Bledsoe had pumped into her system had
made her docile as a lamb. Straightening her clothes, I
walked her barefoot downstairs and out the back door.
The Volkswagen hadn't been towed away, although
some enterprising meter maid had pushed a ticket under
the wiper. It floated off on the freeway.

We were north of Federal Way. She had been half
asleep and I had already shunted her head off my
shoulder more than once. She smelled of beer and spit
and cigarettes and old mattresses. She smelled like
the proverbial horse who'd been ridden hard and put
away wet.

"Why did you run away, Melissa?" I asked.

"Run away? Did I run away?"

"Don't you want to see your little girl?"

When I looked down at her, she was weeping. She
stopped as precipitously as she had begun, like a sloppy
drunk. "Angel needs a real mother. Not me. She needs a
real home. I can't give her anything."

"I think you can."

"What?" she challenged. "What can I give?"

For a few seconds I was afraid to say it. I didn't know how she would take it.

"Love. You can give her more love than anyone else on earth."

It was almost the hook, but not quite. "Me? I'm nothing but trouble for everyone."

"Are you?"

"Look at Aunt Mary. She's dead."

"You didn't do that."

"Maybe I did. Maybe I took the bus up and killed her."

Melissa gazed at the freeway in front of us, her eyes wide and dry and bloodshot, like somebody who had been awake two or three nights in a row and now couldn't sleep no matter what she tried.

"Let's talk about it," I said. "Did you kill your aunt?" She turned and faced me. She was awfully close in that tiny, cramped car. The Polaroids in my pocket were less than an hour old. That fact, combined with her proximity and aroma, made me slightly uncomfortable.

"What about Helen?" she asked. "Did I kill her? Somebody tell me if I'm a murderer. Everyone I need seems to be dying. And you'll die too."

"I won't die. And you're no murderer," I said without conviction. "You're just a sad little mixed-up girl."

"I think I am a murderer. Why else would Auntie Mary be dead? And Helen? I must have done it. Strangers wouldn't do those awful things."

She was still dopey when we arrived at my place. I put my arm under her legs, swept her off her feet, and carried her into the house, spotting Horace next door as he peeped out from behind a venetian blind. No doubt he thought I was buying into the white slave trade. First I was a gigolo and now a white slaver. Start with one or two and gradually build up the inventory until the basement and garage were filled with shackled women I could sell to the Arabs. We would have words next week.

She was drooling and muttering, "Murderer. Murderer."

I stood her in the bathtub and pointed the shower spigot at her head. The lukewarm spray hit her at neck level and quickly drenched her only two articles of clothing, the thin dress and her black bikini briefs. Wet, the odors of her transgressions began to come out. Rolling up my sleeves, I shampooed her hair, peeled off her water-heavy dress and had already soaped and rinsed her when she seemed to realize what was happening for the first time.

"Who are you?" she asked, in a startled voice, shielding every vital part of her body with elbows and splayed hands. In other circumstances it would have been comical. "Who are you and what the hell are you doing to me?"

"I'm Thomas . . ."

"Get the hell out of here!"

"I'm . . ."

"I don't care if you're Santa Claus's little helper. Get out!"

"You're doped up . . ."

"Out! Out!"

I limped into the kitchen and ate an apple. Ten minutes later, she emerged, wrapped in a long, floppy robe that had been hanging on the back of the door, her hair swathed in a towel. She stared at me accusingly.

"Only trying to help," I said.

"Help?"

"Yeah."

"You soaked my clothes. What am I going to wear?"

"You were doped up."

"I don't do dope."

"You recall how you got here?"

Incredulity struck her face like the back of a hand. Slowly, her jaw dropped open and she looked down at the bathrobe as if she couldn't recall how she'd gotten into it, as if perhaps it were alive and had leaped up and wrapped itself about her on its own. She looked around the room.

"You're that detective. You're Kathy's friend."

"That I am."

"You don't have any business undressing me. I think you were taking advantage. Where's Kathy? You were trying to compromise me."

"Compromise?" I pulled a handful of pornographic Polaroids out of my jacket pocket and flung them at her. "Compromise? How's that for compromise? Who are you trying to kid? You did that without any help from me."

One of the Polaroids wafted through the air and stuck on the belt of the terry cloth bathrobe. She reached down and turned it right side up, staring at it for a long while, trying to recognize the performers, trying to recall the performance. I could tell she had finally succeeded when she collapsed onto the floor and began weeping. Stooping, I tried to comfort her. She shied away.

Several minutes later when I came out of the bathroom, after bandaging the teeth marks on my thigh, she was sound asleep, still huddled on the floor. It was only three-thirty in the afternoon, but I had good reason to believe she hadn't slept in forty-eight hours.

Gently, I scooped her up and deposited her on the davenport in the living room, covering her with a comforter Kathy had stitched for me.

Melissa looked like a wilted flower, some drab bloom you'd find on a grave at the end of the week.

When Kathy came home, she went in her own downstairs door, rummaged around for twenty minutes, then came up through my kitchen. I motioned for her to be quiet as she tiptoed into the dark living room.

"You find her in Tacoma?"

I nodded. Kathy winced.

"How long is she going to sleep?"

"Maybe until morning. I don't know. She was higher than a kite."

"I'll watch her for a few hours. You go do whatever you have to do."

I burned the Polaroids one by one, fluttering the remnants of each picture into the toilet bowl where they disappeared in a whirlpool. I watched the ashes swirling around and around, finally whooshing down into the sewer. Metro could have the scraps now. If they could make anything out of them, fine.

Later in the night, Kathy asked, "What was she on?"

"Don't know. I didn't bother to look around the hotel room. I got a little out of control."

Sometimes I caught Kathy gazing at me in an admiring way, her thoughts rambling, taking me in the way an old woman took in a sunset. She looked at me in such a way now. "You got out of control? How?"

"I stuck a knife in a guy's leg."

"The pimp?"

"How did you guess?"

"He the one who gave you that limp?"

"Yeah."

"Tit for tat, I'd say."

"We weren't fighting. The fight was over. He was finished. I just did it. I just picked up the knife and stuck it into his leg. I haven't done anything like that in a long time."

"Forget it," said Kathy. "You got Melissa away from the creep. He deserves whatever he got, maybe more."

"It was demeaning to be the one to give it to him, though."

Kathy and I split shifts sitting up with Melissa. Neither one of us wanted her loping off into the night a second time. During my last watch, from two to four, Melissa stirred and began sniveling into her pillow. Her head bobbed up, and with a start she spotted me, sitting in the darkness across from her.

"Are you Mr. Black?"

My sleepless voice came hard and gravelly. "That's me."

"Is Kathy here?"

"Downstairs."

That seemed to settle her. Her head dropped back onto the pillow, and a few minutes later the quiet went away and I could hear her rhythmic breathing again.

I awoke to the sounds of sausages sizzling outside my bedroom door. Assuming Kathy was cooking up a spot of breakfast, I tugged on a pair of jeans and trudged, shirtless, into the kitchen. Melissa was at the stove. Clad in my robe, she had fried enough sausages and scrambled enough eggs for an army.

She turned to me, gave me a sheepish look, and said, "I hope this is all right. I figured you had to eat. I thought I'd fix it for you."

"Fantastic. I'll be right back."

On my way back into the bedroom, I caught a glimpse of Kathy in the big chair in the living room, curled up like a cat, dead to the world.

The three of us sat around the small kitchen table. Kathy ate sparingly, but Melissa and I fought it out for the pig-of-the-meal award. I guessed it had been a while since the runaway wife had eaten anything substantial, anything more than a pocketful of pills and a tumbler of whiskey. Afterward, Melissa sprang up and began washing the dishes, declining Kathy's assistance. Kathy gave me a pinched look and sat back down at the table. We made strained small talk. When the dishes were stacked and drying, Melissa sat down purposefully.

"I've been thinking," she said. "A lot's happened in the last two weeks. I won't pretend you both don't know I was hooking. I'm not particularly proud of any of it, but I'm not going to blame myself. That's one thing Helen taught me. Instead of living in the past and wasting all my time blaming myself, I'm going to move forward."

"But why?" asked Kathy. "The money?"

"Money? That's a riot. I didn't see any money. Rome took all that. No. He came at exactly the right time, I guess. Helen Gunther had convinced me in order to get better I had to finally confront my father. I tried. I really did try. But . . . I don't know. I guess I wasn't ready for it. I kind of cracked under the pressure. That's when Rome came up. That Sunday. I didn't really know what he was planning, but I didn't want to have to think about my father anymore either. It just got to be too much. That's all. Entirely too much. Rome gave me some pills and I took them."

Kathy, uncomfortable with the confessions, said, "Burton must be home by now. We can go over and get you two back together. Then we can see about retrieving Angel."

Melissa shook her head. "I don't think so."

"Aren't you planning to get Angel?"

"It's Burton. I'm not going to get back together. I don't know why I married him. He's sweet, but we're not really a couple. He goes around on tippytoes trying not to offend me. He's just not right for me."

"What about Angel?" I asked.

"Angel can't stay with her grandfather. I won't allow that. She has to come back with me. If I have to get a job and put her in a daycare, then fine. We can live with that. You said something to me yesterday that shook it all loose, Mr. Black. You said I could give her more love than anyone else on earth. I'm never going to forget that."

After climbing into one of Kathy's shirts, which was too big in the chest, and donning a pair of Kathy's jeans, which were too big all over, Melissa slipped into a pair of sandals and was ready to leave.

I drove her to Ballard in Kathy's bug. Burton was already home. He came to the door. The look on his face was pathetic, a mixture of relief and anxiety. I waited in the car. It was almost half an hour before she emerged, alone. Burton watched her from the window like a waif in an orphanage.

She had showered and put on a pair of slacks and a beige blouse under a blazer. Her hair was pulled back into a crisp ponytail. She looked incredibly younger than she had yesterday at The Last Inn. And she was suddenly extraordinarily pretty.

"Did you tell him?" I asked.

She nodded.

"What did he say?"

"Not much. There's not much fight in Burton," she stated, flatly.

"I think you're underestimating him."

She didn't hear me. Or she didn't listen. "Where are we going?"

"Your folks' place. I figure that's where Angel's bound to be."

"You will come in with me, won't you?"

"I'll do whatever you think is necessary," I promised. The relief was evident in her face.

"The only trouble is you might not believe some of what I have to say to him."

"I don't have to believe it."

"I'm just ... worried that you'll think I'm going hooly-gooly. Father can convince people of just about anything. I have this terrible vision of us going in together and coming out separately, you going to your car and me being dragged away by three men in white."

"Nobody's going to drag you away. Not while I'm around."

The battered Volkswagen bug was an odd contrast to the ritzy Crowell homestead. It stood in front of the door like something a stray dog had dragged up and chewed ragged. The Mexican maid answered the door.

"Hi, Pilar," Melissa said, striding in past the stunned woman. "I've come for my daughter. Go get her, please."

Mouth open, the maid didn't know how to react. She gaped at Melissa, then at me, then Melissa, and finally turned to Muriel Crowell when she marched into the room.

Muriel Crowell spotted me first and zeroed in on me. "You!"

"Good morning," I said jovially.

"Pilar! Call the police!"

"Hello, Mother."

"Melissa!" Though she had been standing beside me, incredibly this was the first time her mother had noticed her daughter. "Where have you been? We've been worried sick. You've kept us worried sick. Where were you?"

"I've come for Angel."

Stupidly, her mother said, "Angel?"

"You know the one," I said. "Blonde hair? About this tall."

"You don't have to talk to me like that."

"Where is she?" Melissa asked.

Muriel Crowell organized her thoughts and attempted to take charge. "She's only in the other room. Don't get into a tizzy. We've been watching her for you."

Melissa bolted from the room past her mother. Muriel Crowell gave me a jaundiced look of pure chagrin and said, "I suppose you're responsible for this?"

"I'd like to think so."

"Angus will have something to say to you."

"I'm looking forward to it. I brought a pen. I'll take notes."

"Smart aleck. Do you know what you're doing? Do you think she's capable of raising a child?"

"Don't you?"

"Of course not. Melissa is barely capable of taking care of herself."

"Whose fault would that be?" I asked, eyeing Muriel Crowell. The question hit her like a spear, impaled her with the sheer force of its logic.

"We can raise the child," she said feebly. From the

other room, bubbling laughter erupted, mother and daughter, then playful shrieks as sharp and as shrill as the breaking of mirrors. Muriel Crowell spoke louder, straining to counter the happy sounds from the other room, as if to drown them out with her own strident and cheerless truths.

"Where's Melissa been hiding? Angus has been worried sick. I suppose she ran off with some man?"

"Where is your husband?" I asked.

Muriel turned her eyes fearfully upon me. "Angus will get you for this. Angus will make you pay. Don't think he won't."

"Pretty serious business," I said. "Getting a mother back together with her daughter. Think they'll put me in the clink?"

"Smart aleck!"

Peals of laughter erupted from the other room before Melissa came through the doorway carrying Angel in her arms, Angel's tiny wan arms wrapped around her mother's neck. Soberly, the blonde tot looked around at the grown-ups and spotted me.

"Mommy. Mommy. You got the nice man."

Melissa looked at me and hugged Angel. "Yes. I've got him for a little while." Then she turned to her mother. "Muriel, where's Angus?"

"You've never called me anything but Mother before," Muriel Crowell said, looking to me for some sort of social support. I grinned like an imbecile on his first pony ride.

"You've never been a mother. I'll call you Muriel. Where's Angus?"

"Your father's going to blow his stack when he hears you talking this way. He's going to blow sky-high."

"That would be in character," said Melissa. "Where is he? Out prospecting?"

"He took the Winnebago to Monroe. He needs a three-day weekend now and then. Your father works awfully hard. Harder than you'll ever know."

"Cut the bullshit . . ." said Melissa. Her mother's face fell like a bum cake. "Honestly. He treats you worse than an old shoe and you talk about him like he's a saint or something. You oughta have your head examined." Mrs. Crowell looked around the room, finally turning on me.

"You!" she said. "If it weren't for you, none of this would have happened."

"Sure," I said. "And I work part-time with the Easter Bunny striping eggs." Angel giggled but cut it off when she read the mood in the room, displaying remarkable instincts for someone her age.

"I wouldn't want to be in your shoes when Angus hears about this," Muriel Crowell warned, as we went out the front door. The maid shuddered in the corner, crossing herself repeatedly like a mechanical mannequin gone mad.

"Goodbye, Muriel."

"When Angus hears about this, you're both going to be sorry you were ever born." The maid nodded rapidly and crossed herself several more times. The last thing I saw through the closing door was her head bobbing up and down.

 "WILL YOU COME TO MONROE with me so I can talk to my father?" Melissa asked timidly, leaning in and strapping Angel into a seat belt in the back seat. "Is that too much to ask?"

"I wouldn't miss it for all the bullets in Texas."

"It's a long drive," she added, twisting around and focusing her pale blues on me.

"If you're trying to talk me out of it, I'll tell you right now, I get car sick," I said. She shrugged, unsure of my meaning, and unsure of herself. She didn't know what she was trying to do. "Until you shake this thing, I'm yours. Today, tomorrow, next week. I'm here for the duration. Don't doubt it."

"Why are you doing this?"

"Initially, because Kathy asked me. But I got caught up in it. I want to help you. I want to see Angel in her right place. And I have some selfish reasons."

"Such as?"

"I want to find out who smacked your aunt with that ketchup bottle. I want to know who strangled your psychologist with her own brassiere. If I hang around long enough, I might get lucky."

We drove to Ballard and dropped Angel off with a jubilant but nonetheless subdued Burton. The child was reluctant to give up her mother so soon after their reunion, but Melissa bribed her with the promise of a pack of gum when she returned. I had forgotten how uncomplicated a child's world was.

Monroe was maybe an hour from Seattle, north and a bit east, nestled just under the foothills of the Cascades. It was a tiny town, famous locally for the prison on the south side of the village. It wasn't until we were almost there that Melissa spoke.

"Kathy said you thought the two murders were connected. But how could they be?"

"For one thing, if you had done it," I said, "that would connect them."

"Me?" She started laughing. "I might kill *myself*. It never occurred to me that anybody would ever think I'd kill someone else."

"Or Burton. You discount him too easily. I've seen people more mild-mannered than Burton kill. When the provocation becomes right, almost anybody can kill. There's also your mother. She hated your aunt. Then there's some hired muscle your father paid, a guy named Holder. Your friend Bledsoe might have had his fingers in it. Was he with you all the time during the past few days?"

"Rome? I don't know where he was. I can't even remember where I was most of last week."

"Or your father. He might have done it."

The pretty blonde in her ponytail and trim blazer touched my arm and said, "Do you know why I have to speak to my father? Why Helen Gunther told me I had to confront him?"

I liked the gentle feel of her hand on my arm. I liked it too much. "I've got a notion."

"What? What is it? What do you know?"

"I'd rather you told me."

Melissa squirmed in her seat. "Would you think I was crazy if I said I saw my father kill somebody when I was a baby?"

Maybe she was crazy. I glanced over at her. "No. Of course not."

"Well, I did."

"A baby? People don't normally recall things that happened before they were two. How old were you?"

"That's just it. I don't know. I suppose I was two and a half. Three?"

"That would make it about twenty years ago, wouldn't it?"

"Twenty-two years ago."

She spoke rapidly, gulping her breath between sentences. The confession was a boulder rolling downhill now and she didn't want to clam up until it was all the way down.

"I guess I was three. Daddy used to take me up poking around in the mines with him. He had a lot of friends in those days. We used to go up with all sorts of people. One time, we went up with this man. All I remember is that the man had a bottle and he was drinking. He was a big man, almost as big as my father. There was a lot of yelling. We were inside the mine. I don't know which mine. Just a mine. The only light was a lantern and it was spooky. They fought. Daddy began socking the other man. Then he picked up a big piece of timber and hit him over the head with it. A lot of times. I was so terrified I wet myself."

"I don't doubt it."

"I've never forgotten that night."

"Do you remember anything else about the struggle or the man?"

"All I remember is the inside of the mine. It was near Christmas. I began having terrible nightmares. And every time I brought it up, or tried to, Daddy would yell at me. He used to scream at me all the time. Thinking back on it, I don't know which of us was the more terrified. Him, fearing that I might blab what I had seen, or me, thinking I really had imagined it all and afraid of what he would accuse me of next. For years, I thought I had imagined it.

"Daddy deliberately played games with me, trying to destroy my credibility. And he did. Oh, how he did. Even *I* used to wonder about myself. He was always forcing me into situations where I had to lie or take the consequences. I remember when I was about six, he used to leave candy lying around the house, tell me not to take it, and then watch from the other room. Sometimes he'd let me take it, and sometimes he'd catch me. If he caught me, he always did it when we had company. It was only when I grew more mature that I realized he did it all purposely."

"Your father seems to be someone who always has to be in control."

"He played psychological games with me the whole time I was growing up. When I was sixteen, he gave me a car for my birthday. One of those little European two-seater sports cars. Along with the keys, he handed me a list of rules. I could drive to school, but I was expected to be home twelve minutes after it let out. He actually drove from school and timed it so he would know how long it took. He would have had the maid time me. I knew he was going to be insufferable. I took the keys and threw them out into the sound. Outwardly, it was a generous gift. Actually, it was another way to catch me doing things wrong. His scheme was always to dangle something I wanted very badly in front of me, then tie so many rules to it there was no way I could obey them all. Of course, he got mileage out of my throwing the keys away, too. He was always telling everyone I had mental problems. And what made it worse was that nobody ever seemed to see my side of it. Inevitably, it became an all-out war."

"What about your mother?"

"You've seen her. He owns her, lock, stock, and barrel. Whatever Angus Crowell thinks, Muriel Crowell thinks."

Staring straight ahead at the highway, the memories pulled her pale cheeks into long, sorry pouts. The look on her face made her seem three years old, the image of her daughter.

It was quite a bit longer before either of us broke the silence. Melissa directed me to drive through the town of Monroe and into the foothills. Before we cleared the burg, though, we had to stop for fuel. As I stood jawing with a gas jockey who couldn't have been older than fifteen, Holder drove past on the main drag, heading in the opposite direction. He did not see us. He was driving a brand-new Toyota Celica. It looked like the sort of car that might belong to a girlfriend. I had every reason to believe our destination was the same place he had just departed.

I tipped the gas jockey and drove away while he twisted his baseball cap sideways and stood gawking at the blonde in my passenger seat. He was in love, was trying to memorize the vision before it faded. I looked over at pretty Melissa sitting ramrod-stiff in the worn, faded Volkswagen seat.

"He owns old mining claims all over the Northwest," she said, feeling my eyes on her. "He tramps all over the country on weekends. Mother thinks he prospects, but I don't believe it. I think he's just out catting."

A side road diverted us north. After a few miles, Melissa told me to slow down while she scanned the woods to our left. It took three miles of slow hunting before she spotted the narrow dirt path that led off the two-lane highway.

Immediately after we turned into the overgrown path, a logging truck roared down the highway behind us, its trailing vacuum rocking the bug. It was the first vehicle we had seen in more than five minutes. I could not even remember how far back the last house had been. Ten miles, maybe.

Melissa must have been reading my mind as she got out of the car and walked up the overgrown path toward a fork in the road. "It's really in the boonies, huh?" she said.

"It seems like the 'Leaving Seattle' sign was only a minute ago."

I got out and followed her to the fork. I was a city boy and I knew it.

"One of these winds down to the river," said Melissa. "The other one goes up to the mine. I can't remember which is which. I was only here a couple of times. Dad liked to come up by himself, and I did my best not to get caught alone with him."

It wasn't difficult to tell which trail was wide enough to allow a Winnebago to pass. There were ruts in the uppermost trail, and it had had the trees and high brush hacked away six months ago to accommodate something large and cumbersome. The tall, wet grass was bent over. Someone had driven it since the last rain. Judging by the condition of the packed soil, I would have to guess the last rain had been yesterday sometime, or maybe even two days ago, though the land undoubtedly remained soggy up here for weeks at a crack.

"That way," said Melissa, spotting the same bowed and wet grasses I was looking at. "I think that's the way to the mine shaft."

"How far?"

"I don't really remember. Quite a ways, I think."

We got back into the car. Out of curiosity, I noted the distance on the odometer as we bumped along on the rutted trail. In several places we saw freshly sheared branches like broken bird wings high above the road where the Winnebago had been too wide for the path. We plowed through two separate places where it looked as if the motor home had bogged down. It was a bumpy 3.2 miles to a clearing beside the road. Melissa asked me to park in it. There was no motor home in sight. And no sign of her father.

"He used to camp right here. I guess he parks it up closer to the shaft now. It might be best if we walked the rest of the way."

We got out and stretched our legs. The ground up here was higher, drier and sandier. The stands of trees had been thick since we'd left the highway and even though at least half of them were deciduous and stripped by the winter, I doubted if one could see more than a hundred feet off the road. Anything could have been out there watching us. Or anyone.

Around a bend, the trail opened up into a pasture about the size of an infield in a ballpark.

The Winnebago sat plunk in the center of the virgin dew-spotted grass. Angus Crowell was nowhere to be seen, off somewhere sorting butterflies. Melissa, who had been leading me up the road, stopped and turned to me. Her face had the blank, drugged look I'd seen two days ago when I'd first met her in Tacoma. For a moment I thought she was suffering a relapse, reverting to a doped-up tramp before my eyes. But she gritted her teeth and pushed on.

I scanned the motor home for signs of life. Nothing. The drapes were uniformly pulled closed, the doors all sealed. It might have been sitting two hours, or two months.

"He's watching us," said Melissa. As far as I could tell—and I was pretty good at that sort of thing—nobody was in any sort of position to be watching anything.

"Don't get paranoid," I said.

"You don't know him. He's watching. I can feel it."

We had climbed in elevation since leaving Seattle, but I could not guess how much. A saucer-shaped cloud hovered a few hundred feet over a mountain behind the clearing. At least an Easterner would call it a mountain. Native Westerners would term it a hill. It was steep and craggy and rigidly picturesque, and I imagined there was at least one man-sized hole drilled into its bowels. The mine.

I let Melissa rap on the rear door of the Winnebago. It was her gig. I was only the support unit. The more small things I let her handle, the more able she would be when it came to the big crunch.

Nobody answered the door. She knocked again, getting

the same negative results. Melissa heeled around brusquely and scanned the woods and mountain behind us.

"He could be anywhere," I said.

"No," said Melissa, turning back to the Winnebago and rattling the door. "He's right here." She knocked a fourth time and a fifth. I began meandering around the clearing. Anybody observing the tightness in her neck and shoulders, anybody with half a gift for interpretation would think Melissa had gone loopy. She had that awkward stiffness, the stiffness of the blind, the adult retarded, the crazed, the damned.

At the edge of the woods, I stumbled onto an ancient debris pile grown over by weeds. Embedded in the grass and dirt were old rusted pick heads, forgotten iron wheels, and broken shovels. The mine probably hadn't been active since the war, maybe even long before that. I wondered whether Crowell ever found traces of what he was looking for up here. I heard a noise behind me. The rear door to the Winnebago had been opened from the inside. By golly, Melissa had been right. He had been burrowed in there all along.

I jogged over to the motor home where Crowell had only cracked the door open. I couldn't hear what they were saying and they both stopped talking when I arrived.

I huffed once or twice, catching my breath, and said, "Afternoon, Crowell."

Angus Crowell did not have time to acknowledge me. He was staring at his daughter, his face a contorted mask. She stared right back, though it was evident she was frightened to death. The snake and the field mouse.

"Father, this is Thomas Black," Melissa said, her voice cracking. "I believe you've already met."

Angus nodded and said, "Ayeah," like some old-time sourdough, all without taking his hard eyes off his daughter. He was almost like one of those absurd boxers trying to psych out his opponent with menacing primate stares. It was an act, and I realized it even if Melissa did not. Angus Crowell infused every day with minor dramas, and sometimes with major theatrics, and he was damn good at it. Obviously, it had been a boon to his business and social life, if not his family life.

Finally, the old man broke the stalemate and said, "Excuse me. I don't know where my manners went. I'm out here in the wilds and I don't know where the hell my mind's been. The last thing I expected was company." He looked more fully at me as if it were difficult for him to see without glasses, and then he laughed. "I come up here to get away from people. Last company I had was a pair of drunken deer hunters. You hunt deer, do you, Mr. Black?"

I shook my head.

"Yeah, well, tell you what. If you two could wait outside a minute, I'll get things shipshape in here." He closed the door and I could hear him rustling around inside.

Walking over to Melissa, who had strolled off a good thirty yards, almost to the woods, I spoke in a low voice. "What were you two talking about?"

The pretty blonde was rigid and formal, as if we were two strangers riding a bus and battling to avoid each other's eyes. "I told him I came to clear the air."

"What did he say?"

Melissa turned away from me again and looked up at the mountain, tears beginning to well up in her eyes. She folded her arms snugly against her small breasts and her shoulders squared themselves up against the mountain.

"Melissa, what did your father say?"

"Don't you understand? This is all for your benefit."

She was choking on her own words, strangling on her own life.

"What is? What's for my benefit?"

"This whole charade. He knew you were up here when we first arrived. He was watching us. He waited until you were out of earshot. Damn. He said what he said because he knew when I told you about it you'd think I was crazy. Why do you think he's leaving us alone right now? He wants to be sure I'll tell you about it."

"If you don't want to say it, don't. I don't have to know."

Melissa pivoted around sharply and grabbed my belt, inserting her fingers down between the belt and my pants. It was a big move for her. She wasn't the type of person who touched others easily, especially members of the opposite sex, at least not in a social setting.

"He said nasty things. Horrible perverted things. They didn't even make sense. He sounded like someone who just escaped from a mental asylum."

"Why would he do that, Melissa?"

"Don't you see? So when I told you about it you'd look at me the way you're looking right now. It worked. He's outsmarted us both. I just should have kept my big mouth shut. Chalk up number one to dear old Dad."

"Don't get all worked up, now," I cautioned.

"Don't you see? If I keep my nerve and go through with this, you're going to be the lone witness and it's going to boil down to my word against his. And Father doesn't relish losing, not at anything. He wants my word tarnished from the outset. The way it's been my whole life." She sniffled. "And it is."

"No," I said. "Don't believe that."

I hugged her. The air rushed out of her lungs like a paper bag underfoot. She was shaky and weak. I hadn't been holding a lot of women lately. This week I'd held two of them, Kathy and Melissa. I couldn't help comparing them, their bodies, their smells, the sway of their hips against my legs, the way they laid their heads against my chest, the manner in which their breasts thrust against me.

I knew he was watching. She was right. The old con artist was crafty. He came barging out of the Winnebago before I released her.

 ARMS SWINGING, MASSIVE,
rounded shoulders rolling, Cro-
well strode toward us like an old grizzly, a smirk on his
coarse, weathered face. It was the smirk of a lifelong professional pressure salesman approaching a customer he
knew he could gull.

"Gawd, it's splendid up here," he boomed. "Look at
this landscape. God's country. No two ways about it. Just
lucky I can afford a slice or two. You own any ground,
Black?"

"Not like this," I said, watching him lumber closer.

"It's cheap now. Hell, it is cheap. You oughta look into
it." He gazed at the weeds around his feet as if they were
an audience. He knew I was watching him the way
George C. Scott knew I was watching him when he per-
formed. The world was full of consummate actors, only a
handful of them holding union cards.

"I'll tell you two. I just gave up on Gurty. I can't clean
her up. I'm an old bachelor at heart, I guess." He looked
at me and snickered. Gurty, I took it, was the nickname
of his Winnebago. He seemed the sort of man who
wanted to be inside a woman as much as possible. A
man's man, so to speak.

241

Melissa inhaled and then spoke timorously. "We did not come up here for small talk, Angus. I have something to say to you and I want Mr. Black to witness it."

"Nonsense," Angus Crowell bellowed, his voice an exquisite timbre in stark contrast to his daughter's rabbit-squeak. "You both hike up with me. Bet you've never seen one of these mines, eh, Black?"

I was struck by the confidence in his voice and by the resolute look in his eyes. It made Melissa seem very much the child. And he very much the father. But then, that was the general idea.

"I'd rather get this over," I said, but Crowell had already started marching.

"We're not coming," shouted Melissa, but her father either did not hear or pretended he did not hear, kept stalking away through the sparse trees at the edge of the clearing. In a few moments he would be out of sight. We looked at each other, both realizing at the same instant that he might not return until after he was certain we had left. It would be dark in a few hours.

"We'd better follow him," I said. Melissa concurred with a jittery sigh. Her pop wasn't making it easy and she was beginning to display signs of faltering.

For an old man, a man in his late sixties, Angus Crowell tramped up the side of that mountain like a son-ofabitch. Either he kept himself in extraordinary shape or he was killing his body to prove a point.

The trees opened up onto a hill and toward a well-defined path leading up the hill.

Though Melissa wore a sensible pair of shoes and tried her best, there was no way she could keep up. I decided to hang back with her. Two sleepless weeks of drinking, drugging, and tricking had drained her stamina. By the time we got halfway up the mountainside to the clearing in front of the mine entrance, she was bushed.

Angus hunkered on a dilapidated, overturned cart buried in knee-deep grass. He watched as Melissa plunked down onto a large angular piece of granite. I thought I saw traces of contempt in his eyes, eyes the color of bitter blackberries.

Scrub pines, rooted into crevices, bearded the face of the mountain. Crushed rock, dirt, and other rubble had been strewn down the hillside over a period of years, forming a smooth bib beneath the mine entrance. A thousand feet up, it would look as if ants had meted it out.

From our vantage point, we could see the clearing, the treetops, and the toothy-white roof of the Winnebago. To the south, more mountains rose up, real mountains, the Cascade range, most of them frosted with snow.

"We're going to talk, Father, if we have to march all the way to Yakima with you."

"Sure, sure," he said glibly. "But don't you want to go inside? You ever been inside a real working mine, Black? You'd be amazed at how far a man can dig into solid rock." He picked up a handful of loose soil from beside his boot and trickled it through his fingers. "Course this stuff is a little crumbly. Some old gummer owned the mine. Did all the work himself. Called it The Hemorrhoid. He lived on beans and varmints. They tell me he stayed up here almost thirty years. Addlepated old coot. Crowd of hunters finally found him. They guessed he'd been dead maybe six months." At the word *dead*, Angus's eyes met mine.

Melissa's father wore an outdated pair of dress trousers, boots, and a yellowed dress shirt. Somehow, hunkered on the cart, playing with the dirt, he didn't fit into the scenery. I looked him over carefully, wondering if he might have a weapon concealed under the shirt.

Melissa blasted him. "You killed someone, Daddy. I know you did. I was little, but I remember as if it happened two minutes ago. You killed some man inside a mine. It was dark and scary and you fought."

She had pretty well caught her breath now and she stood up and walked over beside me. She spat it out again in one big mouthful, as if she were vomiting.

"You killed some jasper inside a mine and I saw it. That's why you treated me like a numbskull all these years. You were afraid I'd someday say what I'm saying right now. So here I am. I'm saying it. And I'm not afraid of you anymore. You killed someone. I know you did."

Angus did not move. He was so motionless he threatened to become a part of the dilapidated cart. I hadn't seen so much quiet power in a man in years. He had the charisma men exhibited only after attaining great fame and wealth. Crowell would have been devastating in politics. Absolutely devastating.

He gave his daughter a distinctly paternal look, acting as if he were going to say something, but saying nothing. His mouth twitched. He wiped his face with his great gnarled bear hands, sighed, and worked his lips as if he had a popcorn kernel in his mouth.

"You know what this is all about?" he asked me, in an unnaturally soft voice.

"I know what it's about."

"Oh, cut the crap," said Melissa. "You know damn well what's going on."

"My dear, I did not raise a daughter to curse in the manner of a longshoreman."

"Of course you didn't." Melissa's mouth grew ugly

and she ejaculated the words like bullets. "You raised a daughter who doesn't know who she is or what she wants or how to do anything. You raised a daughter who's so nutty she'll screw anything in pants!"

Melissa glanced quickly at me as if to ask, Shall we run for it now? I gave her a reassuring look. When I wanted, I could exude a great deal of quiet power myself. I knew she would calm down as soon as she saw the look in my eyes. She put my arm into a quasi hammer-lock, wrenched it down against herself and yelped, "Let's get the hell out of here."

"No, no, no, no, no." Angus spoke patiently, as if calming a horse that wanted to bolt. "It's not going to be that easy. You've made an awfully serious accusation here. Or at least I think you have. I don't know. Maybe these old ears didn't hear right."

"They heard right," said Melissa, her grip on my arm tightening.

Crowell's voice was deep, mellifluous, almost sleepy. "So what is it you're saying?"

"I just told you."

"Put it in plain English."

"In plain English?" Melissa darted a querulous look at me. "What's the matter with you, Father? You're not fooling anyone. Thomas knows what you did. I know what you did. Everyone here knows exactly what you did. Some father. Big pillar of the community!"

Crowell wrinkled his nose and screwed up his face for a few seconds. Then he hawked and spat. "You've been doing a lot of talking, haven't you, Missy?"

"Get off your power trip, Daddy. I've got a big strong man here to guard me and I'm not going to back down.

Not this time. I'm not scared." Maybe she wasn't, but she was shutting off the circulation in my forearm.

"Missy been telling you things, Black?"

"We've talked."

"You believe her?"

I nodded. I was no judge. And certainly I was no psychologist. I wanted to back her up, but I wasn't sure about her mental acuity, any more than I was sure of his. She was making serious allegations.

"I hope you're not foolish enough to repeat anything my little scatterbrain tells you. A man could get into a heap of horse manure repeating things."

"Sure. And sometimes a man can get up to his neck in it not repeating things."

He looked at his daughter. "You're mixed up, Missy. I remember once Todd Sperling and I were up here horsing around. You thought we meant business but we were only horsing around. Is that what you're talking about? You should have brought it up years ago. Todd's still around. We had dinner with him and his second wife not less than a month ago. If this was troubling you so much, you should have brought it up years ago. Missy, you're a troubled girl." Melissa inhaled and it caught in her throat like someone on a crying jag.

"It was not Todd Sperling. I know who Todd is. It was somebody else. Somebody big with red hair. You're not going to talk me out of it or convince me I'm crazy. Not this time."

His lips curled up and he shook his shoulders as though he were laughing, but he wasn't. He wasn't anywhere near a laugh. "If Melissa's been telling you things, Black, did you hear the one about the daughter and the gardener? She tell you that one? It's a doozy. Or how about the one about the daughter and the paper boy who wasn't even fourteen years old, for christsakes!"

"Oh Gawd," said Melissa, tugging on my arm. "I cannot even believe you would try such an obvious smokescreen. I really cannot."

"Let me explain the facts of life, Black. My daughter's been mentally disturbed since she could walk. She's been seeing shrinks for years. Hate to say it, but I think this sort of funny business runs in the family. Her aunt had some problems. And her grandfather, who she never knew . . . he killed himself. I don't pretend to understand how her mind works, but I think this accusation stems from her own guilt over what she's done. Over what she's fantasized."

"You still cannot admit it, can you?" said Melissa.

"Missy. Calm down."

"I don't understand you. Have you really put it out of your mind? Have you convinced yourself over the years that it never happened? Because if you have, I'm here to tell you it did happen. It happened . . . and it ruined me. It's only been the last twenty-four hours that I've held out any hope for myself."

"Melissa, you need counseling. She needs counseling, Black."

"Sure she does," I said. "I think you do, too." He glowered at me. It hit me like a cold wind.

"I suppose we could all use some counseling from time to time," he admitted.

I stared right back at him. Had he been my father in my growing years, there would have been hell to pay. One way or another there would have been hell to pay.

"You don't believe her story, do you? Melissa is disturbed. Ask her mother. She spent nine days at La

Conquistador a few years back. Know what the doctors caught her doing?"

"Father . . ."

"Peddling it. That's right. She was peddling it to the attendants. I don't enjoy telling these things, Missy, but you're forcing my hand."

"You're not going to shock Black," said Melissa, her vanity surfacing. She was proud of the fact that I stood staunchly beside her, despite where I had found her, despite what I had found her doing. "He's seen it all. He knows all about me."

Her father's voice was beginning to fade. The facts of his daughter's life were defeating him. "I'm sorry to hear that, Melissa. I'm sorry to hear you haven't reformed."

"Are you ever going to admit this?" Melissa demanded. "Don't you know? All I want is for you to look at me and say you did it." She tried to stare the old bear down for thirty long seconds, but she didn't have a prayer.

"No. I didn't think so. Well, you can say aloha to your precious daughter. And you can say aloha to Angel, too. You'll not get your filthy hands on her. I'll never forgive you, Daddy. And I'll never forget all those years you tried to rob me of my self-confidence. All those times you tried to convince me and yourself and everybody else that I was a fruitcake, not to be trusted. I'll never forget."

Melissa pivoted and stormed down the hillside. Stomping down the rocky trail, she was slender and frail and pretty. Her ankles bent awkwardly as she crossed the rugged terrain. I hoped she didn't sprain something. I proceeded to leave behind her, but Crowell stopped me.

"Black," he said, "let me have a few words?"

Melissa heard him and glanced over her shoulder

apprehensively, watching me through a veil of tears. I winked at her and sent her on her way.

"Shoot," I said.

He talked for a long while. He rambled, wheedled, conned, and cajoled. I didn't believe much of it. He was a man trying to swim in quicksand. Lots of flailing, but no real movement. He told me how he had adored his daughter as a baby, as a toddler. He tried to assure me she'd been seeing things for years. He tried to convince me he loved her dearly and wanted to see that she got some real competent medical attention. And he told me stories. How he'd caught a man in her room when she was sixteen; how the man, in trying to escape, had knifed Angus so that he came close to bleeding to death.

I strolled about while he talked. Melissa had made it to the car by then. Some time to herself wouldn't hurt. I walked behind him and investigated the opening to the mine. Inside lay a stockpile of modern lamps, a few tools, and a bucket filled with rain water. The bucket gave me an idea. A dangerous idea.

Crowell continued to talk without turning around.

"Listen," he said. "I made a serious mistake letting Penworthy Investigations run on such a long leash. That Holder fellow got out of control. I'll admit that. I don't know what he might have done. But I'd like to make that up to you. Somebody killed my sister and I want to find out who. The cops claim Burton has an alibi. Much as I'd love to see it pinned on him, I'll have to believe them. This Percy joker with the Bellingham police is incompetent. I want you to find out who did do it. It could mean a thousand bucks a day to you."

"I don't think so," I said, wondering why he would

offer so much. He had to realize the going rates were nowhere near that.

"What? Why? Fifteen hundred? Listen, you're done with this case, aren't you? Holder told me you're itching to find out who murdered my sister. Why don't we kill two birds with one stone?"

"I'm a bird lover."

"If that business with Melissa is bothering you, you come back to Seattle with me. I'll show you psychiatric reports that'll curl your hair. In high school she had everyone convinced one of her teachers had seduced her. The man almost went to jail before we found out she was lying. Cost me forty thousand dollars to settle out of court." Crowell cocked around and stared at me for a moment, then turned back. I got the feeling he had squatted on the overturned cart before, had spent a great deal of time in that position, gazing out over the treetops, contemplating.

When he spoke again, he was facing away, looking down at his knees. "She's been a sidewalk stewardess for a number of years. You know that, Black?"

"The way I understand it, it was an on-and-off deal."

"And you still believe her?"

"Prostitutes don't lie any more than the rest of us."

"You're a naive man, Black. But I'll give you your due. Holder says you're damn good at your sort of work. Look, from what I read, if the cops don't find a killer in the first few hours after the event, the likelihood gets smaller and smaller that they ever will. I'm worried. Percy tells me they don't have a clue who murdered Mary Dawn. I need somebody of your caliber to get in and dig, someone who can ferret out all the facts and report directly to me."

"Sorry," I said. Even as I turned down the offer, I began thinking what I might do with the pile of loot I could earn from the case. Much as I liked to think so, I wasn't immune to the lure of filthy lucre. Maybe I could take in next year's boat show with some lettuce in my pocket. I could shop for a video recorder. I could impress my neighbors and pay off the paper boy in cash. And of course, a guy hated to leave loose ends. It might be nice to tidy up the case and find out who the guilty party was. It might even be nicer to get paid a small fortune for doing it.

"I could go as high as eighteen hundred a day, Black."

He remained facing away. I reached inside the mine entrance and lifted out the heavy galvanized bucket spilling over with rain water. Near-freezing liquid slopped over the edges and numbed my fingers.

I hoisted the bucket of icy water, swung it back in both hands, and tossed the frigid contents at Angus Crowell. Bombs away. The water tumbled through the air in a large misshapen silver bubble. With a thwack, it splashed across his shoulders, doused his back, and seeped down into his trousers. A direct hit. Give the bombardier a cigar.

He leaped up, twisted around, planted his heavy legs, and stared at me.

"Muthefucka!"

I smiled a small, wry, sorry smile. "I was afraid you might say that."

**26** "YOU BETTER HAVE A DAMN good explanation for that stunt," Crowell bellowed. "Letting some bonehead toss a bucket of ice water on me in this mountain air is not my idea of fun and games."

I flung the bucket aside. Neither of us watched as it clanked down the hillside.

"No," I said. "Your idea of fun and games runs a bit deeper than a mere prank."

He looked at me carefully. "What do you mean by that?"

"I know who you are; I know what you've been up to."

"You're worse than Melissa. What is this? Some sort of code talk?"

"Five days ago, last Sunday night, somebody broke into my house."

His eyes altered and he gave me a narrow look. "So what? That has nothing to do with me. That has nothing . . ."

"He broke in and he started trashing the place, but Kathy Birchfield, my downstairs renter, interrupted him. You remember Kathy. She talked to you a week ago about your daughter. The guy was big and athletic. He

252

had brown eyes. That was all she could see under the ski mask.

"And he was tall. So tall, in fact, that he bashed his head on one of the low doorways in her apartment. Guess what he said when he bashed his head?"

"I don't know that I care."

Crowell grumbled, but he was growing more and more interested in the point of my story. If he had flubbed up somewhere, he wanted to know where. A successful man made a habit of looking over his shoulder, pinpointing his mistakes, and correcting them.

"He said 'muthefucka.' "

"So?"

"He said it just exactly the way you said it a moment ago."

"A lot of people curse."

"Yes, and most of them have their own little pet phrases."

"What are you getting at?"

"Don't be dense, Crowell. You know what I'm getting at. You broke into my house. You went after Kathy, you bastard."

The tiny impish grin on Crowell's craggy face eroded until it was a full-fledged grimace. His shirt was soaked and sticking to his torso. His trousers were soggy in the seat. It was only when he tugged out his shirttail that I realized what he was grinning about. I saw it before he hauled it out into the light, saw it through the outline of his wet shirt.

It was a forty-five caliber Smith and Wesson revolver, and I was kicking myself for not spotting it sooner.

Angus Crowell lined up the tiny black hole in the end

of the pistol with my sternum and said, "I'd say you're between a rock and a hard place, eh, sonny?"

"You don't shoot a man for tossing a bucket of water on you."

"No, no, no," growled the old man. "Nobody's going to get shot. Not if they behave themselves."

"You broke into my house, didn't you?"

He grinned and I saw gaps in his teeth. "No harm in telling you. It will be your word against mine. Nobody's going to believe you. Sure I did. It's an old business trick. You have to deal with somebody, get them off balance. Do something to their life that takes their concentration away from your dealings. You'd be amazed at how effective it is."

"You wanted me to stop looking for your daughter?"

"That was what I wanted."

"But you had a reward out for her. You had your own detectives looking for her."

"That's right. *My* own detectives. Not some busybody gumshoe doing a favor for a friend. I wanted to talk to Missy first. I didn't need her filling your head with all that hogwash."

"Too late now," I said.

"Yes, isn't it."

"What are you going to do about it?" I asked.

He gestured with the gun. "Not a damn thing. And there's not a damn thing you can do about me, either. If you believe Missy, fine. But what can you do? Not a damn thing."

"What were you planning for Kathy?"

"Kathy?"

"The woman in my house. The one you tied up and slapped around."

"Oh, her. Cute little twitch. Actually, I had some rather elaborate plans for her. You would have enjoyed them. I find a genuine entertainment factor in crime. Too bad you got home and interrupted me."

"You must have killed my dog Saturday night."

"I was scouting your place. Your little twitch, Kathy, visited me and told me you two were going to find Melissa. I believed her. I knew I was going to be wanting to slow you down somehow. I always do my own advance research on a project. So, I was out scouting. Your dog, the little bastard, tore a chunk out of my trousers. He got what he deserved. Seattle's got a leash law, jerk."

"What about your sister?"

"What about her?" His look was not one of superior knowledge. He knew little more than I. And then it hit me. It hit me like the name of an old-time movie star I'd been trying to dredge up all Sunday afternoon for the crossword puzzle. It had been visible all along, but I had been too busy to see it.

As if on cue, she hiked around the bend and trudged up the hillside. Keeping the pistol trained on me, Crowell watched her labor up the rocky trail, a curious look on his craggy face. He was beginning to shiver badly from the breeze on his wet clothes.

She wasn't breathing nearly as hard as one would have suspected. She was in better shape than anybody had realized. She looked at me, revealing a mixture of contempt and relief, flavored with fear. Using the sleeve of her coat, she mopped some of the sudden perspiration off her pale brow.

"Long time no see," I said, being deliberately ironic.

Walking over beside Angus, she said, "How'd you get all wet?"

"This know-it-all gumshoe," said Angus.

"I'm so glad you caught him," she said. "Now you can kill him."

"What the hell are you talking about?"

I was cooked anyway. I might as well jump in with both feet. "She's been protecting you, Angus. She murdered your sister."

Disbelief dappling his hard eyes, Angus stared at her and said, "Muriel? What are you doing up here?"

"Don't you believe me?" I said. "Ask her. She beaned your sister with that ketchup bottle. Didn't you, Muriel?"

"We can't let him live," said Muriel, looking at me as if I were a halibut she needed to chop up for dinner.

"Muriel! What the hell are you talking about? Is he telling the truth? Muriel!"

"Somebody had to do it."

"You stupid, meddling woman!"

She blanched under his onslaught, then plugged on. She had little choice. "I knew about Harry. I've known all these years. You thought I didn't, but I did. I knew you killed him."

"Muriel, keep your goddamned mouth shut!"

She looked at me, then back at her husband. "No. I will not. I've been going way out on a limb to protect you, Angus, and I'm not going to sit still and let you ruin it for the both of us."

"You killed Mary? Why, for godsakes?"

Muriel gulped, jammed her arthritic-looking dishpan hands deep into the pockets of her cloth coat, and shuffled her feet which were caked in mud. She must have lost the trail on the way up. "I knew Melissa was bent on talking to you about what happened when she was three. Oh, don't look at me that way. She told me about it when it happened. She went straight to her mother. Where did you think she would go? I heard you speaking to that detective, Holder, who does work for Taltro. I knew you were worried. When Mary called Monday and said she had to speak to you, I went up instead. Melissa was going to tell Mary what she saw. It's a miracle she didn't do it years ago. And you remember what sort of fixation Mary had on it. She would have had you prosecuted, Angus. You would have gone to jail."

"The butter brickle ice cream was for you, wasn't it?" I said. "Not for Melissa, or for Angus. It was your favorite, too, wasn't it?"

"I hit her," said Muriel Crowell. "I hit her with the first available object. It happened to be that damned bottle from the refrigerator."

"Muriel. You are nuts," said Angus, incredulously. "I don't believe you did that."

"I was protecting you."

"Me? Nobody is ever going to get me."

"Oh, honey. I don't want you in prison."

"Muriel. Nobody would find Harry in a million years."

One of my biggest problems has always been my mouth. I said the most stupid thing I had said all day. They were probably planning to do me in anyway, but if they weren't, I sealed my fate. "Sure they'll find him. He's probably right inside this mine. In a pit, I'd say."

Angus stared at me, then at his wife, trying to divine our thoughts. "You ease on back into that mine," Crowell said, waving the pistol at me.

"I'm afraid of the dark."

"Just do it, jerk."

Suddenly, the open air looked awfully good. "You can't very well leave a witness," I said. "What do you plan to do with Melissa? You already discovered you can't erase her memory."

He gestured with the pistol. "You just back into the mine."

I didn't have any choice. On the way up the trail I'd observed several dozen rusted cans in the creek bed, cans stippled with bullet holes. I had to assume he knew how to use the weapon. And I had to assume he meant business. My hope was that the sopping shirt would cool him off enough to dampen his reaction time and give me a chance to make a move. He was already shivering severely in spurts. The air temperature had to be below thirty-five. The chill factor on a damp body was close to zero.

Inside the mine entrance, I waited in the dark while Crowell put a match to the wick in a glass lantern. I sensed the wary machinations behind his bitter brown eyes.

The lantern dangling from one hand and the pistol from the other, he directed me to walk into the cavern. Muriel followed along without being told, like an obedient cocker spaniel, grasping his arm as if she might get lost without it. We were both tall men and we had to stoop. After about twenty-five feet, the shaft opened up into a wider, higher work area. Two separate tunnels ventured off from the work area, the first branching to the right, the second wending around in a hard left. Crowell ordered me into the second tunnel.

I crouched down and duck-walked through the murk, watching my own lamp-thrown shadow bobble and lunge at me.

Had I known the path the tunnel was taking, I might have outdistanced Crowell. I might have grabbed a rock and laid in ambush for him, but I didn't know beans about mines. I didn't know when the tunnel might open up into a pit or onto a dead end. It was only dumb luck that I retained the presence of mind to count my footsteps. Approximately a hundred yards inside the cool mountain, Crowell ordered me to a halt.

"Right here," Crowell said. "Get in there."

To my right, the tunnel doglegged, while the main shaft continued in what I assumed was a northerly direction. Cobwebs spiraled around my hand when I reached out into the dogleg. The air inside felt colder and damper than the rest of the shaft.

I moved into the dogleg, fending in front of myself, knocking cobwebs out of my face. It wasn't until Crowell reached the mouth of the dogleg carrying the lamp that I could see. Old rotted timbers and one-by-eights were laid out across the floor of the dogleg.

"Keep moving," ordered Crowell. His voice sounded gruffer and more bearlike in the narrow tunnel.

Ancient timbers and one-by-eights took my weight, but not easily, jouncing slightly when I walked. I couldn't discern what was beneath them, but from the cold draft blowing up my pant legs, I had to guess it was a hole of some sort, a vertical shaft, possibly a deep one. Long ago, someone had covered the shaft over using makeshift joists.

The timbers under my feet ended. I found myself walking on solid rock again in an open cavern about twenty feet high and thirty feet in diameter.

Stepping onto the rock floor from the boards, I turned around suddenly and faced the Crowells. He didn't want to get too close, so I was forcing them to stop in the middle of the sagging boards. Angus didn't seem to notice. I could tell from the manner in which he moved that he knew these tunnels like he knew his own heart. He had been across the perilous passage so many times, he no longer thought of it as a hazard. He was like somebody in an apartment on the thirtieth floor leaning over his balcony. The height ceased to seem like a peril after one had lived around it for a spell. And Crowell had lived around it for a spell. Muriel clutched his arm tighter.

Together, the couple weighed at least four hundred pounds, and it showed in the way the one-by-eights bowed under their feet. Crowell set the lantern down in front of himself. Its upward light shaped a monster out of his face, and out of his wife's as well. Two griffins in a cave.

"I'm sorry, Angus," said Muriel. "But I heard you speaking with Melissa on the phone, and you were scared."

"Angus Crowell's never been scared a day in his life. I was cautious. Sure, she called me. I tried to talk her out of this big confrontation she kept insisting on. But it was no dice. This bitch of a psychologist she's been seeing's got her all messed up."

Crowell swatted himself, flapping his free arm, trying to keep warm, then squatted and held his hand out over the squiggles of heat rising from the lantern. His sopping clothes were having an effect.

"I took care of the psychologist for you," Muriel added.

"What?" His voice lowered to an almost inaudible whisper, as if he were talking to his confessor.

"I listened on the extension when that man, Holder,

gave his report to you. He said Black was talking to her. I knew if she was treating Melissa she might know something. Something she had no right to know. I drove over and waited at her apartment. I was planning to wait all day and all night if need be, but she came home for lunch. She refused to answer any of my questions. She refused to talk about it at all. That's when I knew she was hiding something. So I kept her from talking."

Angus Crowell stared incredulously at his wife. They had been married decades and he was just getting to know her.

"Nice job," I said. "Everyone thought a man had done it. Women don't often strangle other women. A nice touch, too, partially disrobing her. But you didn't quite finish the job, did you? So you bashed her over the head, too."

"Muriel," said Angus, angrily. "You idiot. None of that was necessary. Don't you know anything? I've got a load of dynamite in Gurty. Harry's right here underneath us. I'm going to blow this place to hell. They wouldn't find him in a million years. Not even if they knew where to look."

"This must be where it happened," I said. "Twenty some odd years ago, you and your daughter and Harry were standing right about where we are now. Only Harry never left. When Melissa wanted to talk about it, you tried to make people think she was mentally disturbed. You were so good at it, you convinced everyone. Even Melissa."

"Shut up."

"You did it, didn't you?"

"Look, we had a fight. It might not have been anything,

but we had this fight. Harry found out I was misappropriating funds."

"Let me guess. The guy's name was Harry Stubbins."

Crowell's jaw dropped open. "How did you know that?"

"Been doing a little research."

"Poor old Harry. He thought he knew all about everything. He thought I was just an ignoramus who happened to have a few extra bucks to invest in his company. We went in partners, and then the sonofabitch wanted to buy me out for peanuts. Took me for a fool. Said I was ruining things, that I had no business sense. I guess I showed him. Look what I built Taltro into. Look at it, would you?"

"What'd you do? Kill the guy and then fake a suicide note?"

"You want me to go to jail for something that wasn't my fault? He started the rumpus. And then he died. I couldn't show him to anybody. I had to hide him. The suicide note was only a convenience. I went to his office and typed it up. They found it Monday morning. If he'd just disappeared, it might have been years before things got straightened out. I was saving myself a little time, that's all."

"Never mind who it hurt. Your sister had something at stake, too, didn't she?"

"Eh? She thought she was going to marry the jerk. She was too old to get married. I told her that. She was almost forty."

"She was going to tell me something. She thought there was something fishy about Harry's death. She suspected you, didn't she?"

I turned to Muriel. "You were afraid if a detective got

onto it, if he spoke to your sister-in-law, spoke to your daughter, he might piece this jigsaw puzzle together. You were afraid Angus might be found out. What did Mary Dawn threaten? To hire me to find Harry's body? To sick me onto the case to prove Harry Stubbins didn't commit suicide? She thought she was paranoid about the whole affair until Melissa told her she had something serious to talk about, something that had happened years ago. Maybe it was Melissa's tone of voice. Maybe she combined it with hints she'd been unconsciously picking up over the years, but she thought she was finally going to find out how Harry died. Didn't she?"

Angus was shivering like a dog in snow. "Who else knows this? Who else?"

"Sure, I'll hand over a list of names and you two can drive around and strangle all of them. We'll put it in the paper and then you'll have to strangle the whole city. Percy has some prints, but he doesn't have any suspects. You go through with this, and my friends will see that he checks those prints against your fingers. Both of you. There's a rope with the state seal on it waiting for your necks. Maybe they'll get cute and make it a double ceremony."

"Nonsense, boy. I can handle more things than you know. You, for instance. I'm not going to shoot you. Not necessary. I'm merely going to blow out this lantern and make my way back to the mouth of the mine. I can do it in the dark. I doubt whether you'll get ten feet. There are a number of false tunnels along the way and it's very easy in a pitch-dark environment to get completely twisted around. You'll find more than one hole to fall into, too. All I need is one or two minutes' head start."

"What about me?" Muriel asked, in a wee voice.

"I've got my dynamite. Before you know it, I'll have the whole mountain down around your ears. If anyone even knew you were in here, they wouldn't bother to dig. If they started tomorrow, it would take ten years just to find this shaft."

"What about me?" Muriel repeated.

I said, "So you bury me in here, and then what do you do with Melissa?"

"Missy? We'll figure out something."

"Sure you will. Me, and then Melissa. That'll make four murders in a week between the pair of you. Nice, pleasant work, if you can get it. It'll look real good in your dossier. Founder of your church, president of the Boy Scouts, murderer."

Crowell glared at me. "Holder warned me you might try to make me mad."

"You've been mad since you were eighteen."

"Eighteen? What do you know about that?"

"You had a run-in with your father, didn't you? And then he committed suicide? The pattern is beginning to look familiar."

"My father was a completely different situation. That old bastard deserved to die."

"I'll bet you were just the one to make sure he did."

"You should have seen the look on his face."

"You're a couple of moral idiots." I said it low and soft, but still it seemed to reverberate throughout the tunnels. Angus Crowell's breathing stopped and the gun wavered in his fist. For a few seconds he had the look of a man who was about to put a bullet into another man.

Shaking his wife off his wet arm, he pushed her from behind and said, "Over there with him."

"What?"

"You heard me, you stupid, meddling woman. I never would have been caught without your interference. If you'd just stayed out of it. But no. Not you. You bungle everything. Get over there with him."

"You can't be serious," Muriel said, a screeching frog in her throat. It was the sort of shock that comes only once or twice in a lifetime, and is followed closely by swallowing a bottle of sleeping pills or a complete emotional and social retreat from the world. I almost felt sorry for her. She was sniveling loudly. He pushed her again and she resisted. The timbers under their feet bounced slowly and made weak cracking noises. She was much stronger than she looked. But then, she had been a physical therapist. Physical therapists had to be strong.

He cuffed her across the face and she stopped resisting. She didn't come over to where I was standing, but she stopped resisting.

He stooped, picked up the lamp, partially turned around, and began sidling out of the dogleg. He didn't want to turn his back on me, so he walked sideways, crablike. As the light receded, I began to panic. He had pegged it. Without a light I would be worse than helpless. I was beginning to lose perspective already. It would take hours to grope my way out of the tunnels in the pitch black. Maybe days.

I ran at him.

I sprinted to his right, to his blind side. He was cocked halfway around to his left, trying to keep an eye on both me and Muriel at the same time he picked his way across the one-by-eights.

In a split second I had Muriel's bulky body between him and me. I didn't need to get real close, just so I hit those boards hard while his weight was still on them.

They had been spongy under my hundred and eighty pounds. They had bowed and made slight popping sounds under their combined burden. The three of us should collapse the affair.

The noise was stupendous. The lantern flew out of his hands and rolled in front of him onto the solid tunnel floor.

The floor disappeared beneath our feet and I scrabbled onto the ledge that ran along the far side of the pit. His wife disappeared immediately and silently. Crowell slid backward, boards cracking and splitting under him.

He rolled onto his side, reaching out for me. He had realized what I was doing and tried to drag me down with him. He was a day late and a dollar short. He disappeared in a thunder of boards and rocks and powdery dust. He whooped all the way down.

He hit like a wet pillow. Though it wasn't as deep as I thought, about twenty feet, the hole was sheer. Unless a ladder was mounted in the side of the rock wall, neither one of them would be coming up on their own.

Banging my knees on the sides of the pit, I managed to keep my arms and chest on the ledge. Then, when the crashing stopped, I swung first one leg and then the other up onto the ledge. I crawled on my hands and sore knees toward the dying lamp. As soon as I righted it, it burned bright.

Swinging the lantern out in front of me, I could see the hole was fifteen feet across. The remnants of an old wooden ladder were affixed into the rock on the other side. Only the top three or four rungs were still usable. They wouldn't be climbing out on that.

When I leaned over the side, it took me a few seconds to make out the figure of a man among the splintered boards. It took me another few seconds to realize he was conscious and was looking at me. His right hand was combing the darkness. I knew what he was feeling for. I had already searched for it fruitlessly on top. His wife lay beside him, her eyes fixed and buggy. Her head was angled off sharply, twisted and screwed around like a child's doll under a tricycle wheel. Her neck had snapped in the fall. She was dead.

"We kind of got things reversed here, don't we, old timer?" I said.

Crowell did not reply.

"You hurt?" I asked.

"Think I cracked some ribs. My leg might be broken."

"That kind of puts you between a rock and a hard place, eh?"

"Be a sport, Black. Think what you could do with a hundred thousand dollars."

"What? You going to pay me to clam up?"

"A hundred grand. How'd that be?"

"Sure," I said. "That's a splendid idea. I'll take your money and I'll go home with it and next week Holder or some other gumball you hire will slink up behind me with a lead pipe and put stars in my eyes. You must think I'm a dope."

"You might as well take the money. They'll never pin Harry's death on me. I have too many friends. The absolute worst that could happen would be that I'd have to jump bail and leave the country. But I know plenty of places a man can live with my kind of money. Plenty of places where they can't extradite me.

"And that's the worst that can happen. There are other things. Witnesses can change their minds. Or they can disappear altogether. Evidence can be lost. I've pulled strings before and I can pull them again. Jail? Not me. You'd better think again. Now go get some help and yank me out of here."

There were three of them in the pit. Crowell, his dead wife, and a remarkably complete skeleton: Harry Stubbins. They made quite a trio, though the two dead ones had expired twenty-two years apart.

"You got a watch?"

Crowell bent his arm around and peered at his wrist. "Busted."

"Too bad."

"What are you planning to do? Black? Get me some help in here. I can't get out alone."

"You can play three-handed pinochle, eh?"

"Black? You talk a tough game, but you won't do it. You're no assassin. You'd never be able to live with yourself if you abandoned me down here. I've got reports on you, Black. You're no murderer. You wouldn't know how."

"Why don't you give me some quick lessons?"

"Black?" It was a wail, almost a caterwaul, like a sick stir-crazy cat in the zoo.

"I don't know," I said. "You've convinced me justice will never be done any other way."

"Black! Get me out of here!"

Ducking low, I trimmed the lamp so that I wasn't quite as bright. Crowell thought I was skulking away down the tunnels.

"Black? Black! Are you still here? Get me out of this pit."

"So you can have me hit?" My soft voice surprised him as I peered into the pit again. "So you can mess up your daughter's life even more, maybe even kill her? So you can get ahold of your granddaughter? You're a sick man, Crowell. And you're powerful. You know how to get things accomplished. I think Seattle and maybe the rest of the world might be better off if you stayed down there a while."

"A while?" His voice was growing hoarse from screaming. "What do you mean, a while?" He had found the gun, was trying to dig it out of the dirt, using his one good hand.

"I'll come back and see how you're doing later."

"When? When will you come back? I'm freezing. I might be dead by the time you get back."

"Think you can hang on till the Fourth of July?"

"Black!" His scream reverberated down the tunnels.

"Sweet dreams."

The explosion stung my ears and almost sent me into shock. It felt like somebody had sneaked up behind me and clapped their hands hard against both ears. The bullet whirred through my hair. An inch lower and it would have killed me. I flattened myself on the tunnel floor, feeling a twinge where Bledsoe had bit me and another in my knees where they had slammed into the tunnel wall.

He cut loose another salvo.

A bullet struck the rock ceiling and ricocheted down the dogleg, whirring and whining. Bits of lead pinballed down the tunnels looking for a way out. He fired again. A bullet splattered over my head and showered me with particles of rock and lead. He must have fired four times, though the sounds ran so close together it was impossible to count.

"You better leave one in the gun," I said.

I picked up the lamp and forged my way down the

dogleg to the main tunnel. Crowell had been right. I never would have fumbled my way out of the mine in utter darkness. As it was, I had to stop and think long and hard about which way to go at the end of the dogleg. Even with the lantern, I got lost and had to backtrack twice.

When I reached the entrance, I took a deep breath, mildly surprised that it was still daylight. The cold, fresh air felt wonderful as it seared my lungs. Now, outside in the breeze, I could no longer hear his screams, could hear nothing except some raucous crows chasing a hawk down below. According to my wristwatch, we had been inside the mountain only twenty minutes. How time flew when you were having fun.

**27**   In bright, flashy whiteface,
Kathy was doing her clown
schtick. She mimed, mugged, juggled balls, and squirted
guests with water from a plastic lily in her lapel. The
party was being held at my house. She wasn't having
much luck in her attempts to jazz up the gathering.

The guests included Melissa and Burton, still sepa-
rated after several weeks, but on talking terms.

Burton had brought the birthday girl. They swapped
Angel every other week, and it was his week. Pilar was
flopped onto the sofa, giggling to beat the band. Somebody had erroneously informed her the grape punch was
alcoholic and she was reacting accordingly, the perfect
psychological study. Helen Gunther might have been
taking notes, only she had been in the ground for weeks.

Helga Iddins stood in the other corner, sans husband,
her strong arms folded across her breasts, bestowing odd
looks on me that might have been sultry or just plain
mean, while she explicated to a waxy-faced Clarice
Crowell her philosophy of the dance. Clarice was under
the impression Helga was a ballerina. Clarice and
Edward were both attending, having stayed over to help
Pilar with the multitude of arrangements.

271

Kathy sneaked up, hugged me from behind, and whispered into my ear, "Hey, Cisco."

"Hey, Pancho."

"Things have turned out so nicely, Thomas. Burton's working at Boeing. Melissa's back in therapy and doing well. Doesn't she look happy? Well . . . better? You're some sort of genius." Kathy bussed my left ear warmly, wetly.

"Just luck," I said, recalling how close I'd come to getting sealed inside a mountain.

"Luck, schmuck, you stooge. Who do you think is going to believe that?" Arms still twined around my neck, Kathy crabbed around until she was in front of me, her arms making an arbor for us. With her bulb nose, painted eyebrows, and whiteface, the only parts of her I recognized were her violet eyes, eyes the vivid shade of Elizabeth Taylor's. "And Angus? I almost wish you had left him down in that hole."

"I thought about it."

"You must have. You didn't even tell Melissa until you got to Monroe."

"He'll get what's coming to him, one way or another."

"I don't know, Thomas. I worry. After all, he's out on bail. Can you believe that? A man is accused of one murder and two other attempted murders, and they let him off on a bond. It makes you wonder."

"Crowell wasn't fooling when he said he had a lot of pull."

"And he really did kill your dog?"

"He said he hadn't planned it. He came here to scout around, and the mutt attacked him. You had talked to him and given him my name. You have to remember he was a desperate man. He'd been trying to keep a murder covered up for over twenty years and it was about to be exposed. Or so he thought, until he cooked up the idea of dynamiting the mine. After he thought of that, he calmed down significantly."

"And he broke in here?"

"Before he thought of the dynamite. Yes. And when you interrupted him, he decided that since you were implicated in getting me into the case, you should be taught a lesson also."

"What was he going to do?"

"Whatever he had to to upset our lives. Anything to shake us up so we wouldn't go through with our plans."

Spotting Kathy in a compromising position, Angel bounded across the room, dashing to grab a wrapped present jutting from the pocket of Kathy's black clown pants. Kathy had been taunting her with it since she'd arrived. Halfheartedly, Kathy tried to escape, but I hugged her and pinned her while Angel picked her pocket, then ran away tittering. Feigning anger, Kathy crouched down and pretended she was going to give chase. Angel squealed delightedly, hid behind the sofa, and began feverishly unwrapping the gift.

The phone rang. Before I could answer it, Kathy said, "You want a Christmas goose?" The phone rang again.

"What's wrong with turkey?"

"I've had enough turkeys."

"Christmas is a long time away."

"I like to plan ahead."

"Sure. A goose sounds good."

"How about right now?"

The phone rang again. I could see it coming. Before I could cover myself, Kathy goosed my behind, using a noisemaker of some sort. It made a gross noise like a whoopee cushion. Everyone laughed at the look on my face.

I picked up the phone. It was Holder. Julius Caesar Holder. I was so stunned, I almost did not speak. "Black? You there?"

"This is Black," I said, finally, glancing around the room at the modest little party. Nobody in the room was quite as contented as they might have been, nobody except the clown and the child. It was one of those weird birthday parties for a child with only one child in attendance.

"You know, about that Crowell thing. Well, I done it."

"I'm not sure I understand."

"What Crowell done . . . I thought about it."

"Yes?"

"I been tailin' him. Tailed him all week. I tailed him to the airport this afternoon. He had a ticket to Jamaica. When he was waitin' for his plane, I tipped off the cops. He won't be gettin' out on no bail."

Edward Crowell was close enough to hear what I said, so I had to think twice before speaking. I had to think twice about the audaciousness of his brother, too, about the moxie it must have taken to try to skip the country so openly, so unselfconsciously. Or was it merely insolence? A grand disrespect for the police? For the law? And of course, he had almost been right when he bragged he was going to get away scot-free. Had it not been for the work of a pair of interested free-lancers, he would be jetting to a Caribbean isle this moment.

"I'm glad to hear it," I said.

"Yeah, well, I jus' din't think it was right for him to get away with that sort of scam. You know? 'Sides, he give me five grand to take you out."

"Sounds like a cheap date."

"You listening, man? Take you out? He give me five grand to kill you."

"I heard."

"Yeah. I already spent the money."

"I thought you didn't go in for that sort of work."

"Ahhh . . ."

"Are you going to earn it?"

Holder laughed deeply. "I told you, I don't do that sort of gig."

"Sure, that's what you said. But you might have been fibbing."

"I guess Crowell have to report me to the Better Business Bureau." His laugh boomed out.

When I hung up, some clown with a plastic boutonnière squirted me in the eye. The roomful of guests laughed. The clown winked at me. Pilar giggled some more and hiked up her skirt. Edward Crowell, peering over his wire-rimmed spectacles, seemed to be more than mildly interested in what was under the maid's skirt.

Over in the corner, Helga Iddins demonstrated dance steps for Clarice, and Clarice practiced them without realizing she was doing a stripper's routine. Melissa and Burton were off in a corner, heads touching over their punch cups, murmuring and giving each other looks like spontaneous combustion. It was beginning to look as if the hot breath of time and separation was puffing some life into their marriage.

The birthday girl marched over, pulled on my thumbs, and was whirled around into the air, gleefully chirping encouragement to her benefactor. The clown in the center of the room winked at me again. It isn't often a clown with violet Elizabeth Taylor eyes winks at you like that. A guy could get used to it. A guy could grow to like it.